IT AND
OTHER STORIES

IT AND
OTHER STORIES

GOUVERNEUR MORRIS

WILDSIDE PRESS

IT and Other Stories

TO ELSIE

I

Crown the heads of better men
With lilies and with morning-glories!
I'm unworthy of a pen—
These are Bread-and-Butter stories.
Shall I tell you how I know?
Strangers wrote and told me so.

II

He who only toils for fame
I pronounce a silly Billy.
I can't dine upon a name,
Or look dressy in a lily.
And—oh shameful truth to utter!—
I *won't* live on bread and butter.

III

Sometimes now (and sometimes then)
Meat and wine my soul requires.
Satan tempted me—my pen
Fills the house with open fires.
I *must* have a horse or two—
Babies, oh my Love—and you!

G. M.
Aiken, February 10, 1912.

CONTENTS

IT

Prana Beach would be a part of the solid west coast if it wasn't for a half circle of the deadliest, double-damned, orchid-haunted black morass, with a solid wall of insects that bite, rising out of it. But the beach is good dry sand, and the wind keeps the bugs back in the swamp. Between the beach and the swamp is a strip of loam and jungle, where some niggers live and a god.

I landed on Prana Beach because I'd heard — but it wasn't so and it doesn't matter. Anyhow, I landed — all alone; the canoemen wouldn't come near enough for me to land dry, at that. Said the canoe would shrivel up, like a piece of hide in a fire, if it touched that beach; said they'd turn white and be blown away like puffs of smoke. They nearly backed away with my stuff; would have if I hadn't pulled a gun on them. But they made me wade out and get it myself — thirty foot of rope with knots, dynamite, fuses, primers, compass, grub for a week, and — well, a bit of skin in a half-pint flask with a rubber and screw-down top. Not nice, it wasn't, wading out and back and out and back. There was one shark, I remember, came in so close that he grounded, snout out, and made a noise like a pig. Sun was going down, looking like a bloody murder victim, and there wasn't going to be any twilight. It's an uncertain light that makes wading nasty. It might be salt-water soaking into my jeans, but with that beastly red light over it, it looked like blood.

The canoe backed out to the — you can't call 'em a nautical name. They've one big, square sail of crazy-quilt work — raw silk, pieces of rubber boots, rattan matting, and grass cloth, all colors, all shapes of patches. They point into the wind and then go sideways; and they *don't* steer with an oar that Charon discarded thousands of years ago, that's painted crimson and raw violet; and the only thing they'd be good for would be fancy wood-carpets. Mine, or better, ours, was made of satinwood, and was ballasted with scrap-iron, rotten ivory, and ebony. There, I've told you what she was like (except for the live entomological collection aboard), and you may call her what you please. The main point is that she took the canoe aboard, and then disobeyed orders. Orders were to lie at anchor (which was a dainty thing of stone, all carved) till further orders. But she'd gotten rid of me, and she proposed to lie farther off, and come back (maybe) when I'd finished my job. So she pointed straight in for where I was standing amid my duds and chattels, just as if she was going to thump herself ashore — and then she began to slip off sideways like a misbegotten crab, and backward, too — until what with the darkness tumbling down, and a point o' palms, I lost sight of her. Why didn't I shout, and threaten, and jump up and down?

Because I was alone on Prana Beach, between the sea and the swamp. And because the god was beginning to get stirred up; and because now that I'd gone through six weeks' fever and boils to get where I was, I wished I hadn't gotten there. No, I wasn't scared. You wouldn't be if you were alone on a beach, after sundown, deserted you may say, your legs shaky with being wet, and your heart hot and mad as fire because you couldn't digest the things you had to put into your stomach, and if you'd heard that the beach was the most malodorous, ghoul-haunted beach of the seas, and if just as you were saying to yourself that *you* for one didn't believe a word of it — if, I say, just then *It* began to cut loose — back of you — way off to the left — way off to the right — why you'd have been scared.

It wasn't the noise it made so much as the fact that it could make any noise at all. . . . Shut your mouth tight and hum on the letter m-mmmmmmm — that's it exactly. Only It's was ten times as loud, and vibrating. The vibrations shook me where I stood.

With the wind right, that humming must have carried a mile out to sea; and that's how it had gotten about that there was a god loose on Prana Beach. It was an It-god, the niggers all agreed. You'll have seen 'em carved on paddles — shanks of a man, bust of a woman, nose of a snapping-turtle, and mouth round like the letter O. But the Prana Beach one didn't show itself that first night. It hummed awhile — m-m-m-m-m — oh, for maybe a minute — stopped and began again — jumped a major fifth, held it till it must have been half burst for breath, and then went down the scale an octave, hitting every note in the middle, and giving the effect of one damned soul meeting another out in eternity and yelling for pure joy and malice. The finish was a whoop on the low note so loud that it lifted my hair. Then the howl was cut off as sharp and neat and sudden as I've seen a Chinaman's head struck from his body by the executioner at Canton — Big Wan — ever seen him work? Very pretty. Got to perfection what golfers call "the follow through."

Yes. I sauntered into the nearest grove, whistling "Yankee Doodle," lighted a fire, cooked supper, and turned in for the night. Not!... I took to the woods all right, but on my stomach. And I curled up so tight that my knees touched my chin. Ever try it? It's the nearest thing to having some one with you, when you're cold and alone. Adam must have had a hard-shell back and a soft-shell stomach, like an armadillo — how does it run? — "dillowing in his armor." Because in moments of real or imaginary danger it's the first instinct of Adam's sons to curl up, and of Eve's daughters. Ever touch a Straits Settlement Jewess on the back of the hand with a lighted cigarette?...

As I'm telling you, I curled up good and tight, head and knees on the grub sack, Colt and dynamite handy, hair standing perfectly straight up, rope round me on the ground in a circle — I had a damn-fool notion that It mightn't be allowed to cross knotted ropes, and I shook with chills and nightmares and cramps. I could only lie on my left side, for the boils on my right. I couldn't keep my teeth quiet. I couldn't do anything that a Christian ought to do, with a heathen It-god strolling around. Yes, ... the thing came out on the beach, in full view of where I was, but I couldn't see it, because of the pitch dark. It came out, and made noises with its feet in the sand — up and down — up and down — scrunch — scrunch — something like a man walking, and not in a hurry. Something like it, but not exactly. The It's feet (they have seven toes according to the nigger paddles) didn't touch the ground as often as a man's would have done in walking the distance. There'd be one scrunch and then quite a long pause before the next. It sounded like a very, very big man, taking the very longest steps he could. But there wasn't any more mouth work. And for that I'm still offering up prayers of thanksgiving; for, if — say when it was just opposite where I lay, and not fifty yards off — it had let off anything sudden and loud, I'd have been killed as dead as by a stroke of lightning.

Well, I was just going to break, when day did. Broke so sweet, and calm, and pretty; all pink landward over the black jungle, all smooth and baby-blue out to sea. Till the sun showed, there was a land breeze — not really a breeze, just a stir, a cool quiet moving of spicy smells from one place to another — nothing more than that. Then the sea breeze rose and swept the sky and ocean till they were one and the same blue, the blue that comes highest at Tiffany's; and little puffs of shore birds came in on the breeze and began to run up and down on the beach, jabbing their bills into the damp sand and flapping their little wings. It was like Eden — Eden-by-the-Sea — I wouldn't have been surprised if Eve had come out of the woods yawning and stretching herself. And I wouldn't have cared — if I'd been shaved.

I took notice of all this peacefulness and quiet, twenty grains of quinine, some near food out of a can, and then had a good look around for a good place to stop, in case I got started running.

I fixed on a sandy knoll that had a hollow in the top of it, and one twisted beach ebony to shade the hollow. At the five points of a star with the knoll for centre, but at safe blasting distance, I planted dynamite, primed and short-fused. If anything chased me I hoped to have time to spring one of these mines in passing, tumble into my hollow and curl up, with my fingers in my ears.

I didn't believe in heathen gods when the sea and sky were that exclusive blue; but I had learned before I was fifteen years old that day is invariably followed by night, and that between the two there is a time toward the latter end of which you can believe anything. It was with that dusky period in view that I mined the approaches to my little villa at Eden-by-the-Sea.

Well, after that I took the flask that had the slip of skin in it, unscrewed the top, pulled the rubber cork, and fished the skin out, with a salvage hook that I made by unbending and rebending a hair-pin. . . . Don't smile. I've always had a horror of *accidentally* finding a hair-pin in my pocket, and so I carry one on purpose. . . . See? Not an airy, fairy Lillian, but an honest, hard-working Jane ... good to clean a pipe with. So I fished out the slip of skin (with the one I had then) and spread it out on my knee, and translated what was written on it, for the thousandth time.

Can you read that? The old-fashioned S's mix you up. It's straight modern Italian. I don't know what the ink's made of, but the skin's the real article — it's taken from just above the knee where a man can get at himself best. It runs this way, just like a "personal" in the *Herald*, only more so:

Prisoner on Prana Beach will share treasure with rescuing party. Come at once.

Isn't that just like an oil-well-in-the-South-west-Company's prospectus? "Only a little stock left; price of shares will be raised shortly to thirteen cents."

I bit. It was knowing what kind of skin the ad. was written on that got me. I'd seen cured human hide before. In Paris they've got a Constitution printed on some that was peeled off an aristocrat in the Revolution, and I've seen a seaman's upper arm and back, with the tattoos, in a bottle of alcohol in a museum on Fourteenth Street, New York — boys under fourteen not admitted. I wasn't a day over eight when I saw those tattoos. However. . . .

To get that prisoner loose was the duty that I owed to humanity; to share the treasure was the duty that I owed to myself. So I got together some niggers, and the fancy craft I've described (on shares with a Singapore Dutchman, who was too fat to come himself, and too much married), and made a start. . . . You're bothered by my calling them niggers. Is that it? Well, the Mason and Dixon line ran plump through my father's house; but mother's room being in the south gable, I was born, as you may say, in the land of cotton, and consequently in my bright Southern lexicon the word nigger is defined as meaning anything black or brown. I think I said that Prana is on the west coast, and that may have misled you. But Africa isn't the only God-forsaken place that has a west coast; how about Staten Island?

Malaysian houses are built mostly of reed and thatch work standing in shallow water on bamboo stalks, highly inflammable and subject to alterations by a blunt pocket-knife. So a favorite device for holding a man prisoner is a hole in the ground too deep and sheer for him to climb out of. That's why I'd brought a length of knotted rope. The dynamite was instead of men, which we hadn't means to hire or transport, and who wouldn't have landed on that beach anyhow, unless drowned and washed up. Now dynamite wouldn't be a pleasant thing to have round your club or your favorite restaurant; but in some parts of the world it makes the best company. It will speak up for you on occasion louder than your best friend, and it gives you the feeling of being Jove with a handful of thunderbolts. My plan was to find in what settlement there was the most likely prisoner, drive the inhabitants off for two or three days — one blast would do that, I calculated (especially if preceded and followed by blowings on a pocket siren) — let my rope down into his well, lift the treasure with him, and get away with it.

This was a straight ahead job — except for the god. And in daylight it didn't seem as if It could be such an awful devil of a god. But It did have the deuce of a funny spoor, as I made haste to find out. The thing had five toes, like a man, which was a relief. But unlike nigger feet, the thumb toe and the index weren't spread. The thumb bent sharply inward, and mixed its pad mark with that of the index. Furthermore, though the impress of the toes was very deep (downslanting like a man walking on tiptoe), the heel marks were also very deep, and between toe and heel marks there were no other marks at all. In other words, the thing's feet must have been arched like a croquet wicket. And It's heels were not rounded; they were *perfectly* round — absolute circles they were, about the diameter of the smallest sized cans in which Capstan tobacco is sold. If ever a wooden idol had stopped squatting and gone out for a stroll on a beach, it would have left just such a track. Only it might not have felt that it had to take such peculiarly long steps.

My knoll being near the south end of Prana Beach (pure patriotism I assure you), my village hunts must be to the northward. I had one good hunt, the first day, and I got near some sort of a village, a jungle one built over a pool, as I found afterward. The reason I gave up looking that day was because the god got between me and where

I was trying to get; burst out humming, you might say, right in my face, though I couldn't see It, and directly I had turned and was tiptoeing quietly away (I remember how the tree trunks looked like teeth in a comb, or the nearest railroad ties from the window of an express train), It set up the most passionate, vindictive, triumphant vocal fireworks ever heard out of hell. It made black noises like Niagara Falls, and white noises higher than Pike's Peak. It made leaps, lighting on tones as a carpenter's hammer lights on nails. It ran up and down the major and minor diatonics, up and down the chromatic, with the speed and fury of a typhoon, and the attention to detail of Paderewski — at his best, when he makes the women faint — and with the power and volume of a church organ with all the stops pulled out. It shook and It trilled and It quavered, and It gargled as if It had a barrel of glycothermoline in It's mouth and had been exposed to diphtheria, and It finished — just as I tripped on a snake and fell — with a round bar of high C sound, that lasted a good minute (or until I was a quarter of a mile beyond where I had fallen), and was the color of butter, and could have been cut with a knife. And It stopped short — biff — just as if It had been chopped off.

That was the end of my village hunting. Let the prisoner of Prana Beach drown in his hole when the rains come, let his treasure remain unlifted till Gabriel blows his trumpet; but let yours truly bask in the shade of the beach ebony, hidden from view, and fortified by dynamite — until the satinwood shallop should see fit to return and take him off.

Except for a queer dream (queer because of the time and place, and because there seemed absolutely nothing to suggest it to the mind asleep), I put in six hours' solid sleep. In my dream I was in Lombardy in a dark loft where there were pears laid out to ripen; and we were frightened and had to keep creepy-mouse still — because the father had come home sooner than was expected, and was milking his goats in the stable under the loft, and singing, which showed that he was in liquor, and not his usual affable, bland self. I could hear him plainly in my dream, tearing the heart out of that old folk-song called *La Smortina* — "The Pale Girl":

"T' ho la scia to e son contento
Non m'in cresca niente, niente
Altro giovine hogià in mente
Pin belino assai di te."

And I woke up tingling with the remembered fear (it was a mixed feeling, half fright, and half an insane desire to burst out laughing to see what the old man would do), and I looked over the rim of my hat, and there walking toward me, in the baby-blue and pink of the bright dawn (but a big way off), came a straggling line of naked niggers, headed by the It-god, Itself.

One look told me that, one look at a great bulk of scarletness, that walked upright like a man. I didn't look twice, I scuttled out to my nearest mine, lighted the fuse, tumbled back into the hollow, fingers in ears, face screwed up as tight as a face can be screwed, and waited.

When it was over, and things had stopped falling, I looked out again. The tropic dawn remained as before, but the immediate landscape was somewhat altered for the worse, and in the distance were neither niggers nor the god. It is possible that I stuck my thumbs into my armpits and waggled my fingers. I don't remember. But it's no mean sensation to have pitted yourself against a strange god, with perfectly round heels, and to have won out.

About noon, though, the god came back, fortified perhaps by reflection, and more certainly by a nigger who walked behind him with a spear. You've seen the donkey boys in Cairo make the donkeys trot?... This time I put my trust in the Colt forty-five; and looked the god over, as he came reluctantly nearer and nearer, singing a magic.

Do you know the tragedian walk as taken off on the comic opera stage, the termination of each strutting, dragging step accentuated by cymbals smashed together F-F-F? That was how the god walked. He was all in scarlet, with a long feather sticking straight up from a scarlet cap. And the magic he sang (now that you knew the sounds he made were those of a tenor voice, you knew that it was a glorious tenor voice) was a magic out of "Aïda." It was the magic that what's-his-name sings when he is appointed commander-in-chief of all the Egyptian forces. Now the niggers may have thought that their god's magics were stronger than my dynamite. But the god, though very, very simple, was not so simple as that. He was an Italian colored man, black bearded, and shaped like Caruso, only more so, if that is possible; and he sang, because he was a singing machine, but he couldn't have talked. I'll bet on that. He was too plumb afraid.

When he reached the hole that the dynamite had made in the landscape — I showed myself; trying to look as much like a dove of peace as possible.

"Come on alone," I called in Italian, "and have a bite of lunch."

That stopped his singing, but I had to repeat. Well he had an argument with the nigger, that finished with all the gestures that two monkeys similarly situated would have made at each other, and after a time the nigger sat down, and the god came on alone, puffing and indignant.

We talked in Dago, but I'll give the English of it, so's not to appear to be showing off.

"Who and what in the seventh circle of hell *are* you?" I asked.

He seemed offended that I should not have known. But he gave his name, sure of his effect. "Signor —" and the name sounded like that tower in Venice that fell down the other day.

"You don't mean it!" I exclaimed joyfully. "Be seated," and, I added, being silly with joy and relief at having my awful devil turn into a silly child — "there may be some legacy — though trifling."

Well, he sat down, and stuck his short, immense hirsute legs out, all comfy, and I, remembering the tracks on the beach, had a look at his feet. And I turned crimson with suppressed laughter. He had wooden cylinders three inches high strapped to his bare heels. They made him five feet five inches high instead of five feet two. They were just such heels (only clumsier and made of wood instead of cork and crimson morocco or silk) as *Siegfried* wears for mountain climbing, dragon fighting, or other deeds of derring-do. And with these heels to guide me, I sighed, and said:

"Signor Recent-Venetian-Tower, you have the most beautiful pure golden tenor voice that I have ever heard in my life."

Have you ever been suddenly embraced by a pile-driver, and kissed on both cheeks by a blacking-brush? I have. Then he held me by the shoulders at arm's length, and looked me in the eyes as if I had been a long-lost son returned at last. Then he gathered a kiss in his finger tips and flung it to the heavens. Then he asked if by any chance I had any spaghetti with me. He cried when I said that I had not; but quietly, not harassingly. And then we got down to real business, and found out about each other.

He was the prisoner of Prana Beach. The treasure that he had to share with his rescuer was his voice. Two nights a week during the season, at two thousand a night. But — There was a great big But.

Signor What-I-said-before, his voice weakened by pneumonia, had taken a long travelling holiday to rest up. But his voice, instead of coming back, grew weaker and weaker, driving him finally into a suicidal artistic frenzy, during which he put on his full suit of evening clothes, a black pearl shirt stud, a tall silk hat, in the dead of night, and flung himself from the stern of a P. & O. boat into the sea. He had no knowledge of swimming and expected to drown at once. But he was not built for drowning. The laws of buoyancy and displacement caused him to float upon his back, high out of the water, like an empty barrel. Nor was the water into which he had fallen as tepid as he had expected. From his description, with its accompaniment of shudderings and shiverings, the temperature must have been as low as 80° Fahrenheit, which is pretty sharp for dagoes. Anyhow, the double shock of the cold and of not drowning instantly acted on his vocal chords. Without even trying, he said, he knew that his voice had come back. Picture the poor man's despair — overboard in the ocean, wanting to die because he had nothing to live for, and suddenly discovering that he had everything to live for. He asserts that he actually forgot the cold, and thought only of how to preserve that glorious instrument, his voice; not for himself but for mankind. But he could not think out a way, and he asserted that a passion of vain weeping and delirium, during which he kicked himself warm, was followed by a noble and godlike calm, during which, lying as easily upon the sea as on a couch, and inspired by the thought that some ear might catch the notes and die the happier for it, he lifted his divine voice and sang a swan song. After that he sang twenty-nine others. And then, in the very midst of *La Bella Napoli*, with which he intended to close (fearing to strain his voice if he sang any more), he thought of sharks.

Spurred by that thought, he claims to have kicked and beaten with his hands until he was insensible. Otherwise, he would, he said, have continued to float about placidly, singing swan songs at intervals until, at last, thinned by starvation to the sinking point, he would have floated no more.

To shorten up. Signor You-know-what, either owing to his struggles, or to the sea breeze pressing against his stomach, came ashore on Prana Beach; was pounced upon by the niggers, stripped of his glad rags (the topper had been lost in the shuffle), and dropped into a hole eight feet deep, for safe-keeping. It was in this hole, buried in sand, that he found the flask I have told you about. Well, one day, for he had a bit of talent that way, he fell to sketching on his legs, knees, upper thigh and left forearm, using for ink something black that they had given him for breakfast. That night it rained; but next morning his drawings were as black and sharp as when he had made them; this, coupled with the flask, furnished him with an idea, a very forlorn and hopeless one, but an idea for all that. He had, however, nothing to write his C Q D on but himself, none of which (for he held himself in trust for his Maker as a complete whole, he explained) he intended to part with.

It was in trying to climb out of the hole that he tore a flap of skin from his left thigh just above the knee, clean off, except for one thread by which it hung. In less than two days he had screwed up his courage to breaking that thread with a sudden jerk. He cured his bit of hide in a novel way. Every morning he cried on it, and when the tears had dried, leaving their minute residue of salt, he would work the raw skin with his thumb and a bit of stick he had found. Then a nigger boy, one beast of a hot day, lowered him a gourd of sea-water as a joke, and Signor What-we-agreed-on, made salt of that while the sun shone, and finished his job of tanning.

The next time he was given a black breakfast, he wrote his hurry-call message and corked it into the flask. And there only remained the somewhat herculean task of getting that flask flung into the sea.

You'll never believe how it got there finally. But I'll tell you for all that. A creek flowed near the dungeon in which the famous tenor was incarcerated. And one night of cloud-burst that creek burst its cerements, banks I mean, filled the singing man's prison in two jerks of a lamb's tail, and floated both him and his flask out of it. He grounded as usual, but the flask must have been rushed down to the sea. For in the sea it was found, calmly bobbing, and less than two years later. A nigger fisherman found it, and gave it to me, in exchange for a Waterbury watch. He tried to make me take his daughter instead, but I wouldn't.

Signor What-you-would-forget-if-I-told-you wasn't put back in his dungeon till the rainy season was at an end. Instead he was picketed. A rope ran from his wrists, which were tied behind his back, and was inserted through the handles (it had a pair of them like ears just above the trunnions) of a small bronze cannon, that had Magellan's name and the arms of Spain engraved around the touch-hole. And thus picketed, he was rained on, joked on, and abused until dry weather. Then, it was the first happiness that he had had among them, they served him one day with a new kind of fish that had begun to run in the creek. It tasted like Carlton sole, he said. And it made him feel so good that, being quite by himself and the morning blue and warm, he began, sitting on his little cannon, to hum an aria. Further inspirited by his own tunefulness, he rose (and of course struck an attitude) and opened his mouth and sang.

Oh, how good it was to hear — as he put it himself — after all those months of silence!

Well, the people he belonged to came running up with eyes like saucers and mouths open, and they squatted at his feet in a semi-circle, and women came and children. They had wonder in their faces and fear. Last came the old chief, who was too old to walk, and was carried always in a chair which two of his good-natured sons-in-law made with their hands. And the old chief, when he had listened awhile with his little bald monkey head cocked on one side, signed to be put down. And he stood on his feet and walked.

And he took out a little khris and walked over to the Divo, and cut the ropes that bound him, and knelt before him and kowtowed, and pressed the late prisoner's toes with his forehead. Then — and this was terribly touching, my informant said, and reminded him of St. Petersburg — one of the old chief's granddaughters, a little brown slip of a girl, slender and shapely as a cigar, flung her arms round his neck, and hung — just hung. When they tried to get her away she kicked at them, but she never so much as once changed the expression of her upturned face, which was one of adoration. Well, the people hollered and made drums of their cheeks and beat on them, and the first thing Signor Recent-Disaster knew he was being dressed in a scarlet coat that had belonged to a British colonel dead this hundred years. The girl by now had had to let go and had dropped at his feet like a ripe guava — and he was being ushered into the largest bamboo-legged house that the place boasted, and told as plainly as round eyes, gesticulations, and moans can, that the house was his to enjoy. Then they began to give him things. First his own dress suit, ruined by sea-water and shrinking, his formerly boiled shirt, his red silk underwear still wearable, his black pearl stud and every stiver of gold, silver, copper, and English banknotes that had been found in his pockets. They gave him knives, rough silver bangles, heaps of elaborate mats, a handful of rather disappointing pearls, a scarlet head-dress with a feather that had been a famous chief's, a gun without a lock, and, what pleased him most (must have), a bit of looking-glass big enough to see half of his face in at a time. They allowed him to choose his own house-keeper; and, although several beauties were knocked down in the ensuing riot, he managed to satisfy them that his unalterable choice rested upon the little lady who had been the most convincing in her recognition of his genius, and — what's the line? — "Hang there like fruit, my soul, till the tree die."

Well, he offered to put me up, and show me how the gods keep house. I counter-offered to keep him with me, by force of dynamite, carry him back to civilization, and go shares on his voice, as per circular. And this is where the big But comes in. My offer was pestilential; he shunned it.

"You shall have my black pearl stud for your trouble," he said. "I bought her years ago in a pawnshop at Aix. But *me* — no. I have found my niche, and my temple. But you shall be the judge of that."

"You don't *want* to escape?"

His mouth curled in scorn at the very idea.

"Try to think of how much spaghetti you could buy for a song."

His eyes and mouth twitched. But he sighed, and shook his head.

"Do you know," said he, "when you demonstrated against us with your dynamite it was instantly concluded that you were some new kind of a god come to inhabit the beach. It was proposed that I go against you singing a charm that should drive you away. But, as you saw, I came only at the spear's point. Do you think I was afraid? I was; but not of your godship. I had seen your tracks, I had seen the beach rise to your explosive, and I knew that as one Christian gentleman I had nothing on the lines of violence to fear from another. Your explosion was like a note, asking me when I should next call to bring fewer attendants. I *was* afraid; I was afraid that you were not one, alone, but several, and that you would compel me to return with you to a world in which, take it for all and all, the good things, such as restaurants, artificial heat, Havana cigars, and Steinway pianos, are nullified by climatic conditions unsuited to vocal chords, fatal jealousies among members of the same artistic professions, and a public that listens but does not hear; or that hears and does not listen. But you shall stop with me a few days, in my house. You shall see for yourself that among all artists I alone enjoy an appreciation and solicitude that are better than gold."

Signor Shall-we-let-it-go-at-that had not lied to me. And all he asked was, with many apologies, that I should treat him with a certain reverence, a little as if he were a conqueror. So all the way to the village I walked two paces right flank rear, and wore a solemn and subdued expression. My host approached the dwellings of his people with an exaggeration of tragi-comic stride, dragging his high-heeled feet as Henry Irving used, raising and advancing his chest to the bursting point, and holding his head so proudly that the perpendicular feather of his cap leaned backward at a sharp angle. With his scarlet soldier's coat, all burst along the seams, and not meeting by a yard over his red silk undershirt, with his bit of broken mirror dangling at his waist like a lady's jewelled "vanity set," with his china-ink black mustache and superb beard, he presented for all the purposes of the time and place an appearance in keeping with the magnificence of his voice and of his dreams.

When we got among the houses, from which came a great peeping of shy eyes, the Signor suddenly raised his fingers to his throat and sounded a shocking b-r-rr-rrr of alarm and anxiety. Then there arose a murmur, almost pitiful it was so heartfelt, as of bees who fear an irreparable tragedy in the hive. The old chief came out of the council-house upon the hands of his good-natured sons-in-law, and he was full of tenderness and concern. I saw my friend escorted into his own dwelling by ladies who sighed and commiserated. But already the call for help had reached the tenor's slip of a wife; and she, with hands that shook, was preparing a compress of leaves that smelt of cinnamon and cloves. I, too, showed solicitude, and timidly helped my conqueror to the heaped mats upon which he was wont to recline in the heat of the day. He had made himself a pair of very round terrified eyes, and he had not taken the compress from his throat. But he spoke quietly, and as one possessed of indomitable fortitude. In Malay he told his people that it was "nothing, just a little — brrr — soreness and thickening," and he let slip such a little moan as monkeys make. To me he spoke in Italian.

"I shall have to submit to a bandage," said he. "But there is nothing the matter with my throat" (slight monkey moan here for benefit of adorers), "absolutely nothing. I have invented a slight soreness so — so that you could see for yourself ... so that you could see for yourself. . . . If you were to count those here assembled and those assembled without, you would number our entire population, including children and babes in arms" (a slight moan while compress is being readjusted over Adam's apple by gentle, tremulous brown fingers), "and among these, my friend, are no dissenters. There is none here to stand forth and say that on Tuesday night Signor And-he-pronounced-it's singing was lacking in those golden tones for which we used to look to him. His voice, indeed, is but a skeleton of its former self, and shall we say that the public must soon tire of a singer with so pronounced a tendency to flat?

"Here in this climate," he continued, "my voice by dint of constant and painstaking care and practice has actually improved. I should not have said that this was possible; but a man must believe experience. . . . And then these dear, amiable people are one in their acclaim of me; although I sometimes grieve, not for myself, but for them, to think that they can never *really* know what they've got. . . ."

I sometimes wonder how the god of Prana Beach will be treated when he begins to age and to lose his voice. It worries me — a little.

The black pearl stud? Of course not, you wretched materialist. I sold it in the first good market I came to. No good ever came of material possessions, and always much payment of storage bills. But I have a collection of memories that I am fond of.

Still, on second thought, and if I had the knack of setting them straight on paper, I'd part even with them for a consideration, especially if I felt that I could reach such an appreciative audience as that of Prana Beach, which sits upon its heels in worship and humility and listens to the divine fireworks of Signor I-have-forgotten-too.

TWO BUSINESS WOMEN

They engaged themselves to be married when they were so young they couldn't tell anybody about it for fear of being laughed at; and if I mentioned their years to you, you would laugh at me. They thought they were full-grown, but they weren't even that. When they were finally married they couldn't either of them have worn the clothes they got engaged in. The day they got engaged they wore suits made of white woollen blankets, white knitted toques, and white knitted sashes. It was because they were dressed exactly alike that they first got excited about each other. And Cynthia said: "You look just like a snowman." And G. G. — which was his strange name — said: "You look just like a snowbird."

G. G. was in Saranac for his health. Cynthia had come up for the holidays to skate and to skee and to coast, and to get herself engaged before she was full-grown to a boy who was so delicate that climate was more important for him than education. They met first at the rink. And it developed that if you crossed hands with G. G. and skated with him you skated almost as well as he did. He could teach a girl to waltz in five minutes; and he had a radiant laugh that almost moved you to tears when you went to bed at night and got thinking about it. Cynthia had never seen a boy with such a beautiful round head and such beautiful white teeth and such bright red cheeks. She always said that she loved him long before he loved her. As a matter of fact, it happened to them both right away. As one baby, unabashed and determined, embraces a strange baby — and is embraced — so, from their first meeting in the great cold stillness of the North Woods, their young hearts snuggled together.

G. G. was different from other boys. To begin with, he had been born at sea. Then he had lived abroad and learned the greatest quantity of foreign languages and songs. Then he had tried a New England boarding-school and had been hurt playing games he was too frail to play. And doctors had stethoscoped him and shaken their heads over him. And after that there was much naming of names which, instead of frightening him, were magic to his ear — Arizona, California, Saranac — but, because G. G.'s father was a professional man and perfectly square and honest, there wasn't enough money to send G. G. far from New York and keep him there and visit him every now and then. So Saranac was the place chosen for him to get well in; and it seemed a little hard, because there was almost as much love of sunshine and warmth and flowers and music in G. G. as there was patience and courage.

The day they went skeeing together — which was the day after they had skated together — he told Cynthia all about himself, very simply and naturally, as a gentleman farmer should say: "This is the dairy; this is the blacksmith shop; this is the chicken run." And the next day, very early, when they stood knee-deep in snow, armed with shot-guns and waiting for some dogs that thought they were hounds to drive rabbits for them to shoot at, he told her that nothing mattered so long as you were happy and knew that you were happy, because when these two stars came into conjunction you were bound to get well.

A rabbit passed. And G. G. laid his mitten upon his lips and shook his head; and he whispered:

"I wouldn't shoot one for anything in the world."

And she said: "Neither would I."

Then she said: "If you don't shoot why did you come?"

"Oh, Miss Snowbird," he said, "don't I look why I came? Do I have to say it?"

He looked and she looked. And their feet were getting colder every moment and their hearts warmer. Then G. G. laughed aloud — bright, sudden music in the forest. Snow, balanced to the fineness of a hair, fell from the bowed limbs of trees. Then there was such stillness as may be in Paradise when souls go up to the throne to be forgiven. Then, far off, one dog that thought he was a hound began to yap and thought he was belling; but still G. G. looked into the snowbird's eyes and she into his, deeper and deeper, until neither had any secret of soul from the other. So, upon an altar cloth, two wax candles burn side by side, with clear, pure light.

Cynthia had been well brought up, but she came of rich, impatient stock, and never until the present moment had she thought very seriously about God. Now, however, when she saw the tenderness there was in G. G.'s eyes and the smile of serene joyousness that was upon his lips, she remembered the saying that God has made man — and boys — in His image — and understood what it meant.

She said: "I know why you think you've come."

"Think?" he said. "Think!"

And then the middle ends of his eyebrows rose — all tender and quizzical; and with one mitten he clutched at his breast — just over his heart. And he said:

"If only I could get it out I would give it to you!"

Cynthia, too, began to look melting tender and wondrous quizzical; and she bent her right arm forward and plucked at its sleeve as if she were looking for something. Then, in a voice of dismay:

"Only three days ago it was still there," she said; "and now it's gone — I've lost it."

"Oh!" said G. G. "You don't suspect me of having purloined —"
His voice broke.

"We're only kids," said Cynthia.

"Yes," said he; "but you're the dearest kid!"

"Since you've taken my heart," said she, "you'll not want to give
it back, will you? I think that would break it."

"I oughtn't to have taken it!" said G. G.

And then on his face she saw the first shadow that ever he had
let her see of doubt and of misgiving.

"Listen!" he said. "My darling! I think that I shall get well. . . . I
think that, once I am well, I shall be able to work very hard. I have
nothing. I love you so that I think even angels don't want to do right
more than I do. Is that anything to offer? Not very much."

"Nobody in all the world," said she, "will ever have the chance
to offer me anything else — just because I'm a kid doesn't mean that
I don't know the look of forever when I see it."

"Is it really forever?" he said. "For you too?"

"For me — surely!"

"Ah," said he, "what shall I think of to promise you?"
His face was a flash of ecstasy.

"You don't even have to promise that you will get well," she
said. "I know you will try your hardest. No matter what happens —
we're final — and I shall stick to you always, and nothing shall take
you from me, and nobody. . . . When I am of age I shall tell my papa
about us and then we shall be married to each other! And meanwhile you shall write to me every day and I shall write to you three
times every day!" Her breath came like white smoke between her
parted lips and she stood valiant and sturdy in the snow — a strong,
resolute girl, built like a boy — clean-cut, crystal-pure, and steel-
true. A shot sounded and there came to them presently the pungent,
acid smell of burnt powder.

"And we shall never hurt things or kill them," said G. G. "And
every day when I've been good I shall kiss your feet and your
hands."

"And when I've been good," she said, "you'll smile at me the
way you're smiling now — and it won't be necessary to die and go to
Heaven to see what the gentlemen angels look like."

"But," cried G. G., "whoever heard of going to Heaven? It
comes to people. It's here."

"And for us," she said, "it's come to stay."

All the young people came to the station to see Cynthia off and
G. G. had to content himself with looking things at her. And then he

went back to his room and undressed and went to bed. Because for a week he had done all sorts of things that he shouldn't have done, just to be with Cynthia — all the last day he had had fever and it had been very hard for him to look like a joyous boy angel — he knew by experience that he was in for a "time." It is better that we leave him behind closed doors with his doctors and his temperature. We may knock every morning and ask how he is, and we shall be told that he is no better. He was even delirious at times. And it is only worth while going into this setback of G. G's because there are miracles connected with it — his daily letter to Cynthia.

Each day she had his letter — joyous, loving, clearly writ, and full of flights into silver-lined clouds and the plannings of Spanish castles. Each day G. G. wrote his letter and each day he descended a little farther into the Valley of the Shadow, until at last he came to Death Gate — and then rested, a voyager undecided whether to go on or to go back. Who may know what it cost him to write his letter, sitting there at the roadside!

His mother was with him. It was she who took the letter from his hands when he sank back into his pillows; and they thought for a little that he had gone from that place — for good and all. It was she who put it into the envelope and who carried it with her own hands to the post-office. Because G. G. had said: "To get there, it must go by the night's mail, Mumsey."

G. G.'s mother didn't read the letter; but you may be sure she noted down the name and address in her heart of hearts, and that for the girl who seemed to mean so much to G. G. she developed upon the spot a heavenly tenderness, mixed with a heavenly jealousy.

II

One day there came to G. G., in convalescence — it was after his mother had gone back to New York — a great, thick package containing photographs and a letter. I think the letter contained rouge — because it made G. G.'s cheeks so red.

Cynthia had collected all the pictures she could find of herself in her father's house and sent them to G. G. There were pictures of her in the longest baby clothes and in the shortest. There were pictures posed for occasions, pictures in fancy clothes, and a quart of kodaks. He had her there on his knees — riding, driving, diving, skating, walking, sitting on steps, playing with dogs, laughing, looking sad, talking, dimpling, smiling. There were pictures that looked right at G. G., no matter at what angle he held them. There were pictures so delicious of her that he laughed aloud for delight.

All the stages of her life passed before his eyes — over and over — all day long; and, instead of growing more and more tired, he grew more and more refreshed. He made up his spotless mind to be worthy of her and to make, for her to bear, a name of which nobody should be able to say anything unkind.

If G. G. had had very little education he had made great friends with some of the friendliest and most valuable books that had ever been written. And he made up his mind, lying at full length — the livelong day — in the bright, cold air — his mittened hands plunged into deep pockets full of photographs — that, for her sake and to hasten that time when they might always be together, he would learn to write books, taking infinite pains. And he determined that these books should be as sweet and clean and honorable as he could make them. You see, G. G. had been under the weather so much and had suffered so much all alone by himself, with nobody to talk to, that his head was already full of stories about make-believe places and people that were just dying to get themselves written. So many things that are dead to most people had always been alive to him — leaves, flowers, fairies. He had always been a busy maker of verses, which was because melody, rhythm, and harmony had always been delicious to his ear. And he had had, as a little boy, a soprano voice that was as true as truth and almost as agile as a canary bird's.

He decided, then, very deliberately — lying upon his back and healing that traitor lung of his — to be a writer. He didn't so decide entirely because that was what he had always wanted to be, but for many reasons. First place, he could say things to her through prose and verse that could not be expressed in sculpture, music, painting, groceries, or dry-goods. Second place, where she was, there his heart was sure to be; and where the heart is, there the best work is done. And, third place, he knew that the chances were against his ever living in dusty cities or in the places of business thereof.

"I am so young," he wrote to her, "that I can begin at the beginning and learn to be anything — in time to be it! And so every morning now you shall think of G. G. out with his butterfly net, running after winged words. That's nonsense. I've a little pad and a big pencil, and a hot potato in my pocket for to warm the numb fingers at. And father's got an old typewriter in his office that's to be put in order for me; and nights I shall drum upon it and print off what was written down in the morning, and study to see why it's all wrong. I think I'll never write anything but tales about people who love each other. 'Cause a fellow wants to stick to what he knows about. . . ."

Though G. G. was not to see Cynthia again for a whole year he didn't find any trouble in loving her a little more every day. To his mind's eye she was almost as vivid as if she had been standing right there in front of him. And as for her voice, that dwelt ever in his ear, like those lovely airs which, once heard, are only put aside with death. You may have heard your grandmother lilting to herself, over her mending, some song of men and maidens and violets that she had listened to in her girlhood and could never forget.

And then, of course, everything that G. G. did was a reminder of Cynthia. With the help of one of Doctor Trudeau's assistants, who came every day to see how he was getting on, he succeeded in understanding very well what was the matter with him and under just what conditions a consumptive lung heals and becomes whole. To live according to the letter and spirit of the doctor's advice became almost a religion with him.

For six hours of every day he sat on the porch of the house where he had rooms, writing on his little pad and making friends with the keen, clean, healing air. Every night the windows of his bedroom stood wide open, so that in the morning the water in his pitcher was a solid block. And he ate just the things he was told to — and willed himself to like milk and sugar, and snow and cold, and short days!

In his writing he began to see progress. He was like a musical person beginning to learn an instrument; for, just as surely as there are scales to be run upon the piano before your virtuoso can weave music, binding the gallery gods with delicious meshes of sound, so in prose-writing there must be scales run, fingerings worked out, and harmonies mastered. For in a page of *lo bello stile* you will find trills and arpeggios, turns, grace notes, a main theme, a sub theme, thorough-bass, counterpoint, and form.

Music is an easier art than prose, however. It comes to men as a more direct and concrete gift of those gods who delight in sound and the co-ordination of parts. The harmonies are more quickly grasped by the well-tuned ear. We can imagine the boy Mozart discoursing lovely music at the age of five; but we cannot imagine any one of such tender years compiling even a fifth-rate paragraph of prose.

Those men who have mastered *lo bello stile* in music can tell us pretty clearly how the thing is done. There be rules. But your prose masters either cannot formulate what they have learned — or will not.

G. G. was very patient; and there were times when the putting together of words was fascinating, like the putting together of those picture puzzles which were such a fad the other day. And such reading as he did was all in one book — the dictionary. For hours, guided by his nice ear for sound, he applied himself to learning the derivatives and exact meanings of new words — or he looked up old words and found that they were new.

As for his actual compositions, he had only the ambition to make them as workmanlike as he could. He made little landscapes; he drew little interiors. He tried to get people up and down stairs in the fewest words that would make the picture. And when he thought that he had scored a little success he would count the number of words he had used and determine to achieve the same effect with the use of only half that number.

Well, G. G.'s lung healed again; and this time he was very careful not to overdo. He had gained nine pounds, he wrote to Cynthia — "saved them" was the way he put it; and he was determined that this new tissue, worth more than its weight in gold, should go to bank and earn interest for him — and compound interest.

"Shall I get well?" he asked that great dreamer who dreamed that there was hope for people who had never hoped before — and who has lived to see his dream come true; and the great dreamer smiled and said:

"G. G., if growing boys are good boys and do what they are told, and have any luck at all — they always get well!"

Then G. G. blushed.

"And when I am well can I live where I please — and — and get married — and all that sort of thing?"

"You can live where you please, marry and have children; and if you aren't a good husband and a good father I dare say you'll live to be hanged at ninety. But if I were you, G. G., I'd stick by the Adirondacks until you're old enough to — know better."

And G. G. went back to his rooms in great glee and typewrote a story that he had finished as well as he could, and sent it to a magazine. And six days later it came back to him, with a little note from the editor, who said:

"There's nothing wrong with your story except youth. If you say so we'll print it. We like it. But, personally, and believing that I have your best interests at heart, I advise you to wait, to throw this story into your scrap basket, and to study and to labor until your mind and your talent are mature. For the rest, I think you are going to do some fine things. This present story isn't that — it's not fine. At the same time, it is so very good in some ways that we are willing to leave its publication or its destruction to your discretion."

G. G. threw his story into the scrap basket and went to bed with a brand-new notion of editors.

"Why," said he to the cold darkness — and his voice was full of awe and astonishment — "they're — alive!"

III

Cynthia couldn't get at G. G. and she made up her mind that she must get at something that belonged to him — or die. She had his letter, of course, and his kodaks; and these spoke the most eloquent language to her — no matter what they said or how they looked — but she wanted somehow or other to worm herself deeper into G. G.'s life. To find somebody, for instance, who knew all about him and would enjoy talking about him by the hour. Now there are never but two people who enjoy sitting by the hour and saying nice things about any man — and these, of course, are the woman who bore him and the woman who loves him. Fathers like their sons well enough — sometimes — and will sometimes talk about them and praise them; but not always. So it seemed to Cynthia that the one and only thing worth doing, under the circumstances, was to make friends with G. G.'s mother. To that end, Cynthia donned a warm coat of pony-skin and drove in a taxicab to G. G.'s mother's address, which she had long since looked up in the telephone book.

"If she isn't alone," said Cynthia, "I shan't know what to say or what to do."

And she hesitated, with her thumb hovering about the front-door bell — as a humming-bird hovers at a flower.

Then she said: "What does it matter? Nobody's going to eat me." And she rang the bell.

G. G.'s mother was at home. She was alone. She was sitting in G. G.'s father's library, where she always did sit when she was alone. It was where she kept most of her pictures of G. G.'s father and of G. G., though she had others in her bedroom; and in her dressing-room she had a dapple-gray horse of wood that G. G. had galloped about on when he was little. She had a sweet face, full of courage and affection. And everything in her house was fresh and pretty, though there wasn't anything that could have cost very much. G. G.'s father was a lawyer. He was more interested in leaving a stain-less name behind him than a pot of money. And, somehow, fruit doesn't tumble off your neighbor's tree and fall into your own lap — unless you climb the tree when nobody is looking and give the tree a sound shaking. I might have said of G. G., in the very beginning, that he was born of poor *and* honest parents. It would have saved all this explanation.

G. G.'s mother didn't make things hard for Cynthia. One glance was enough to tell her that dropping into the little library out of the blue sky was not a pretty girl but a blessed angel — not a rich man's daughter but a treasure. It wasn't enough to give one hand to such a maiden. G. G.'s mother gave her two. But she didn't kiss her. She felt things too deeply to kiss easily.

"I've come to talk about G. G.," said Cynthia. "I couldn't help it. I think he's the *dearest* boy!"

She finished quite breathless — and if there had been any Jacqueminot roses present they might have hung their lovely heads in shame and left the room.

"G. G. has shown me pictures of you," said his mother. "And once, when we thought we were going to lose him, he used his last strength to write to you. I mailed the letter. That is a long time ago. Nearly two years.

"And I didn't know that he'd been ill in all that time," said Cynthia; "he never told me."

"He would have cut off his hand sooner than make you anxious. That was why he *would* write his daily letter to you. That one must have been almost as hard to write as cutting off a hand."

"He writes to me every day," said Cynthia, "and I write to him; but I haven't seen him for a year and I don't feel as if I could stand it much longer. When he gets well we're going to be married. And if he doesn't get well pretty soon we're going to be married anyway."

"Oh, my dear!" exclaimed G. G.'s mother. "You know that wouldn't be right!"

"I don't know," said Cynthia; "and if anybody thinks I'm going to be tricked out of the man I love by a lot of silly little germs they are very much mistaken!"

"But, my dear," said G. G.'s mother, "G. G. can't support a wife — not for a long time anyway. We have nothing to give him. And, of course, he can't work now — and perhaps can't for years."

"I, too," said Cynthia — with proper pride — "have parents. Mine are rolling in money. Whenever I ask them for anything they always give it to me without question."

"You have never asked them," said G. G.'s mother, "for a sick, penniless boy."

"But I shall," said Cynthia, "the moment G. G.'s well — and maybe sooner."

There was a little silence.

Then G. G.'s mother leaned forward and took both of Cynthia's hands in hers.

"I don't wonder at him," she said — "I don't. I was ever so

jealous of you, but I'm not any more. I think you're the *dearest* girl!"

"Oh!" cried Cynthia. "I am so glad! But will G. G.'s father like me too?"

"He has never yet failed," said G. G.'s mother, "to like with his whole heart anything that was stainless and beautiful."

"Is he like G. G.?"

"He has the same beautiful round head, but he has a rugged look that G. G. will never have. He has a lion look. He might have been a terrible tyrant if he hadn't happened, instead, to be a saint."

And she showed Cynthia, side by side, pictures of the father and the boy.

"They have such valiant eyes!" said Cynthia.

"There is nothing base in my young men," said G. G.'s mother.

Then the two women got right down to business and began an interminable conversation of praise. And sometimes G. G.'s mother's eyes cried a little while the rest of her face smiled and she prattled like a brook. And the meeting ended with a great hug, in which G. G.'s mother's tiny feet almost parted company with the floor.

And it was arranged that they two should fly up to Saranac and be with G. G. for a day.

IV

It wasn't from shame that G. G. signed another name than his own to the stories that he was making at the rate of one every two months. He judged calmly and dispassionately that they were "going to be pretty good some day," and that it would never be necessary for him to live in a city. He signed his stories with an assumed name because he was full of dramatic instinct. He wanted to be able — just the minute he was well — to say to Cynthia:

"Let us be married!" Then she was to say: "Of course, G. G.; but what are we going to live on?" And G. G. was going to say: "Ever hear of so-and-so?"

CYNTHIA: Goodness gracious! Sakes alive! Yes; I should think I had! And, except for you, darlingest G. G., I think he's the very greatest man in all the world!

G. G.: Goosey-Gander, know that he and I are one and the same person — and that we've saved seventeen hundred dollars to get married on!

(Tableau not to be seen by the audience.)

So far as keeping Cynthia and his father and mother in ignorance of the fledgling wings he was beginning to flap, G. G. succeeded admirably; but it might have been better to have told them all in the beginning.

Now G. G.'s seventeen hundred dollars was a huge myth. He was writing short stories at the rate of six a year and he had picked out to do business with one of the most dignified magazines in the world. Dignified people do not squander money. The magazine in question paid G. G. from sixty to seventy dollars apiece for his stories and was much too dignified to inform him that plenty of other magazines — very frivolous and not in the least dignified — would have been ashamed to pay so little for anything but the poems, which all magazines use to fill up blank spaces. So, even in his own ambitious and courageous mind, a "married living" seemed a very long way off.

He refused to be discouraged, however. His health was too good for that. The doctor pointed to him with pride as a patient who followed instructions to the letter and was not going to die of the disease which had brought him to Saranac. And they wrote to G. G's father — who was finding life very expensive — that, if he could keep G. G. at Saranac, or almost anywhere out of New York, for another year or two, they guaranteed — as much as human doctors can — that G. G. would then be as sound as a bell and fit to live anywhere.

This pronouncement was altogether too much of a good thing for Fate. As G. G's father walked up-town from his office, Fate raised a dust in his face which, in addition to the usual ingredients of city dust, contained at least one thoroughly compatible pair of pneumonia germs. These went for their honey-moon on a pleasant, warm journey up G. G's father's left nostril and to house-keeping in his lungs. In a few hours they raised a family of several hundred thousand bouncing baby germs; and these grew up in a few minutes and began to set up establishments of their own right and left.

G. G.'s father admitted that he had a "heavy cold on the chest." It was such a heavy cold that he became delirious, and doctors came and sent for nurses; and there was laid in the home of G. G.'s father the corner-stone of a large edifice of financial disaster.

He had never had a partner. His practice came to a dead halt. The doctors whom G. G.'s mother called in were, of course, the best she had ever heard of. They would have been leaders of society if their persons had been as fashionable as their prices. The corner drug store made its modest little profit of three or four hundred per cent on the drugs which were telephoned for daily. The day nurse rolled up twenty-five dollars a week and the night nurse thirty-five. The servant's wages continued as usual. The price of beef, eggs, vegetables, etc., rose. The interest on the mortgage fell due. And it is a wonder, considering how much he worried, that G. G.'s father ever lived to face his obligations.

Cynthia, meanwhile, having heard that G. G. was surely going to get well, was so happy that she couldn't contain the news. And she proceeded to divulge it to her father.

"Papa," she said, "I think I ought to tell you that years ago, at Saranac — that Christmas when I went up with the Andersons — I met the man that I am going to marry. He was a boy then; but now we're both grown up and we feel just the same about each other."

And she told her father G. G.'s name and that he had been very delicate, but that he was surely going to get well. Cynthia's father, who had always given her everything she asked for until now, was not at all enthusiastic.

"I can't prevent your marrying any one you determine to marry, Cynthia," he said. "Can this young man support a wife?"

"How could he!" she exclaimed — "living at Saranac and not being able to work, and not having any money to begin with! But surely, if the way *we* live is any criterion, you could spare us some money — couldn't you?"

"You wish me to say that I will support a delicate son-in-law whom I have never seen? Consult your intelligence, Cynthia."

"I have my allowance," she said, her lips curling.

"Yes," said her father, "while you live at home and do as you're told."

"Now, papa, don't tell me that you're going to behave like a lugubrious parent in a novel! Don't tell me that you are going to cut me off with a shilling!"

"I shan't do that," he said gravely; "it will be without a shilling." But he tempered this savage statement with a faint smile.

"Papa, dear, is this quite definite? Are you talking in your right mind and do you really mean what you say?"

"Suppose you talk the matter over with your mother — she's always indulged you in every way. See what she says."

It developed that neither of Cynthia's parents was enthusiastic at the prospect of her marrying a nameless young man — she had told them his name, but that was all she got for her pains — who hadn't a penny and who had had consumption, and might or might not be sound again. Personally they did not believe that consumption can be cured. It can be arrested for a time, they admitted, but it always comes back. Cynthia's mother even made a physiological attack on Cynthia's understanding, with the result that Cynthia turned indignantly pink and left the room, saying:

"If the doctor thinks it's perfectly right and proper for us to marry I don't see the least point in listening to the opinions of excited and prejudiced amateurs."

The ultimatum that she had from her parents was distinct, final, and painful.

"Marry him if you like. We will neither forgive you nor support you."

They were perfectly calm with her — cool, affectionate, sensible, and worldly, as it is right and proper for parents to be. She told them they were wrong-headed, old-fashioned, and unintelligent; but as long as they hadn't made scenes and talked loud she found that she couldn't help loving them almost as much as she always had; but she loved G. G. very much more. And having definitely decided to defy her family, to marry G. G. and live happily ever afterward, she consulted her check-book and discovered that her available munition of war was something less than five hundred dollars — most of it owed to her dress-maker.

"Well, well!" she said; "she's always had plenty of money from me; she can afford to wait."

And Cynthia wrote to her dress-maker, who was also her friend!

MY DEAR CELESTE: I have decided that you will have to afford to wait for your money. I have an enterprise in view which calls for all the available capital I have. Please write me a nice note and say that you don't mind a bit. Otherwise we shall stop being friends and I shall always get my clothes from somebody else. Let me know when the new models come. . . .

V

On her way down-town Cynthia stopped to see G. G.'s mother and found the whole household in the throes occasioned by its head's pneumonia.

"Why haven't you let me know?" exclaimed Cynthia. "There must be so many little things that I could have done to help you."

Though the sick man couldn't have heard them if they had shouted, the two women talked in whispers, with their heads very close together.

"He's better," said G. G.'s mother, "but yesterday they wanted me to send for G. G. 'No,' I said. 'You may have given him up, but I haven't. If I send for my boy it would look as if I had surrendered,' And almost at once, if you'll believe it, he seemed to shake off something that was trying to strangle him and took a turn for the better; and now they say that, barring some long names, he will get well. . . . It does look, my dear, as if death had seen that there was no use facing a thoroughly determined woman."

At this point, because she was very much overwrought, G. G.'s mother had a mild little attack of hysteria; and Cynthia beat her on the back and shook her and kissed her until she was over it. Then G. G.'s mother told Cynthia about her financial troubles.

"It isn't us that matters," she said, "but that G. G. ought to have one more year in a first-rate climate; and it isn't going to be possible to give it to him. They say that he's well, my dear, absolutely well; but that now he should have a chance to build up and become strong and heavy, so that he can do a man's work in the world. As it is, we shall have to take him home to live; and you know what New York dust and climate can do to people who have been very, very ill and are still delicate and high-strung."

"There's only one thing to do for the present," said Cynthia — "anybody with the least notion of business knows that — we must keep him at Saranac just as long as our credit holds out, mustn't we? — until the woman where he boards begins to act ugly and threatens to turn him out in the snow."

"Oh, but that would be dreadful!" said G. G.'s mother. Cynthia smiled in a superior way.

"I don't believe," she said, "that you understand the first thing about business. Even my father, who is a prude about bills, says that all the business of the country is done on credit. . . . Now you're not going to be silly, are you? — and make G. G. come to New York before he has to?"

"It will have to be pretty soon, I'm afraid," said G. G.'s mother.

"Sooner than run such risks with any boy of mine," said Cynthia, with a high color, "I'd beg, I'd borrow, I'd forge, I'd lie — I'd steal!"

"Don't I know you would!" exclaimed G. G.'s mother. "My darling girl, you've got the noblest character — it's just shining in your eyes!"

"There's another thing," said Cynthia: "I have to go down-town now on business, but you must telephone me around five o'clock and tell me how G. G.'s father is. And you must spend all your time between now and then trying to think up something really useful that I can do to help you. And" — here Cynthia became very mysterious — "I forbid you to worry about money until I tell you to!"

Cynthia had a cousin in Wall Street; his name was Jarrocks Bell. He was twenty years older than Cynthia and he had been fond of her ever since she was born. He was a great, big, good-looking man, gruff without and tender within. Clever people, who hadn't made successful brokers, wondered how in the face of what they called his "obvious stupidity" Jarrocks Bell had managed to grow rich in Wall Street. The answer was obvious enough to any one who knew him intimately. To begin with, his stupidity was superficial. In the second place, he had studied bonds and stocks until he knew a great deal about them. Then, though a drinking man, he had a head like iron and was never moved by exhilaration to mention his own or anybody else's affairs. Furthermore, he was unscrupulously honest. He was so honest and blunt that people thought him brutal at times. Last and not least among the elements of his success was the fact that he himself never speculated.

When the big men found out that there was in Wall Street a broker who didn't speculate himself, who didn't drink to excess, who was absolutely honest, and who never opened his mouth when it was better shut, they began to patronize that man's firm. In short, the moment Jarrocks Bell's qualities were discovered, Jarrocks Bell was made. So that now, in speculative years, his profits were enormous.

Cynthia had always been fond of her big, blunt cousin, as he of her; and in her present trouble her thoughts flew to him as straight as a homing aeroplane to the landing-stage.

Even a respectable broker's office is a noisome, embarrassing place, and among the clients are men whose eyes have become popped from staring at paper-tapes and pretty girls; but Cynthia had no more fear of men than a farmer's daughter has of cows, and she flashed through Jarrocks's outer office — preceded by a very small boy — with her color unchanged and only her head a little higher than usual.

Jarrocks must have wondered to the point of vulgar curiosity what the deuce had brought Cynthia to see him in the busiest hour of a very busy day; but he said "Hello, Cynthia!" as naturally as if they two had been visiting in the same house and he had come face to face with her for the third or fourth time that morning.

"I suppose," said Cynthia, "that you are dreadfully busy; but, Jarrocks dear, my affairs are so much more important to me than yours can possibly be to you — do you mind?"

"May I smoke?"

"Of course."

"Then I don't mind. What's your affair, Cynthia — money or the heart?"

"Both, Jarrocks." And she told him pretty much what the reader has already learned. As for Jarrocks's listening, he was a perfect study of himself. He laughed gruffly when he ought to have cried; and when Cynthia tried to be a little humorous he looked very solemn and not unlike the big bronze Buddha of the Japanese. Inside, however, his big heart was full of compassion and tenderness for his favorite girl in all the world. Nobody will ever know just how fond Jarrocks was of Cynthia. It was one of those matters on which — owing, perhaps, to his being her senior by twenty years — he had always thought it best to keep his mouth shut.

"What's your plan?" he asked. "Where do I come in? I'll give you anything I've got." Cynthia waived the offer; it was a little unwelcome.

"I've got about five hundred dollars," she said, "and I want to speculate with it and make a lot of money, so that I can be independent of papa and mamma."

"Lots of people," said Jarrocks, "come to Wall Street with five hundred dollars, more or less, and they wish to be independent of papa and mamma. They end up by going to live in the Mills Hotel."

"I know," said Cynthia; "but this is really important. If G. G. could work it would be different."

"Tell me one thing," said Jarrocks: "If you weren't in love with G. G. what would you think of him as a candidate for your very best friend's hand?"

Cynthia counted ten before answering.

"Jarrocks, dear," she said — and he turned away from the meltingness of her lovely face — "he's so pure, he's so straight, he's so gentle and so brave, that I don't really think I can tell you what I think of him."

There was silence for a moment, then Jarrocks said gruffly:

"That's a clean-enough bill of health. Guess you can bring him into the family, Cynthia."

Then he drummed with his thick, stubby fingers on the arm of his chair.

"The idea," he said at last, "is to turn five hundred dollars into a fortune. You know I don't speculate."

"But you make it easy for other people?"

He nodded.

"If you'd come a year ago," he said, "I'd have sent you away. Just at the present moment your proposition isn't the darn-fool thing it sounds."

"I knew you'd agree with me," said Cynthia complacently. "I knew you'd put me into something that was going 'way up."

Jarrocks snorted.

"Prices are at about the highest level they've ever struck and money was never more expensive. I think we're going to see such a tumble in values as was never seen before. It almost tempts me to come out of my shell and take a flyer — if I lose your five hundred for you, you won't squeal, Cynthia?"

"Of course not."

"Then I'll tell you what I think. There's nothing certain in this business, but if ever there was a chance to turn five hundred dollars into big money it's now. You've entered Wall Street, Cynthia, at what looks to me like the psychological moment."

"That's a good omen," said Cynthia. "I believe we shall succeed. And I leave everything to you."

Then she wrote him a check for all the money she had in the world. He held it between his thumb and forefinger while the ink dried.

"By the way, Cynthia," he said, "do you want the account to stand in your own name?"

She thought a moment, then laughed and told him to put it in the name of G. G.'s mother. "But you must report to me how things go," she said.

Jarrocks called a clerk and gave him an order to sell something or other. In three minutes the clerk reported that "it" — just some letter of the alphabet — had been sold at such and such a price.

For another five minutes Jarrocks denied himself to all visitors. Then he called for another report on the stock which he had just caused to be sold. It was selling "off a half."

"Well, Cynthia," said Jarrocks, "you're fifty dollars richer than when you came. Now I've got to tell you to go. I'll look out for your interests as if they were my own."

And Jarrocks, looking rather stupid and bored, conducted Cynthia through his outer offices and put her into an elevator "going down." Her face vanished and his heart continued to mumble and grumble, just the way a tooth does when it is getting ready to ache.

Cynthia had entered Wall Street at an auspicious moment. Stocks were at that high level from which they presently tumbled to the panic quotations of nineteen-seven. And Jarrocks, whom the unsuccessful thought so very stupid, had made a very shrewd guess as to what was going to happen.

Two weeks later he wrote Cynthia that if she could use two or three thousand dollars she could have them, without troubling her balance very perceptibly.

"I thought you had a chance," he wrote. "I'm beginning to think it's a sure thing! Keep a stiff upper lip and first thing you know you'll have the laugh on mamma and papa. Give 'em my best regards."

VI

If it is wicked to gamble Cynthia was wicked. If it is wicked to lie Cynthia was wicked. If the money that comes out of Wall Street belonged originally to widows and orphans, why, that is the kind of money which she amassed for her own selfish purposes. Worst of all, on learning from Jarrocks that the Rainbow's Foot — where the pot of gold is — was almost in sight, this bad, wicked girl's sensations were those of unmixed triumph and delight!

The panic of nineteen-seven is history now. Plenty of people who lost their money during those exciting months can explain to you how any fool, with the least luck, could have made buckets of it instead.

As a snowball rolling down a hill of damp snow swells to gigantic proportions, so Cynthia's five hundred dollars descended the long slopes of nineteen-seven, doubling itself at almost every turn. And when, at last, values had so shrunk that it looked to Jarrocks as if they could not shrink any more, he told her that her account — which stood in the name of G. G.'s mother — was worth nearly four hundred thousand dollars. "And I think," he said, "that, if you now buy stocks outright and hold them as investments, your money will double again."

So they put their heads together and Cynthia bought some Union Pacific at par and some Steel Common in the careless twenties, and other standard securities that were begging, almost with tears in their eyes, to be bought and cared for by somebody. She had the certificates of what she bought made out in the name of G. G.'s mother. And she went up-town and found G. G.'s mother alone, and said:

"Oh, my dear! If anybody ever finds out *you* will catch it!"

G. G.'s mother knew there was a joke of some kind preparing at her expense, but she couldn't help looking a little puzzled and anxious.

"It's bad enough to do what you have done," continued Cynthia; "but on top of it to be going to lie up and down — that does seem a little too awful!"

"What are you going to tell me?" cried G. G.'s mother. "I know you've got some good news up your sleeve!"

"Gambler!" cried Cynthia — "cold-blooded, reckless Wall

Street speculator!" And the laughter that was pent up in her face burst its bonds, accompanied by hugs and kisses.

"Now listen!" said Cynthia, as soon as she could. "On such and such a day, you took five hundred dollars to a Wall Street broker named Jarrocks Bell — you thought that conditions were right for turning into a Bear. You went short of the market. You kept it up for weeks and months. Do you know what you did? You pyramided on the way down!"

"Mercy!" exclaimed G. G.'s mother, her eyes shining with wonder and excitement.

"First thing you knew," continued Cynthia, "you were worth four hundred thousand dollars!"

G. G.'s mother gave a little scream, as if she had seen a mouse.

"And you invested it," went on Cynthia, relenting, "so that now you stand to double your capital; and your annual income is between thirty and forty thousand dollars!"

After this Cynthia really did some explaining, until G. G.'s mother really understood what had really happened. It must be recorded that, at first, she was completely flabbergasted.

"And you've gone and put it in my name!" she said. "But why?"

"Don't you see," said Cynthia, "that if I came offering money to G. G. and G. G.'s father they wouldn't even sniff at it? But if you've got it — why, they've just got to share with you. Isn't that so?"

"Y-e-e-s," admitted G. G.'s mother; "but, my dear, I can't take it. Even if I could, they would want to know where I'd gotten it and I'd have nothing to say."

"Not if you're the one woman in a million that I think you are," said Cynthia. "Tell me, isn't your husband at his wit's end to think how to meet the bills for his illness and all and all? And wouldn't you raise your finger to bring all his miserable worries to an end? Just look at the matter from a business point of view! You must tell your husband and G. G. that what has really happened to me happened to you; that you were desperate; that you took the five hundred dollars to speculate with, and that this is the result."

"But that wouldn't be true," said G. G.'s mother.

"For mercy's sake," said Cynthia, "what has the truth got to do with it! This isn't a matter of religion or martyrdom; it's a matter of business! How to put an end to my husband's troubles and to enable my son to marry the girl he loves? — that's your problem; and the solution is — lie! Whom can the money come from if not from you? Not from me certainly. You must lie! You'd better begin in the dark, where your husband can't see your face — because I'm afraid you don't know how very well. But after a time it will get easy; and when you've told him the story two or three times — with details — you'll end by believing it yourself. . . . And, of course," she added, "you must make over half of the securities to G. G., so that he will have enough money to support a wife."

For two hours Cynthia wrestled with G. G.'s mother's conscience; but, when at last the struggling creature was thrown, the two women literally took it by the hair and dragged it around the room and beat it until it was deaf, dumb, and blind.

And when G. G.'s father came home G. G.'s mother met him in the hall that was darkish, and hid her face against his — and lied to him! And as she lied the years began to fall from the shoulders of G. G.'s father — to the number of ten.

VII

Cynthia was also met in a front hall — but by her father.

"I've been looking for you, Cynthia," he said gravely. "I want to talk to you and get your advice — no; the library is full of smoke — come in here."

He led her into the drawing-room, which neither of them could remember ever having sat in before.

"I've been talking with a young gentleman," said her father without further preliminaries, "who made himself immensely interesting to me. To begin with, I never saw a handsomer, more engaging specimen of young manhood; and, in the second place, he is the author of some stories that I have enjoyed in the past year more than any one's except O. Henry's. He doesn't write over his own name — but that's neither here nor there.

"He came to me for advice. Why he selected me, a total stranger, will appear presently. His family isn't well off; and, though he expects to succeed in literature — and there's no doubt of it in my mind — he feels that he ought to give it up and go into something in which the financial prospects are brighter. I suggested a rich wife, but that seemed to hurt his feelings. He said it would be bad enough to marry a girl that had more than he had; but to marry a rich girl, when he had only the few hundreds a year that he can make writing stories, was an intolerable thought. And that's all the more creditable to him because, from what I can gather, he is desperately in love — and the girl is potentially rich."

"But," said Cynthia, "what have I to do with all this?"

Her father laughed. "This young fellow didn't come to me of his own accord. I sent for him. And I must tell you that, contrary to my expectations, I was charmed with him. If I had had a son I should wish him to be just like this youngster."

Cynthia was very much puzzled.

"He writes stories?" she said.

"Bully stories! But he takes so much pains that his output is small."

"Well," said she, "what did you tell him?"

"I told him to wait."

"That's conservative advice."

"As a small boy," said her father, "he was very delicate; but now he's as sound as a bell and he looks as strong as an elk."

Cynthia rose to her feet, trembling slightly.

"What was the matter with him — when he was delicate?"

"Consumption."

She became as it were taller — and vivid with beauty.

"Where is he?"

"In the library."

Cynthia put her hands on her father's shoulders.

"It's all right," she said; "his family has come into quite a lot of money. He doesn't know it yet. They're going to give him enough to marry on. You still think he ought to marry — don't you?"

They kissed.

Cynthia flew out of the room, across the hall, and into the library.

They kissed!

THE TRAP

The animals went in two by two.

Hurrah! Hurrah!

Given Bower for a last name, the boys are bound to call you "Right" or "Left." They called me "Right" because I usually held it, one way or another. I was shot with luck. No matter what happened, it always worked out to my advantage. All inside of six months, for instance, the mate fell overboard and I got his job; the skipper got drunk after weathering a cyclone and ran the old *Boldero* aground in "lily-pad" weather — and I got his. Then the owner called me in and said: "Captain Bower, what do you know about Noah's Ark?" And I said: "Only that 'the animals went in two by two. Hurrah! Hurrah!'" And the owner said: "But how did he feed 'em — specially the meat-eaters?" And I said: "He got hold of a Hindu who had his arm torn off by a black panther and who now looks after the same at the Calcutta Zoo — and he put it up to him."

"The Bible doesn't say so," said the owner.

"Everything the Bible says is true," said I. "But there're heaps of true sayings, you know, that aren't in it at all."

"Well," says the owner, "you slip out to yon Zoo and you put it up to yon one-armed Hindu that a white Noah named Bower has been ordered to carry pairs of all the Indian fauna from Singapore to Sydney; and you tell him to shake his black panther and 'come along with.'"

"What will you pay?" I asked.

The owner winked his eye. "What will I promise?" said he. "I leave that to you."

But I wasn't bluffed. The owner always talked pagan and practised Christian; loved his little joke. They called him "Bond" Hadley on the water-front to remind themselves that his word was just as good.

I settled with Yir Massir in a long confab back of the snake-house, and that night Hadley blew me to Ivy Green's benefit at the opera-house.

Poor little girl! There weren't fifty in the audience. She couldn't act. I mean she couldn't draw. The whole company was on the bum and stone-broke. They'd scraped out of Australia and the Sandwich Islands, but it looked as if they'd stay in Calcutta, doing good works, such as mending roads for the public, to the end of time.

"Ivy Green is a pretty name for a girl," said the owner.

"And Ivy Green is a pretty girl," I said; "and I'll bet my horned soul she's a good girl."

To tell the truth, I was taken with her something terrible at first sight. I'd often seen women that I wanted, but she was the first girl — and the last. It's a different sort of wanting, that. It's the good in you that wants — instead of the bad.

Her little face was like the pansies that used to grow in mother's dooryard; and a dooryard is the place for pansies, not a stage. When her act was over the fifty present did their best; but I knew, when she'd finished bobbing little curtsies and smiling her pretty smile, she'd slip off to her dressing-room and cry like a baby. I couldn't stand it. There were other acts to come, but I couldn't wait.

"If Ivy Green is a pretty name for a girl, Ivy Bower is a prettier name for a woman," I said. "I'm going behind."

He looked up, angry. Then he saw that I didn't mean any harm and he looked down. He said nothing. I got behind by having the pull on certain ropes in that opera-house, and I asked a comedian with a face like a walrus which was Miss Green's dressing-room.

"Friend of hers?" he says.

"Yes," says I, "a friend."

He showed me which door and I knocked. Her voice was full of worry and tears.

"Who's there?" she said.

"A friend," said I.

"Pass, friend," said she.

And I took it to mean "Come in," but it didn't. Still, she wasn't so dishabilled as to matter. She was crying and rubbing off the last of her paint.

"Miss Green," I said, "you've made me feel so mean and miserable that I had to come and tell you. My name is Bower. The boys call me 'Right' Bower, meaning that I'm lucky and straight. It was lucky for me that I came to your benefit, and I hope to God that it will be lucky for you."

"Yes?" she says — none too warm.

"As for you, Miss Green," I said, "you're up against it, aren't you? The manager's broke. You don't know when you've touched any salary. There's been no balm in your benefit. What are you going to do?"

This time she looked me over before she spoke.

"I don't know," she said.

"I don't have to ask," said I, blushing red, "if you're a good girl. It's just naturally obvious. I guess that's what put me up to butting in. I want to help. Will you answer three questions?"

She nodded.

"Where," said I, "will you get breakfast tomorrow? — lunch tomorrow? — and dinner tomorrow?"

"We disband tonight," she said, "and I don't know."

"I suppose you know," said I, "what happens to most white girls who get stranded in Indian cities?"

"I know," she said, "that people get up against it so hard that they oughtn't to be blamed for anything they do."

"They aren't," I said, "by — Christians; but it's ugly just the same. Now —"

"And you," she said, flaring up, "think that, as long as it's got to be, it might as well be you! Is that your song and dance, Mr. Smarty?"

I shook my head and smiled.

"Don't be a little goat!" I said; and that seemed to make her take to me and trust me.

"What do you want me to do?" she asked.

"I'll tell you," I said; and I found that it wasn't easy. "First place," I said, "I've got some money saved up. That will keep you on Easy Street till I get back from Sydney. If by that time nothing's turned up that you want of your own free heart and will, I'll ask you to pay me back by — by changing your name."

She didn't quite follow.

"That," said I, "gives you a chance to look around — gives you one small chance in a million to light on some man you can care for and who'll care for you and take care of you. Failing that, it would be fair enough for you to take me, failing a better. See?"

"You mean," she said, "that if things don't straighten out, it would be better for me to become Mrs. Bower than walk the streets? Is that it?"

I nodded.

"But I don't see your point of view," she cried. "Just because you're sorry for a girl don't mean you want to make her your wife."

"It isn't sorrowing," I said. "It's wanting. It's the right kind of wanting. It's the wanting that would rather wait than hurt you; that would rather do without you than hurt you."

"And you'll trust me with all your savings and go away to Australia — and if I find some other man that I like better you'll let me off from marrying you? Is that it?"

"That's about it," I said.

"And suppose," says she, "that you don't come back, and nobody shows up, and the money goes?"

That was a new point of view.

"Well," said I, "we've got to take some chances in this world."

"We have," said she. "And now look here — I don't know how much of it's wanting and how much of it's fear — but if you'll take chances I will."

She turned as red as a beet and looked away.

"In words of two syllables," said I, "what do you mean?"

"I mean," she said — and she was still as red as a beet, but this time she looked me in my eyes without a flinch in hers — "that if you're dead sure you want me — are you? — if you're dead sure, why, I'll take chances on my wanting you. I believe every word you've said to me. Is that right?"

"Every word," I said. "That is right."

Then we looked at each other for a long time.

"What a lot we'll have to tell each other," she said, "before we're really acquainted. But you're sure? You're quite sure?"

"Sure that I want you? Yes," I said; "not sure that you ought not to wait and think me over."

"You've begun," she said, "with everything that's noble and generous. I could never look myself in the face again if I felt called upon to begin by being mean."

"Hadn't you better think it over?" I said. "Hadn't you?"

But she put her hands on my shoulders.

"If an angel with wings had come with gifts," she said, "would I have thought them over? And just because your wings don't show —"

"It isn't fair," I mumbled. "I give you a choice between the streets and me and you feel forced to choose me."

But she pulled my head down and gave me a quick, fierce kiss.

"There," said she — "was that forced? Did you force me to do that? No," she said; "you needn't think you're the only person in the world that wants another person. . . . If you go to Australia I don't wait here. I go too. If you sink by the way, I sink. And don't you go to thinking you've made me a one-sided bargain. . . . I can cook for you and mend for you and save for you. And if you're sick I can nurse you. And I can black your boots."

"I thought," said I, "that you were just a little girl that I wanted, but you turn out to be the whole world that I've got to have. Slip the rest of your canvas on and I'll hook it up for you. Then we'll find some one to marry us — 'nless you'd rather wait."

"Wait?" said she, turning her back and standing still, which most women haven't sense enough to do when a man's ten thumbs are trying to hook them up. "I've been waiting all my life for this — and you!"

"And I," said I, splitting a thumb-nail, "would go through an eternity of hell if I knew that this was at the end of it — and you!"

"What is your church?" she asked of a sudden.

"Same as yours," I said, "which is —"

"Does it matter," said she, "if God is in it? Do you pray?"

"No," said I; "do you?"

"Always," she said, "before I go to bed."

"Then I will," said I; "always — before we do."

"Sometimes," she said, "I've been shaken about God. Was to-night — before you came. But He's made good — hasn't He?"

"He has," I said. "And now you're hooked up. And I wish it was to do all over again. I loved doing it."

"Did you?" said she.

Her eyes were bright and brave like two stars. She slipped her hand through my arm and we marched out of the opera-house. Half a dozen young globe-trotters were at the stage-door waiting to take a chance on Miss Green as she came out, but none of them spoke. We headed for the nearest city directory and looked up a minister.

II

I had married April; she cried when she thought she wasn't good enough for me; she smiled like the sun when I swore she was.

I had married June; she was like an armful of roses.

We weren't two; we were one. What alloy does gold make mixed with brass? We were that alloy. I was the brass.

We travelled down to Singapore first-class, with one-armed Yir Massir to look after us — down the old Hoogli with the stubs of half-burned Hindus bobbing alongside, crows sitting on 'em and tearing off strips. We ran aground on all the regular old sand-bars that are never twice in the same place; and one dusk we saw tigers come out of the jungle to drink. We'd both travelled quite some, but you wouldn't have thought it. Ivy Bower and Right Bower had just run away from school for to see the world "so new and all."

Some honey-moons a man keeps finding out things about his wife that he don't like — little tricks of temper and temperature; but I kept finding out things about mine that I'd never even dared to hope for. I went pretty near crazy with love of her. At first she was a child that had had a wicked, cruel nightmare — and I'd happened to be about to comfort her when she waked and to soothe her. Then she got over her scare and began to play at matrimony, putting on little airs and dignities — just like a child playing grown-up. Then all of a sudden it came to her, that tremendous love that some women have for some of us dogs of men. It was big as a storm, but it wasn't too big for her. Nothing that's noble and generous was too big for her; nor was any way of showing her love too little. Any little mole-hill of thoughtfulness from me was changed — presto! — into a chain o' mountains; but she thought in mountains and made mole-hills of 'em.

We steamed into Singapore and I showed her the old *Boldero*, that was to be our home, laid against the Copra Wharf, waiting to be turned into an ark. The animals weren't all collected and we had a day or two to chase about and enjoy ourselves; but she wasn't for expensive pleasures.

"Wait," she said, "till you're a little tired of me; but now, when we're happy just to be together walking in the dust, what's the use of disbursing?"

"If we save till I'm tired of you," says I, "we'll be rich."

"Rich it is, then," said she, "for those who will need it more."

"But," says I, "the dictionary says that a skunk is a man that economizes on his honey-moon."

"If you're bound to blow yourself," says she, "let's trot down to the Hongkong-Shanghai Bank and buy some shares in something."

"But," says I, "you have no engagement ring."

"And I'm not engaged," says she. "I'm a married woman."

"You're a married child."

"My husband's arm around my waist is my ring," says she; "his heart is my jewel."

Even if it had been broad daylight and people looking, I'd have put her ring on her at that. But it was dark, in a park of trees and benches — just like Central Park.

"With this ring," says I, "I thee guard from all evil."

"But there is no evil," said she. "The world's all new; it's been given a fresh start. There's no evil. The apple's back on the tree of knowledge. Eden's come back — and it's spring in Eden."

"And among other items," says I, "that we've invoiced for Sydney is a python thirty feet long."

"Look!" says she.

A girl sat against one of the stems of a banyan, and a Tommy lay on his back with his head in her lap. She was playing with his hair. You could just see them for the dark.

"'And they lived on the square like a true married pair,'" says I.

"Can't people be naughty and good?" says she.

"No," says I; "good and naughty only."

"Suppose," says she, "you and I felt about each other the way we do, but you were married to a rich widow in Lisbon and I was married to a wicked old Jew in Malta — would that make you Satan and me Jezebel?"

"No," says I; "only me. Nothing could change you." She thought a little.

"No," says she; "I don't think anything could. But there isn't any wicked old Jew. You know that."

"And you know about the rich widow?"

"What about her?" This said sharp, with a tug at my arm to unwrap it.

"She was born in Singapore," said I, "of a silly goose by an idle thought. And two minutes later she died."

"There's nothing that can ever hurt us — is there? — nothing that's happened and gone before?"

Man that is born of woman ought not to have that question put up to him; but she didn't let me answer.

"Because, if there is," she said, "it's lucky I'm here to look after us."

"Could I do anything that you wouldn't forgive?"

"If you turned away from me," she said, "I'd die — but I'd forgive."

Next daylight she was leaning on the rail of the *Boldero* watching the animals come over the side and laughing to see them turn their heads to listen to what old Yir Massir said to them in Hindustani. He spoke words of comfort, telling them not to be afraid; and they listened. Even Bahut, the big elephant, as the slings tightened and he swung dizzily heavenward, cocked his moth-eaten ears to listen and refrained from whimpering, though the pit of his stomach was cold with fear; and he worked his toes when there was nothing under them but water.

"The elephant is the strongest of all things," I said, "and the most gentle."

Her little fingers pressed my arm, which was like marble in those days.

"No," said she — "the man!"

III

That voyage was good, so far as it went, but there's no use talking about it, because what came afterward was better. We'd no sooner backed off the Copra Wharf and headed down the straits, leaving a trail of smoke and tiger smell, than Ivy went to house-keeping on the *Boldero*. There are great house-keepers, just as there are great poets and actors. It takes genius; that's all. And Ivy had that kind of genius. Yir Massir had a Hindu saying that fitted her like a glove. He looked in upon her work of preparing and systematizing for the cramped weeks at sea and said: "The little memsahib is a born woman."

That's just what she is. There are born idiots and born leaders. Some are born male and some female; but a born woman is the rarest thing in the world, the most useful and the most precious. She had never kept house, but there was nothing for her to learn. She worked things so that whenever I could come off duty she was at leisure to give all her care and thought to me.

There was never a millionaire who had more speckless white suits than I had, though it's a matter almost of routine for officers to go dirty on anything but the swell liners. Holes in socks grew together under her fingers, so that you had to look close to see where they'd been. She even kept a kind of dwarf hibiscus, with bright red flowers, alive and flourishing in the thick salt air; and she was always slipping into the galley to give a new, tasty turn to the old sea-standbys.

The crew, engineer, and stokers were all Chinks. Hadley always put his trust in them and they come cheap. We had forty coolies who berthed forward, going out on contract to work on a new government dry-dock at Paiulu. I don't mind a Chink myself, so long as he keeps his habits to himself and doesn't over-smoke; but they're not sociable. Except for Yir Massir and myself, there was no one aboard for Ivy to talk to. Yir Massir's duty kept him busy with the health of the collection for the Sydney Zoo, and Ivy found time to help, to advise, and to learn. They made as much fuss between them over the beasts as if they had been babies; and the donkey-engine was busy most of the day hoisting cages to the main-deck and lowering them again, so that the beasts could have a better look at the sea and a bit of sun and fresh air. As it was, a good many of the beasts and all the birds roomed on the main-deck all the time. Sometimes Yir Massir would take out a chetah — a nasty, snarling, pin-headed piece of long-legged malice — and walk him up and down on a dog-chain, same as a woman walks her King Charlie. He gave the monkeys all the liberty they could use and abuse; it was good sport to see them chase themselves and each other over the masts and upper-works.

The most you can say of going out with a big tonnage of beasts is that, if you're healthy and have no nerves, you can just stand it. Sometimes they'll all howl together for five or six hours at a time; sometimes they'll all be logy and still as death, except one tiger, who can't make his wants understood and who'll whine and rumble about them all round the clock. I don't know which is worse, the chorus or the solo. And then, of course, the smell side to the situation isn't a matter for print. If I say that we had twenty hogsheads of disinfectants and deodorizers along it's all you need know. Anyhow, according to Yir Massir, it was the smell that killed big Bahut's mate. And she'd been brought up in an Indian village and ought to have been used to all the smells, from A to Z.

One elephant more or less doesn't matter to me, especially when it's insured, but Yir Massir's grief and self-reproach were appalling; and Ivy felt badly too. It was as much for her sake as Yir Massir's that I read a part of the burial service out of the prayer-book and committed the body of "this our sister" to the deep. It may have been sacrilegious, but I don't care. It comforted Ivy some and Yir Massir a heap. And it did this to me, that I can't look at a beast now without thinking that — well, that there's not such an awful lot of difference between two legs and four, and that maybe God put Himself out just as much to make one as the other.

We swung her overside by heavy tackle. What with the roll of the ship and the fact that she swung feet down, she looked alive; and the funeral looked more like a drowning than a burial.

We had no weights to sink her; and when I gave the word to cut loose she made a splash like a small tidal wave and then floated.

We could see her for an hour, like a bit of a slate-colored island with white gulls sitting on it.

And that night Yir Massir waited on us looking like some old crazy loon out of the Bible. He'd made himself a prickly shirt of sackcloth and had smeared his black head and brown face with gray ashes. Big Bahut whimpered all night and trumpeted as if his heart were broken.

IV

I've often noticed that when things happen it's in bunches. The tenth day south of the line we had a look at almost all the sea-events that are made into woodcuts for the high-school geographies. For days we'd seen nothing except sapphire-blue sea, big swells rolling under a satin finish without breaking through, and a baby-blue sky. On the morning of the tenth the sea was streaked with broad, oily bands, like State roads, and near and far were whales travelling south at about ten knots an hour, as if they had a long way to go.

We saw heaps of porpoises and heaps of flying-fish; some birds; unhewn timber — a nasty lot of it — and big floats of sea-weed. We saw a whale being pounded to death by a killer; and in the afternoon as perfect an example of a brand-new coral island as was ever seen. It looked like a ring of white snow floating on the water, and inside the ring was a careened two-master — just the ribs and stumps left. There was a water-spout miles off to port, and there was a kind of electric jump and thrill to the baked air that made these things seem important, like omens in ancient times. Besides, the beasts, from Bahut the elephant to little Assam the mongoose, put in the whole day at practising the noises of complaint and uneasiness. Then, directly it was dark, we slipped into a "white sea." That's a rare sight and it has never been very well explained. The water looks as though it had been mixed with a quantity of milk, but when you dip it up it's just water.

About midnight we ran out of this and Ivy and I turned in. The sky was clear as a bell and even the beasts were quiet. I hadn't been asleep ten minutes and Ivy not at all, when all at once hell broke loose. There was a bump that nearly drove my head through a bulk-head; though only half awake I could feel to the cold marrow of my bones that the old *Boldero* was down by the head. The beasts knew it and the Chinks. Never since Babel was there such pandemonium on earth or sea. By a struck match I saw Ivy running out of the cabin and slipping on her bath-wrapper as she went. I called to her, but she didn't answer. I didn't want to think of anything but Ivy, but I had to let her go and think of the ship.

There wasn't much use in thinking. The old *Boldero* was set-tling by the head and the pumps couldn't hold up the inflood. In fif-teen minutes I knew that it was all up with us — or all down, rather — and I ordered the boats over and began to run about like a maniac, looking for Ivy and calling to her. And why do you suppose I couldn't find her? She was hiding — hiding from me!

She'd heard of captains of sinking ships sending off their wives and children and sweethearts and staying behind to drown out of a mistaken notion of duty. She'd got it into her head that I was that kind of captain and she'd hid so that she couldn't be sent away; but it was all my fault really. If I'd hurried her on deck the minute I did find her we'd have been in time to leave with the boats. But I stopped for explanations and to give her a bit of a lecture; so when we got on deck there were the boats swarming with Chinks slipping off to windward — and there at our feet was Yir Massir, lying in his own blood and brains, a wicked, long knife in his hand and the thread outpiece of a Chink's pigtail between his teeth.

I like to think that he'd tried to make them wait for us, but I don't know. Anyhow, there we were, alone on a sinking deck and all through with earthly affairs as I reckoned it. But Ivy reckoned dif-ferently.

"Why are they rowing in that direction?" she says. "They won't get anywhere."

"Why not?" says I.

She jerked her thumb to leeward.

"Don't you feel that it's over there? — the land?" she says. "Just over there."

"Why, no, bless you!" says I. "I don't have any feeling about it. . . . Now then, we've got to hustle around and find something that will float us. We want to get out of this before the old *Boldero* goes and sucks us down after."

"There's the life-raft," says she; "they left that."

"Yes," says I; "if we can get it overboard. It weighs a ton. You make up a bundle of food on the jump, Ivy, and I'll try to rig a tackle."

When the raft was floating quietly alongside I felt better. It looked then as if we were to have a little more run for our money.

We worked like a couple of furies loading on food and water, Ivy lowering and I lashing fast.

"There," says I at last; "she won't take any more. Come along. I can help you down better from here."

"We've got to let the beasts loose," says she.

"Why?" says I.

"Oh, just to give 'em a chance," she says.

So I climbs back to where she was standing.

"It's rot!" I says. "But if you say so —"

"There's loads of time," says she — "we're not settling so fast. Besides, even if I'm wrong about the land, they'll know. They'll show us which way to go. Big Bahut, he knows."

"It don't matter," I says. "We can't work the raft any way but to leeward — not one man can't."

"If the beasts go the other way," says she, "one man must try and one woman."

"Oh, we'll try," says I, "right enough. We'll try."

The first beast we loosed was the python. Ivy did the loosing and I stood by with a big rifle to guard against trouble; but, bless you, there was no need. One and all, the beasts knew the old *Boldero* was doomed, and one and all they cried and begged and made eyes and signs to be turned loose. As for knowing where the nearest land was — well, if you'd seen the python, when he came to the surface, make a couple of loopy turns to get his bearings and his wriggles in order, and then hike off to leeward in a bee-line — you'd have believed that he — well, that he knew what he was talking about.

And the beasts, one and all, big and little, the minute they were loosed, wanted to get overboard — even the cats; and off they went to leeward in the first flush of dawn, horned heads, cat heads, pig heads — the darnedest game of follow-my-leader that ever the skies looked down on. And the birds, white and colored, streaked out over the beasts. There was a kind of wonder to it all that eased the pinch of fear. Ivy clapped her hands and jumped up and down like a child when it sees the grand entry in Buffalo Bill's show for the first time — or the last, for that matter.

There was some talk of taking a tow-line from around Bahut's neck to the raft; but the morning breeze was freshening and with a sail rigged the raft would swim pretty fast herself. Anyway, we couldn't fix it to get big Bahut overboard. The best we could do was to turn him loose, open all the hatches, and trust to his finding a way out when the *Boldero* settled.

He did, bless him! We weren't two hundred yards clear when the *Boldero* gave a kind of shudder and went down by the bows, Bahut yelling bloody murder. Then, just when we'd given him up for lost, he shot up from the depths, half-way out of water. After blowing his nose and getting his bearings he came after the raft like a good old tugboat.

We stood up, Ivy and I did, and cheered him as he caught up with us and foamed by.

The worst kind of remembering is remembering what you've forgotten. I got redder and redder. It didn't seem as if I could tell Ivy; but I did. First I says, hopeful:

"Have you forgotten anything?"

She shakes her head.

"I have," says I. "I've left my rifle, but I've got plenty of cartridges. I've got a box of candles, but I've forgotten to bring matches. A nice, thoughtful husband you've got!"

V

The beasts knew.

There was land just around the first turn of the world — land that had what might be hills when you got to 'em and that was pale gray against the sun, with all the upper-works gilded; but it wasn't big land. You could see the north and south limits; and the trees on the hills could probably see the ocean to the east.

They were funny trees, those; and others just like them had come down to the cove to meet us when we landed. They were a kind of pine and the branches grew in layers, with long spaces between. Since then I've seen trees just like them, but very little, in florists' windows; only the florists' trees have broad scarlet sashes round their waists, by way of decoration, maybe, or out of deference to Anthony Comstock.

The cove had been worked out by a brook that came loafing down a turfy valley, with trees single and in spinneys, for all the world like an English park; and at the upper end of the valley, cutting the island in half lengthwise, as we learned later, the little wooded hills rolled north and south, and low spurs ran out from them, so as to make the valley a valley instead of a plain.

There were flocks of goats in the valley, which was what made the grass so turfy, I suppose; and our own deer and antelopes were browsing near them, friendly as you please. Near at hand big Bahut, who had been the last but us to land, was quietly munching the top of a broad-leafed tree that he'd pulled down; but the cats and riff-raff had melted into the landscape. So had the birds, except a pair of jungle-fowl, who'd found seed near the cove and were picking it up as fast as they could and putting it away.

"Well," says I, "it's an island, sure, Ivy. The first thing to do is to find out who lives on it, owns it, and dispenses its hospitality, and make up to them."

But she shook her head and said seriously:

"I've a feeling, Right," she says — "a kind of hunch — that there's nobody on it but us."

I laughed at her then, but half a day's tramping proved that she was right. I tell you women have ways of knowing things that we men haven't. The fact is, civilization slides off 'em like water off a duck; and at heart and by instinct they are people of the cave-dwelling period — on cut-and-dried terms with ghosts and spirits, all the unseen sources of knowledge that man has grown away from.

I had sure proofs of this in the way Ivy took to the cave we found in a bunch of volcano rock that lifted sheer out of the cove and had bright flowers smiling out of all its pockets. No society lady ever entered her brand-new marble house at Newport with half the happiness.

Ivy was crazy about the cave and never tired of pointing out its advantages. She went to house-keeping without any of the utensils, as keen and eager as she'd gone to it on the poor old *Boldero*, where at least there were pots and pans and pepper.

We had grub to last a few weeks, a pair of blankets, the clothes we stood in, and an axe. I had, besides, a heavy clasp-knife, a watch, and seven sovereigns. The first thing Ivy insisted on was a change of clothes.

"These we stand in," says she, "are the only presentable things we've got, and Heaven only knows how long they've got to last us for best."

"We could throw modesty to the winds," I suggested.

"Of course you can do as you please," she said. "I don't care one way or the other about the modesty; but I've got a skin that looks on the sun with distinct aversion, and I don't propose to go through a course of yellow blisters — and then turn black."

"I've seen islanders weave cloth out of palm fibre — most any kind," I said. "It's clumsy and airy; but if you think it would do —"

"It sounds scratchy."

"It is, but it's good for the circulation."

Well, we made a kind of cloth and cut it into shapes, and knotted the shapes together with more fibre; then we folded up our best and only Sunday-go-to-meeting suits and put the fibre things on; and then we went down to the cove to look at ourselves in the water. And Ivy laughed.

"We're not clothed," she said; "we're thatched; and yet — and yet — it's accident, of course, but this skirt has got a certain hang that —"

"Whatever that skirt's got," I said, "these pants haven't; but if you're happy I am."

Well, there's worse situations than desert-islanding it with the one woman in the world. I even know one man who claims he was cast away with a perfect stranger that he hated the sight of at first — a terribly small-minded, conventional woman — and still he had the time of his life. They got to like each other over a mutual taste for cribbage, which they played for sea-shells, yellow with a pink edge, until the woman went broke and got heavily in debt to the man. He was nice about it and let her off. He says the affair must have ended in matrimony, only she took a month to think it over; during that month they were picked up and carried to Honolulu; then they quarrelled and never saw each other again.

"Ivy," said I one day, "we'll be picked up by a passing steamer some day, of course, but meanwhile I'd rather be here with you than any place I can name."

"It's Eden," she said, "and I'd like to live like this always. But —"

"But what?"

"But people grow old," she said, "and one dies before another. That's what's wrong with Eden."

I laughed at her.

"Old! You and I? We'll cross that bridge when we come to it, Ivy Bower."

"Right Bower," says she, "you don't understand —"

"How not understand?"

"You don't understand that Right Bower and Ivy Bower aren't the only people on this island."

She didn't turn a fiery red and bolt — the way young wives do in stories. She looked at me with steady, brave, considering eyes.

"Don't worry, dear," she says after a time; "everything will be all right. I know it will."

"I know it too." I lied.

Know it? I was cold with fright.

"Don't be afraid," said she. "And — and meanwhile there's dinner to be got ready — and you can have a go at your firesticks."

It was my ambition to get fire by friction. Now and then I got the sticks to smoke and I hoped that practice would give me the little extra speed and cunning that makes for flame. I'd always been pretty good at games, if a little slow to learn.

VI

You'd think anxiety about Ivy'd have been the hardest thing to bear in the life we were living; and so it would have been if she'd showed any anxiety about herself. Not she. You might have thought she was looking forward to a Christmas-box from home. If she was ever scared it was when I wasn't looking. No — it was the beasts that made us anxious.

At first we'd go for long walks and make explorations up and down the island. The beasts hid from us according to the wild nature that's in them. You could only tell from fresh tracks in damp places that they hadn't utterly disappeared. Now and then we saw deer and antelopes far off; and at night, of course, there was always something doing in the way of a chorus. Beasts that gave our end of the island the go-by daytimes paid us visits nights and sat under the windows, you may say, and sang their songs.

It seemed natural after a time to be cooped up in a big green prison with a lot of loose wild things that could bite and tear you to pieces if they thought of it. We were hard to scare. What scared me first was this: When we got to the island it was alive with goats. Well, these just casually disappeared. Then, one morning, bright and early, I came on the big python in the act of swallowing a baby antelope. It gave me a horrid start and set me thinking. How long could the island support a menagerie? What would the meat-eaters do when they'd killed off all the easy meat — finished up the deer and antelopes and all? Would they fight it out among themselves — big tiger eat little tiger — until only the fittest one survived? And what would that fittest one do if he got good and hungry and began to think that I'd make a square meal for him — or Ivy?

I reached two conclusions — and the cave about the same time. First, I wouldn't tell Ivy I was scared. Second, I'd make fire by friction or otherwise — or bust. Once I got fire, I'd never let it go out. I set to work with the firesticks right off, and Ivy came and stood by and looked on.

"Never saw you put so much elbow-grease into anything," she said. "What's the matter with you, anyway?"

"It's a game," I grunted, "and these two fellows will have me beat if I don't look lively."

"Right Bower," she says then, slow and deliberate, "I can see you're upside down about something. Tell Ivy."

"Look," says I — "smoke! I never got it so quick before." I spun the pointed stick between the palms of my hands harder than ever and gloated over the wisp of smoke that came from where it was boring into the flat stick.

"Make a bow," says Ivy. "Loop the bowstring round the hand-piece and you'll get more friction with less work."

"By gorry!" says I; "you're right. I remember a picture in a geography — 'Native Drilling a Conch Shell.' Fool that I am to forget!"

"Guess you and I learned out of the same geography," said Ivy.

"Only I didn't learn," said I. "I'm off to cut something tough to make the bow."

"Don't go far," she says.

"Why not?" said I — the sporty way a man does when he pretends that he's going to take a night off with the boys and play poker.

"Because," she says smiling, "I'm afraid the beasts will get me while you're gone."

"Rats!" says I.

"Tigers!" says she. "Oh, Right, you unplumbable old idiot! Do you think you can come into this cave and hide anything from me under that transparent face of yours? The minute you came in and hemmed and hawed, and said as you had nothing to do you guessed you'd have a go with the firesticks — I knew. What scared you?"

I surrendered and told her.

"... And then," she said, "you think maybe they'll hurt — us?" I nodded.

"Why, it's war," she said. "I've read enough about war to know that there are two safe rules to follow. First, declare war yourself while the other fellow's thinking about it; and then strike him before he's even heard that you have declared it. That sounds mixed, but it's easy enough. We'll declare war on the dangerous beasts while I'm still in the months of hop, skip, and jump."

"A certain woman," said I, "wouldn't let the beasts go down in the old *Boldero*, as would have been beneficial for all parties."

"This is different," she said. "This island's got to be a safe place for a little child to play in or Ivy Bower's got to be told the reason why."

"You're dead right, Ivy dear," I says, "and always was. But how? I'm cursed if I know how to kill a tiger without a rifle. . . . Let's get fire first and put the citadel in a state of siege. Then we'll try our hand at traps, snares, and pitfalls. I'm strong, but I'm cursed if I want to fall on a tiger with nothing in my hands but a knife or an axe."

"All I care about," said Ivy, "is to get everything settled, so that when the time comes we can be comfortable and plenty domestic."

She sat in the mouth of the cave and looked over the smooth cove to the rolling ocean beyond; and she had the expression of a little girl playing at being married with a little boy friend in the playhouse that her father had just given her for her birthday.

I got a piece of springy wood to make a bow with, and sat by her shaping it with my knife. That night we got fire. Ivy caught some fish in the cove and we cooked them; and — thanks, O Lord! — how good they were! We sat up very late comparing impressions, each saying how each felt when the smoke began to show sparks and when the tinder pieces finally caught, and how each had felt when the broiled smell of the fish had begun to go abroad in the land. We told each other of all the good things we had eaten in our day, but how this surpassed them all. And later we told each other all our favorite names — boy names in case it should be a boy and girl names in case it shouldn't.

Then, suddenly, something being hunted by something tore by in the dark — not very far off. The sweat came off me in buckets, and I heaped wood on the fire and flung burning brands into the night, this way and that, as far as I could fling them. Ivy said I was like Jupiter trying to hurl thunder-bolts, after the invention of Christianity, and not rightly understanding why they wouldn't explode any more.

VII

The pines of the island were full of pitch and a branch would burn torch-like for a long time. I kept a bundle of such handy, the short ends sharpened so's you could stick 'em round wherever the ground was soft enough and have an effect of altar candles in a draughty church. If there was occasion to leave the cave at night I'd carry one of the torches and feel as safe as if it had been an elephant rifle.

We made a kind of a dooryard in front of the cave's mouth, with a stockade that we borrowed from Robinson Crusoe, driving pointed stakes close-serried and hoping they'd take root and sprout; but they didn't. Between times I made finger-drawings in the sand of plans for tiger traps and pitfalls. I couldn't dig pits, but I knew of two that might have been made to my order, a volcano having taken the contract. They were deep as wells, sheer-sided; anything that fell in would stay in. I made a wattle-work of branches and palm fibre to serve as lids for these nature-made tiger jars. The idea was to toss dead fish out to the middle of the lids for bait; then for one of the big cats to smell the fish, step out to get it, and fall through. Once in, it would be child's work to stone him to death.

Another trap I made was more complicated and was a scheme to drop trees heavy enough to break a camel's back or whatever touched the trigger that kept them from falling. It was the devil's own job to make that trap. First place, I couldn't cut a tree big enough and lift it to a strategic position; so I had to fell trees in such a way that they'd be caught half-way to the ground by other trees. Then I'd have to clear away branches and roots so that when the trees did fall the rest of the way it would be clean, plumb, and sudden. It was a wonderful trap when it was finished and it was the most dangerous work of art I ever saw. If you touched any of a dozen triggers you stood to have a whole grove of trees come banging down on top of you — same as if you went for a walk in the woods and a tornado came along and blew the woods down. If the big cats had known how frightfully dangerous that trap was they'd have jumped overboard and left the island by swimming. I made two other traps something like it — the best contractor in New York wouldn't have undertaken to build one just like it at any price — and then it came around to be the seventh day, so to speak; and, like the six-day bicycle rider, I rested.

"Days," is only a fashion of speaking. I was months getting my five death-traps into working order. I couldn't work steadily because there was heaps of cavework to do besides, fish to be caught, wood to be cut for the fire, and all; and then, dozens of times, I'd suddenly get scared about Ivy and go running back to the cave to see if she was all right. I might have known better; she was always all right and much better plucked than I was.

Well, sir, my traps wouldn't work. The fish rotted on the wattle-lids of the pitfalls, but the beasts wouldn't try for 'em. They were getting ravenous, too — ready to attack big Bahut even; but they wouldn't step out on those wattles and they wouldn't step under my balanced trees. They'd beat about the neighborhood of the danger and I've found many a padmark within six inches of the edge of things. I even baited with a live kid. It belonged to the Thibet goats and I had a hard time catching it; and after it had bleated all night and done its baby best to be tiger food I turned it loose and it ran off with its mammy. She, poor soul, had gone right into the trap to be with her baby and, owing to the direct intervention of Providence, hadn't sprung the thing.

The next fancy bait I tried was a chetah — dead. I found him just after his accident, not far from the cave. He was still warm; and he was flat — very flat, like a rug made of chetah skin. He had some shreds of elephant-hide tangled in his claws. It looked to me as if he'd gotten desperate with hunger and had pounced on big Bahut — pshaw! the story was in plain print: "Ouch!" says big Bahut. "A flea has bitten me. Here's where I play dead," and — rolls over. Result: one neat and very flat rug made out of chetah.

I showed the rug to Ivy and then carried it off to the woods and spread it in my first and fanciest trap. Then I allowed I'd have a look at the pitfalls, which I hadn't visited for a couple of days — and I was a fool to do it. I'd told Ivy where I was going to spread the chetah and that after that I'd come straight home. Well, the day seemed young and I thought if I hurried I could go home the roundabout way by the pitfalls in such good time that Ivy wouldn't know the difference. Well, sir, I came to the first pitfall — and, lo and behold! something had been and taken the bait and got away with it without so much as putting a foot through the wattling. I'd woven it too strong. So I thought I'd just weaken it up a little — it wouldn't take five minutes. I tried it with my foot — very gingerly. Yes, it was too strong — much too strong. I put more weight into that foot — and bang, smash, crash — bump! There I was at the bottom of the pit, with half the wattling on top of me.

The depth of that hole was full twenty-five feet; the sides were as smooth as bottle-glass; dusk was turning into dark. But these things weren't the worst of it. I'd told Ivy that I'd do one thing — and I'd gone and done another. I'd lied to her and I'd put her in for a time of anxiety, and then fright, that might kill her.

VIII

I wasted what little daylight was left trying to climb out, using nothing but hands and feet. And then I sat down and cursed myself for a triple-plated, copper-riveted, patent-applied-for fool.

Nothing would have been easier, given light, than to take the wattling that had fallen into the pit with me to pieces, build a pole — sort of a split-bamboo fishing-rod on a big scale — shin up and go home. But to turn that trick in the dark wasn't any fun. I did it though — twice. I made the first pole too light and it smashed when I was half-way up. A splinter jabbed into my thigh and drew blood. That complicated matters. The smell of the blood went out of the pit and travelled around the island like a sandwich man saying: "Fine supply of fresh meat about to come out of Right Bower's pet pitfall; second on the left."

When I'd shinned to the top of the second pole I built and crawled over the rim of the pit — there was a tiger sitting, waiting, very patient. I could just make him out in the starlight. He was mighty lean and looked like a hungry gutter-cat on a big scale. Some people are afraid to be alone in the dark. I'm not. Well, I just knelt there — I'd risen to my knees — and stared at him. And then I began to take in a long breath — I swelled and swelled with it. It's a wonder I didn't use up all the air on the island and create a vacuum — in which case the tiger would have blown up. I remember wondering what that big breath was going to do when it came out. I didn't know. I had no plan. I looked at the tiger and he looked at me and whined — like a spoiled spaniel asking for sugar. That was too much. I thought of Ivy, maybe needing me as she'd never needed any one before — and I looked at that stinking cat that meant to keep me from her. I made one jump at him — 'stead of him at me — and at the same time I let out the big breath I'd drawn in a screech that very likely was heard in Jericho.

The tiger just vanished like a Cheshire cat in a book I read once, and I was running through the night for home and Ivy. But the fire at the cave was dying, and Ivy was gone.

Well, of course she'd have gone to look for me. . . . It was then that I began to whimper and cry. I lit a pine-torch, flung some wood on the embers, and went out to look for her — whimpering all the time. I'd told her that I was going out to bait a certain trap and would then come straight home. So of course she'd have gone straight to that trap — and it was there I found her.

The torch showed her where she sat, right near the dead chetah, in the very centre of the trap — triggers all about her — to touch one of which spelt death; and all around the trap, in a ring — like an audience at a one-ring circus — were the meat-eaters — the tigers — the lions — the leopards — and, worst of all, the pigs. There she sat and there they sat — and no one moved — except me with the torch.

She lifted her great eyes to me and she smiled. All the beasts looked at me and turned away their eyes from the light and blinked and shifted; and the old he-lion coughed. They wouldn't come near me because of the torch — and they wouldn't go near Ivy because of the trap. They knew it was a trap. They always had known it and so had Ivy. That was why she had gone into it when so many deaths looked at her in so many ways — because she knew that in there she'd be safe. All along she'd known that my old traps and pitfalls wouldn't catch anything; but she'd never said so — and she'd never laughed at them or at me. I could find it in my heart to call her a perfect wife — just by that one fact of tact alone; but there are other facts — other reasons — millions of them.

Suddenly from somewhere near Ivy there came a thin, piping sound.

"It's your little son talking to you," says Ivy, as calm as if she was sitting up in a four-poster.

"My little son!" I says. That was all for a minute. Then I says: "Are you all right?"

And she says:

"Sure I am — now that I know you are."

I turned my torch fire-end down and it began to blaze and sputter and presently roar. Then I steps over to the lion and he doesn't move; and I points the torch at his dirty face — and lunges.

Ever see a kitten enjoying a fit? That was what happened to him. Then I ran about, beating and poking and shouting and burning. It was like Ulysses cleaning the house of suitors and handmaids. All the beasts ran; and some of 'em ran a long way, I guess, and climbed trees.

I stuck the torch point-end in the ground, stepped into the trap, and lifted my family out. All the time I prayed aloud, saying: "Lord on high, keep Right Bower from touching his blamed foot against any of these triggers and dropping the forest on top of all he holds in his arms!" Ivy, she rubbed her cheek against mine to show confidence — and then we were safe out and I picked up the torch and carried the whole kit and boodle, family, torch, happiness — much too big to tote — and belief in God's goodness, watchfulness, and mercy, home to our cave.

Right Bower added some uneventful details of the few days following — the ship's boat that put into the island for water and took them off, and so on. Then he asked me if I'd like to meet Mrs. Bower, and I went forward with him and was presented.

She was deep in a steamer-chair, half covered with a somewhat gay assortment of steamer-rugs. I had noticed her before, in passing, and had mistaken her for a child.

Bower beamed over us for a while and then left us and we talked for hours — about Bower, the children, and the home in East Orange to which they were returning after a holiday at Aix; but she wouldn't talk much about the island. "Right," she said, "was all the time so venturesome that from morning till night I died of worry and anxiety. Right says the Lord does just the right thing for the right people at the right time — always. That's his creed. . . . Sometimes," she said, "I wonder what's become of big Bahut. He was such a — white elephant!"

Mrs. Gordon-Colfax took me to task for spending so much of the afternoon with Mrs. Bower.

"Who," said she, "was that common little person you were flirting with? — and why?"

"She's a Mrs. Bower," I said. "She has a mission."

"I could tell that," said Mrs. Gordon-Colfax, "from the way she turned up her eyes at you."

"As long as she doesn't turn up her nose at me —" I began; but Mrs. Gordon-Colfax put in:

"The Lord did that for her."

"And," I said, "so she was saying. She said the Lord does just the right thing for the right person at the right time. . . . Now, your nose is beautifully Greek; but, to be honest, it turns up ever so much more than hers does."

"Oh, well," said Mrs. Gordon-Colfax, "I hate common people — and I can't help it. Let's have a bite in the grill."

"Sorry," I said; "I'm dining with the Bowers."

"You have a strong stomach," said she.

"I have," I said, "but a weak heart — and they are going to strengthen it for me."

And there arose thenceforth a coolness between Mrs. Gordon-Colfax and me, which proves once more that the Lord does just the right thing for the right people at the right time.

SAPPHIRA

Mr. Hemingway had transacted a great deal of business with Miss Tennant's father; otherwise he must have shunned the proposition upon which she came to him. Indeed, wrinkling his bushy brows, he as much as told her that he was a banker and not a pawnbroker.

Outside, the main street of Aiken, broad enough to have made five New England streets, lay red and glaring in the sun. The least restless shifting of feet by horses and mules tied to hitching-posts raised clouds of dust, immense reddish ghosts that could not be laid. In the bank itself, ordinarily a cool retreat, smelling faintly of tobacco juice deposited by some of its clients, the mercury was swelling toward ninety. It was April Fools' day, and unless Miss Tennant was cool, nobody was. She looked cool. If the temperature had been 40° below zero she would have looked warm; but she would have been dressed differently.

It was her great gift always to look the weather and the occasion; no matter how or what she really felt. On the present occasion she wore a very simple, inexpensive muslin, flowered with faint mauve lilacs, and a wide, floppy straw-hat trimmed with the same. She had driven into town, half a mile or more, without getting a speck of dust upon herself. Even the corners of her eyes were like those of a newly laundered baby. She smelled of tooth-powder (precipitated chalk and orris root), as was her custom, and she wore no ring or ornament of any value. Indeed, such jewels as she possessed, a graceful diamond necklace, a pearl collar, a pearl pendant, and two cabochon sapphire rings, lay on the table between her and Mr. Hemingway.

"I'm not asking the bank to do this for me," she said, and she looked extra lovely (on purpose, of course). "I'm asking you —"

Mr. Hemingway poked the cluster of jewels very gingerly with his forefinger as if they were a lizard.

"And, of course," she said, "they are worth twice the money; maybe three or four times."

"Perhaps," said Mr. Hemingway, "you will take offence if I suggest that your father —"

The muslin over her shoulders tightened the least in the world. She had shrugged them.

"Of course," she said, "papa would do it; but he would insist on reasons. My reasons involve another, Mr. Hemingway, and so it would not be honorable for me to give them."

"And yet," said the banker, twinkling, "your reasons would

tempt me to accommodate you with the loan you ask for far more than your collateral."

"Oh," she said, "you are a business man. I could give you reasons, and be sure they would go no further — even if you thought them funny. But if papa heard them, and thought them funny, as he would, he would play the sieve. I don't want this money for myself, Mr. Hemingway."

"They never do," said he.

She laughed.

"I wish to lend it in turn," she said, "to a person who has been reckless, and who is in trouble, but in whom I believe. . . . But perhaps," she went on, "the person, who is very proud, will take offence at my offer of help. . . . In which case, Mr. Hemingway, I should return you the money tomorrow."

"This person —" he began, twinkling.

"Oh," she said, "I couldn't bear to be teased. The person is a young gentleman. Any interest that I take in him is a business interest, pure and simple. I believe that, tided over his present difficulties, he will steady down and become a credit to his sex. Can I say more than that?" She smiled drolly.

"Men who are a credit to their sex," said Mr. Hemingway, "are not rare, but young gentlemen —"

"This one," said she, "has in him the makings of a man. Just now he is discouraged."

"Is he taking anything for it?" asked Mr. Hemingway with some sarcasm.

"Buckets," said Miss Tennant simply.

"Was it cards?" he asked.

"Cards, and betting — and the hopeless optimism of youth," said she.

"And you wish to lend him five thousand dollars, and your interest in him is platonic?"

"Nothing so ardent," said she demurely. "I wish him to pay his debts, to give me his word that he will neither drink nor gamble until he has paid back the debt to me, and I shall suggest that he go out to one of those big Western States and become a man."

"If anybody," said Mr. Hemingway with gallantry, "could lead a young gentleman to so sweeping a reform, it would be yourself."

"There is no sequence of generations," said Miss Tennant, "long enough to eradicate a drop of Irish blood."

Mr. Hemingway swept the jewels together and wrapped them in the tissue-paper in which she had brought them.

"Are you going to put them in your safe — or return them to

me?" she asked plaintively.

Mr. Hemingway affected gruffness.

"I am thanking God fervently, ma'am," said he, "that you didn't ask me for more. You'll have to give me your note. By the way, are you of age?"

Her charming eyes narrowed, and she laughed at him.

"People," she said, "are already beginning to say, 'she will hardly marry now.' But it's how old we feel, Mr. Hemingway, isn't it?"

"I feel about seven," said he, "and foolish at that."

"And I," said she, "will be twenty-five for the second time on my next birthday."

"And, by the way," she said, when the details of the loan had been arranged and she had stuffed the five thousand dollars into the palm of a wash glove, "nobody must know about this, because I shall have to say that — my gewgaws have been stolen."

"But that will give Aiken a black eye," said he.

"I'm afraid it can't be helped, Mr. Hemingway. Papa will ask point-blank why I never wear the pearls he gave me, and I shall have to anticipate."

"How?" he asked.

"Oh," she said demurely, "tonight or tomorrow night I shall rouse the household with screams, and claim that I woke and saw a man bending over my dressing-table — a man with a beautiful white mustache and imperial."

Mr. Hemingway's right hand flew to his mouth as if to hide these well-ordered appendages, and he laughed.

"Is the truth nothing to you?" he said.

"In a business matter pure and simple," she said, after a moment's reflection, "it is nothing — absolutely nothing."

"Not being found out by one's parents is hardly a business matter," said Mr. Hemingway.

"Oh," said she with a shiver, "as a little girl I went into the hands of a receiver at least once a month —"

"A hand of iron in a velvet glove," murmured Mr. Hemingway.

"Oh, no," she said, "a leather slipper in a nervous hand. . . . But how can I thank you?"

She rose, still demure and cool, but with a strong sparkling in her eyes as from a difficult matter successfully adjusted.

"You could make the burglar a clean-shaven man," Mr. Hemingway suggested.

"I will," she said. "I will make him look like anybody you say."

"God forbid," said he. "I have no enemies. But, seriously, Miss

Tennant, if you possibly can, will you do without a burglary, for the good name of Aiken?"

"I will do what I can," she said, "but I can't make promises."

When she had gone, one of the directors pushed open the door of Mr. Hemingway's office and tiptoed in.

"Well," said he, "for an old graybeard! You've been flirting fifty minutes, you sinner."

"I haven't," said Mr. Hemingway, twisting his mustache and looking roguish. "I've been discussing a little matter of business with Miss Tennant."

"*What* business?"

"Well, it wasn't any of yours, Frank, at the time, and I'm dinned if I think it is now. But if you must know, she came in to complain of the milk that your dairy has been supplying lately. She said it was the kind of thing you'd expect in the North, but for a Southern gentleman to put water in anything —"

"You go to Augusta," said the director (it is several degrees hotter than Aiken). "Everybody knows that spoons stand up in the milk from my dairy, and as for the cream —"

In the fall from grace of David Larkin there was involved no great show of natural depravity. The difference between a young man who goes right and a young man who goes wrong may be no more than the half of one per cent. And I do not know why we show the vicious such contempt and the virtuous such admiration. Larkin's was the case of a young man who tried to do what he was not old enough, strong enough, or wise enough to "get away with," as the saying is. Aiken did not corrupt him; he was corrupt when he came, with a bank account of thirty-five hundred dollars snatched from the lap of Dame Fortune, at a moment when she was minding some other small boy. Horses running up to their form, spectacular bridge hands (not well played), and bets upon every subject that can be thought of had all contributed. Then Larkin caught a cold in his nose, so that it ran all day and all night; and because the Browns had invited him to Aiken for a fortnight whenever he cared to come, he seized upon the excuse of his cold and boarded the first train. He was no sooner in Aiken than Dame Fortune ceased minding the other small boy, and turned her petulant eyes upon Larkin. Forthwith he began to lose.

Let no man who does not personally know what a run of bad luck is judge another. What color is a lemon? Why, it is lemon-colored, to be sure. And behold, fortune produces you a lemon black as the ace of spades. When fortune goes against you, you cannot be right. The favorite falls down; the great jockey uses bad judgment for the first time in his life; the foot-ball team that ought to win is overtrained; the yacht carries away her bowsprit; your four kings are brought face to face, after much "hiking," with four aces; the cigarette that you try to flick into the fireplace hits the slender and-iron and bounces out upon the rug; the liquor that you carried so amiably and sensibly in New York mixes with the exciting air of the place where the young lady you are attentive to lives, and you make four asses of yourself and seven fools, and wake up with your first torturing headache and your first humiliating apology. Americans (with the unfortunate exception of us who make a business of it) are the greatest phrase-makers the world has ever known. Larkin's judgment was good; he was a modest young fellow of very decent instincts, he was neither a born gambler nor a born drinker; but, in the American phrase, "he was *in* wrong."

Bad luck is not a good excuse for a failure in character; but God knows how wickedly provocative thereof it can be. The elders of the Aiken Club did not notice that Larkin was slipping from grace, because his slipping was gradual; but they noticed all of a sudden, with pity, chagrin (for they liked him), and kindly contempt, that he had fallen. Forthwith a wave of reform swept over the Aiken Club, or it amounted to that. Rich men who did not care a hang about what they won or lost refused to play for high stakes; Larkin's invitations to cocktails were very largely refused; no bets were made in his presence (and I must say that this was a great cause of languishment in certain men's conversation), and the young man was mildly and properly snubbed. This locking of the stable door, however, had the misfortune to happen just after the horse had bolted. Larkin had run through the most of his money; he did not know how he was to pay his bed and board at Willcox's, where he was now stopping; his family were in no position to help him; he knew that he was beginning to be looked on with contempt; he thought that he was seriously in love with Miss Tennant. He could not see any way out of anything; knew that a disgraceful crash was imminent, and for all these troubles he took the wrong medicine. Not the least foolish part of this was that it was medicine for which he would be unable to pay when the club bill fell due. From after breakfast until late at night he kept himself, not drunk, but stimulated. . . . And then one day the president of the club spoke to him very kindly — and the next day wouldn't speak to him at all.

The proper course would have been for Larkin to open his heart to any of a dozen men. Any one of them would have straightened him out mentally and financially in one moment, and forgotten about it the next. But Larkin was too young, too foolish, and too full of false pride to make confessions to any one who could help him; and he was quite ignorant of the genuine kindness and wisdom that lurks in the average rich man, if once you can get his ear.

But one night, being sure they could not be construed into an appeal for help, or anything but a sympathetic scolding, which he thought would be enjoyable (and because of a full moon, perhaps, and a whole chorus of mocking-birds pouring out their souls in song, and because of an arbor covered with the yellow jasmine that smells to heaven, and a little sweeter), he made his sorry confessions into the lovely pink hollow of Miss Tennant's ear.

Instead of a scolding he received sympathy and understanding; and he misconstrued the fact that she caught his hand in hers and squeezed it very hard; and did not know that he had misconstrued that fact until he found that it was her cheek that he had kissed instead of her hastily averted lips.

This rebuff did not prevent him from crowning the story of his young life with further confessions. And it is on record that when Larkin came into the brightly lighted club there was dust upon the knees of his trousers.

"I *am* fond of you, David," she had said, "and in spite of all the mess you have made of things, I believe in you; but even if I were fonder than fondest of you, I should despise myself if I listened to you — now."

But she did not sleep all night for thinking how she could be of real, material help to the young man, and cause him to turn into the straight, narrow path that always leads to success and sometimes to achievement.

Every spring the Mannings, who have nothing against them except that they live on the wrong side of town, give a wistaria party. The Mannings live for the blossoming of the wistaria which covers their charming porticoed house from top to toe and fills their grounds. Ever since they can remember they have specialized in wistaria; and they are not young, and wistaria grows fast. The fine old trees that stand in the Mannings' grounds are merely lofty trellises for the vines, white and mauve, to sport upon. The Mannings' garden cost less money, perhaps, than any notable garden in Aiken; and when in full bloom it is, perhaps, the most beautiful garden in the world. To appreciate wistaria, one vine with a spread of fifty feet bearing ten thousand racemes of blossoms a foot long is not enough; you must enter and disappear into a region of such vines, and then loaf and stroll with an untroubled nose and your heart's desire.

Even Larkin, when he paused under the towering entrance vines, a mauve and a white, forgot his troubles. He filled his lungs with the delicious fragrance, and years after the consciousness of it would come upon him suddenly. And then coming upon tea-tables standing in the open and covered with good things, and finding, among the white flannel and muslin guests, Miss Tennant, very obviously on the lookout for him, his cup was full. When they had drunk very deep of orangeade, and eaten jam sandwiches followed by chicken sandwiches and walnut cake, they went strolling (Miss Tennant still looking completely ethereal — a creature that lived on the odor of flowers and kind thoughts rather than the more material edibles mentioned above), and then Larkin felt that his cup was overflowing.

Either because the day was hot or because of the sandwiches, they found exclusive shade and sat in it, upon a white seat that looked like marble — at a distance. Larkin once more filled his lungs with the breath of wistaria and was for letting it out in further confessions of what he felt to be his heart's ultimate depths. But Miss Tennant was too quick for him. She drew five one-thousand-dollar bills from the palm of her glove and put them in his hand.

"There," she said.

Larkin looked at the money and fell into a dark mood.

"What is this for?" he said presently.

"This is a loan," said she, "from me to you; to be a tiding over of present difficulties, a reminder of much that has been pleasant in the past, and an earnest of future well-doing. Good luck to you, David."

"I wish I could take it," said the young man with a swift, slanting smile. "And at least I can crawl upon my stomach at your feet, and pull my forelock and heap dust upon my head. . . . God bless you!" And he returned the bills to her.

She smiled cheerfully but a little disdainfully.

"Very well, then," said she. "I tear them up."

"Oh!" cried Larkin. "Don't make a mess of a beautiful incident."

"Then take them."

"No."

"Why not?"

"Oh, you know as well as I do that a man can't borrow from a girl."

"A man?" asked Miss Tennant simply, as if she doubted having heard correctly. Then, as he nodded, she turned a pair of eyes upon him that were at once kind, pained, and deeply thoughtful. And she began to speak in a quiet, repressed way upon the theme that he had suggested.

"A man," she said; "what is a man? I can answer better by telling you what a man is not. A man is not a creature who loafs when he ought to be at work, who loses money that he hasn't got, who drinks liquor that he cannot carry, and who upon such a noble ground-work feels justified in making love to a decent, self-respecting girl. That is not a *man*, David. A man would have no need of any help from me. . . . But you — you are a child that has escaped from its nurse, a bird that has fallen out of its nest before it has learned to fly, and you have done nothing but foolish things. . . . But somehow I have learned to suspect you of a better self, where, half-strangled with foolishnesses and extravagance, there lurks a certain contrition and a certain sweetness. . . . God knows I should like to see you a man. . . ."

Larkin jumped to his feet, and all of him that showed was crimson, and he could have cried. But he felt no anger, and he kept his eyes upon hers.

"Thank you," he said; "may I have them?"

He stuffed the bills into his pocket.

"I have no security," he said. "But I will give you my word of honor neither to drink, neither to gamble, neither to loaf, nor to make love until I have paid you back interest and principal."

"Where will you go? What will you do, David?"

"West — God knows. I *will* do something. . . . You see that I can't say any thanks, don't you? That I am almost choking, and that at any moment I might burst into sobs?"

They were silent, and she looked into his face unconsciously while he mastered his agitation. He sat down beside her presently, his elbows on his knees, his chin deep in his hands.

"Is God blessing you by any chance?" he said. "Do you feel any-thing of the kind? Because I am asking Him to — so very hard. I shall ask Him to a million times every day until I die. . . . Would it be possible for one who has deserved nothing, but who would like it for the strengthingest, beautifulest memory. . . ."

"Quick, then," said she, "some one's coming."

That very night screams pierced to every corner of the Tennants' great house on the Whiskey Road. Those whom screams affect in one way sprang from bed; those whom they affect in another hid under the bedclothes. Mr. Tennant himself, a man of sharp temper and implacable courage, dashed from his room in a suit of blue-and-white pajamas, and overturned a Chippendale cabinet worth a thousand dollars; young Mr. Tennant barked both shins on a wood-box and dropped a loaded Colt revolver into the well of the stair; Mrs. Tennant was longer in appearing, having tarried to try the effect upon her nerves and color sense of three divers wrappers. The butler, an Admirable Crichton of a man, came, bearing a bucket of water in case the house was on fire. Mrs. Tennant's French maid carried a case of her mistress's jewels, and seemed determined to leave.

Miss Tennant stood in the door-way of her room. She was pale and greatly agitated, but her eyes shone with courage and resolve. Her arched, blue-veined feet were thrust into a pair of red Turkish slippers turning up at the toes. A mandarin robe of dragoned blue brocade was flung over her night-gown. In one hand she had a golf club — a niblick.

"Oh!" she cried, when her father was sufficiently recovered from overturning the cabinet to listen, "there was a man in my room."

Mr. Tennant }		{ furiously.
Young Mr. Tennant }		{ sleepily.
The butler }	"A man?"	{ as if he thought she meant to say a fire.
The French maid }		{ blushing crimson.

Then, and again all together:

Mr. Tennant —	"Which way did he go?"
Young Mr. Tennant —	"Which man?"
The butler—	"A white man?"
The French maid (with a kind of ecstacy) —	"A man!"

"Out the window!" cried Miss Tennant.

Her father and brother dashed downstairs and out into the grounds. The butler hurried to the telephone (still carrying his bucket of water) and rang Central and asked for the chief of police. Central answered, after a long interval, that the chief of police was out of order, and rang off.

Meanwhile, Mrs. Tennant arrived, and, having coldly recovered her jewel-case from the custody of the French maid, prepared to be told the details of what hadn't happened.

"He was bending over my dressing-table, mamma," said Miss Tennant. "I could see him plainly in the moonlight; he had a mask, and was smooth shaven, and he wore gloves."

"I wonder why he wore gloves," mused Mrs. Tennant.

"I suppose," said Miss Tennant, "that he had heard of the Bertillon system, and was afraid of being tracked by his finger-marks."

"Did he say anything?"

"Not to me, I think," said Miss Tennant, "but he kept mumbling to himself so I could hear: 'Slit her damn throat if she makes a move; slit it right into the backbone.' So, of course, I didn't make a move — I thought he was talking to a confederate whom I couldn't see."

"Why a *confederate*?" asked Mrs. Tennant. "Oh, I see — you mean a sort of partner."

"But there was only the one," said Miss Tennant. "And when he had filled his pockets and was gone by the window — I thought it was safe to scream, and I screamed."

"Have you looked to see what he took?"

"No. But my jewels were all knocking about on the dressing-table. I suppose he got them."

"Well," said Mrs. Tennant, "let's be thankful that he didn't get mine."

"And only to think," said Miss Tennant, "that only last night papa asked me why I had given up wearing my pearls, and was put out about it, and I promised to wear them oftener!"

"Never mind, my dear," said her mother confidentially; "if you are sorry enough long enough your father will buy you others. He can be wonderfully generous if you keep at him."

"Oh," said Miss Tennant, "I feel sure that they will be recovered some day — it may not be tomorrow, or next day — but somehow — some time I feel sure that they will come back. Of course papa must offer a reward."

"I wonder how much he will offer!"

"Oh, a good round sum. I shall suggest five thousand dollars, if he asks me."

The next day Miss Tennant despatched the following note to Mr. Hemingway:

Dear, kind Mr. Hemingway:

You have heard of the great robbery and of my dreadful fright. But there is no use crying about it. It is one of those dreadful things, I suppose, that simply *have* to happen. The burglar was smooth-shaven. How awful that this should have to happen in Aiken of all cities. In Aiken where we never have felt hitherto that it was ever necessary to lock the door. I suppose Mr. Powell's nice hardware store will do an enormous business now in patent bolts. Papa is going to offer five thousand dollars' reward for the return of my jewels, and no questions asked. Do you know, I have a feeling that you are going to be instrumental in finding the stolen goods. I have a feeling that the thief (if he has any sense at all) will negotiate through you for their return. And I am sure the thief would never have taken them if he had known how badly it would make me feel, and what a blow he was striking at the good name of Aiken.

I am, dear Mr. Hemingway, contritely and sincerely yours,

SAPPHIRA TENNANT
(formerly Dolly Tennant).

But Mr. Hemingway refused to touch the reward, and Miss Tennant remained in his debt for the full amount of her loan. She began at once to save what she could from her allowance. And she called this fund her "conscience money."

Miss Tennant and David Larkin did not meet again until the moment of the latter's departure from Aiken. And she was only one of a number who drove to the station to see him off. Possibly to guard against his impulsive nature, she remained in her runabout during the brief farewell. And what they said to each other might have been (and probably was) heard by others.

Aiken felt that it had misjudged Larkin, and he departed in high favor. He had paid what he owed, so Aiken confessed to having misjudged his resources. He had suddenly stopped short in all evil ways, so Aiken confessed to having misjudged his strength of character. He had announced that he was going out West to seek the bubble wealth in the mouth of an Idaho apple valley, so Aiken cheered him on and wished him well. And when Aiken beheld the calmness of his farewells to Miss Tennant, Aiken said: "And he seems to have gotten over that."

But Larkin had done nothing of the kind, and he said to himself, as he lay feverish and restless in a stuffy upper berth: "It isn't because she's so beautiful or so kind; it's because she always speaks the truth. Most girls lie about everything, not in so many words, perhaps, but in fact. She doesn't. She lets you know what she thinks, and where you stand ... and I didn't stand very high."

Despair seized him. How is it possible to go into a strange world, with only nine hundred dollars in your pocket, and carve a fortune? "When can I pay her back? What must I do if I fail?..." Then came thoughts that were as grains of comfort. Was her lend-ing him money philanthropy pure and simple, an act emanating from her love of mankind? Was it not rather an act emanating from affection for a particular man? If so, that man — misguided boy, bird tumbled out of the nest, child that had escaped from its nurse — was not hard to find. "I could lay my finger on him," thought Larkin, and he did so — five fingers, somewhat grandiosely upon the chest. A gas lamp peered at him over the curtain pole; snores shook the imprisoned atmosphere of the car. And Larkin's thoughts flitted from the past and future to the present.

A question that he now asked himself was: "Do women snore?" And: "If people cannot travel in drawing-rooms, why do they travel at all?" The safety of his nine hundred dollars worried him; he knelt up to look in the inside pocket of his jacket, and bumped his head, a dull, solid bump. Pale golden stars, shaped like the enlarged pictures of snow-flakes, streamed across his consciousness. But the money was safe.

Already his nostrils were irritable with cinders; he attempted to blow them clear, and failed. He was terribly thirsty. He wished very much to smoke. Whichever way he turned, the frogs on the uppers of his pajamas made painful holes in him. He woke at last with two coarse blankets wrapped firmly about his head and shoulders and the rest of him half-naked, gritty with cinders, and as cold as a well curb. Through the ventilators (tightly closed) daylight was struggling with gas-light. The car smelled of stale steam and man. The car wheels played a headachy tune to the metre of the Phœbe-Snow-upon-the-road-of-anthracite verses. David cursed Phœbe Snow, and determined that if ever God vouchsafed him a honeymoon it should be upon the clean, fresh ocean.

There had been wistaria in Aiken. There was snow in New York. There was a hurricane in Chicago. But in the smoker bound West there was a fine old gentleman in a blue-serge suit and white spats who took a fancy to David, just when David had about come to the conclusion that nothing in the world looked friendly except suicide.

If David had learned nothing else from Miss Tennant, he had learned to speak the truth. "Any employer that I am ever to have," he resolved, "shall know all that there is to be known about me. I shall not try to create the usual impression of a young man seeking his fortune in the West purely for amusement." And so, when the preliminaries of smoking-room acquaintance had been made — the cigar offered and refused, and one's reasons for or against smoking plainly stated — David was offered (and accepted) the opportunity to tell the story of his life.

David shook his head at a brilliantly labelled cigar eight inches long.

"I love to smoke," he said, "but I've promised not to."

"Better habit than liquor," suggested the old gentleman in the white spats.

"I've promised not to drink."

"Men who don't smoke and who don't drink," said the old gentleman, "usually spend their time running after the girls. My name is Uriah Grey."

"Mine is David Larkin," said David, and he smiled cheerfully, "and I've promised not to make love."

"What — never?" exclaimed Mr. Grey.

"Not until I have a right to," said David.

Mr. Grey drew three brightly bound volumes from between his leg and the arm of his chair, and intimated that he was about to make them a subject of remark.

"I love stories," he said, "and in the hope of a story I paid a dollar and a half for each of three novels. This one tells you how to prepare rotten meat for the market. This one tells you when and where to find your neighbor's wife without being caught. And in this one a noble young Chicagoan describes the life of society persons in the effete East."

"Whom he does not know from Adam," said David.

"Whom he does not distinguish from Adam," corrected Mr. Grey. "But I was thinking that I am disappointed in my appetite for stories, and that just now you made a most enticing beginning as — 'I, Roger Slyweather of Slyweather Hall, Blankshire, England, having at the age of twenty-two or thereabouts made solemn promise neither to smoke nor to drink, nor to make love, did set forth upon a blustering day in April. . . .'"

"Oh," said David, "if it's my story you want, I don't mind a bit. It will chasten me to tell it, and you can stop me the minute you are bored."

And then, slip by slip and bet by bet, he told his story, withholding only the sex of that dear friend who had loaned him the five thousand dollars, and to whom he had bound himself by promises.

"Well," said Mr. Grey, when David had finished, "I don't know your holding-out powers, Larkin, but you do certainly speak the truth without mincing."

"That," said David, "is a promise I have made to myself in admiration of and emulation of my friend. But I have had my little lesson, and I shall keep the other promises until I have made good."

"And then?" Mr. Grey beamed.

"Then," said David, "I shall smoke and I shall make love."

"But no liquor."

David laughed.

"I have a secret clause in my pledge," said he; "it is not to touch liquor except on the personal invitation of my future father-in-law, whoever he may be." But he had Dolly Tennant's father in his mind, and the joke seemed good to him.

"Well," said Mr. Grey, "I don't know as I'd go into apple-growing. You haven't got enough capital."

"But," said David, "I intend to begin at the bottom and work up."

"When I was a youngster," said Mr. Grey, "I began at the bottom of an apple tree and worked my way to the top. There I found a wasp's nest. Then I fell and broke both arms. That was a lesson to me. Don't go up for your pile, my boy. Go down. Go down into the beautiful earth, and take out the precious metals."

"Good Heavens!" exclaimed David; "you're *the* Mr. Grey of Denver."

"I have a car hitched on to this train," said the magnate; "I'd be very glad of your company at dinner — seven-thirty. It's not every young man that I'd invite. But seeing that you're under bond not to make love until you've made good, I can see no objection to introducing you to my granddaughter."

"Grandpa," said Miss Violet Grey, who was sixteen, spoiled, and exquisite, "make that poor boy stop off at Denver, and do something for him."

"Since when," said her grandfather, "have you been so down on apples, miss?"

"Oh," said she with an approving shudder, "all good women fear them — like so much poison."

"But," said Mr. Grey (Mr. "Iron Grey," some called him), "if I take this young fellow up, it won't be to put him down in a drawing-room, but in a hole a thousand feet deep, or thereabouts."

"And when he comes out," said she, "I shall have returned from being finished in Europe."

"Don't know what there is so attractive about these young Eastern ne'er-do-weels," said the old gentleman, "but this one has got a certain something. . . ."

"It's his inimitable truthfulness," said she.

"Not to me," said her grandfather, "so much as the way he says *w* instead of *r* and at the same time gives the impression of having the makings of a man in him. . . ."

"Oh," she said, "make him, grandpa, do!"

"And if I make him?" The old gentleman smiled provokingly.

"Why," said she, "then I'll break him."

"Or," said her grandfather, who was used to her sudden fancies and subsequent disenchantments, "or else you'll shake him."

Then he pulled her ears for her and sent her to bed.

In one matter David was, from the beginning of his new career, firmly resolved. He would in no case write Miss Tennant of his hopes and fears. If he was to be promoted she was not to hear of it until after the fact; and she should not be troubled with the sordid details of his savings-bank account. As to fears, very great at first, these dwindled, became atrophied, and were consumed in the fire of work from the moment when that work changed from a daily nuisance to a daily miracle, at once the exercise and the reward of intelligence. His work, really light at first, seemed stupendous to him because he did not understand it. As his understanding grew, he was given heavier work, and behold! it seemed more light. He discovered that great books had been written upon every phase of bringing forth metal from the great mother earth; and he snatched from long days of toil time for more toil, and burned his lamp into the night, so that he might add theory to practice.

I should like to say that David's swift upward career owed thanks entirely to his own good habits, newly discovered gifts for mining engineering, and industry; but a strict regard for the truth prevents. Upon his own resources and talents he must have succeeded in the end; but his success was the swifter for the interest, and presently affection, that Uriah Grey himself contributed toward it. In short, David's chances came to him as soon as he was strong enough to handle them, and were even created on purpose for him; whereas, if he had had no one behind him, he must have had to wait interminably for them. But the main point, of course, is that, as soon as he began to understand what was required of him, he began to make good.

His field work ended about the time that Miss Violet Grey returned from Europe "completely finished and done up," as she put it herself, and he became a fixture of growing importance in Mr. Grey's main offices in Denver and a thrill in Denver society. His baby *w*'s instead of rolling *r*'s thrilled the ladies; his good habits coupled with his manliness and success thrilled the men.

"He doesn't drink," said one.

"He doesn't smoke," said another.

"He doesn't bet," said a third.

"He can look the saints in the face," said a fourth; and a fifth, looking up, thumped upon a bell that would summon a waiter, and with emphasis said:

"And we *like* to have him around!"

Among the youngest and most enthusiastic men it even became the habit to copy David in certain things. He was responsible for a small wave of reform in Denver, as he had once been in Aiken; but for the opposite cause. Little dialogues like the following might frequently be heard in the clubs:

"Have a drink, Billy?"

"Thanks; I don't drink."

"Cigar, Sam?"

"Thanks (with a moan); don't smoke."

"Betcherfivedollars, Ned."

"Sorry, old man; I don't bet."

Or, in a lowered voice:

"Say, let's drop round to —"

"I've (chillingly) cut out all that sort of thing."

Platonic friendships became the rage. David himself, as leader, maintained a dozen such, chiefest of which was with the newly finished Miss Grey. At first her very soul revolted against a friendship of this sort. She was lovely, and she knew it; with lovely clothes she made herself even lovelier, and she knew this, too. She was young, and she rejoiced in it. And she had always been a spoiled darling, and she wished to be made much of, to cause a dozen hearts to beat in the breast where but one beat before, to be followed, waited on, adored, bowed down to, and worshipped. She wished yellow-flowering jealousy to sprout in David's heart instead of the calm and loyal friendliness to which alone the soil seemed adapted. She knew that he often wrote letters to a Miss Tennant; and she would have liked very much to have this Miss Tennant in her power, and to have scalped her there and then.

This was only at first, when she merely fancied David rather more than other young men. But a time came when her fancy was stronger for him than that; and then it seemed to her that even his platonic friendship was worth more than all the great passions of history rolled into one. Then from the character of that spoiled young lady were wiped clean away, as the sponge wipes marks from a slate, vanity, whims, temper, tantrums, thoughtlessness, and arrogance, and in their places appeared the opposites. She sought out hard spots in people's lives and made them soft; sympathy and gentleness radiated from her; thoughtfulness and steadfastness.

Her grandfather, who had been reading Ibsen, remarked to himself: "It may be artistically and dramatically inexcusable for the ingénue suddenly to become the heroine — but *I* like it. As to the cause —" and the old gentleman rested in his deep chair till far into the night, twiddling his thumbs and thinking long thoughts. Finally, frowning and troubled, he rose and went off to his bed.

"Is it," thought he, "because he gave his word not to make love until he had made good — or is it because he really doesn't give a damn about poor little Vi? If it's the first reason, why he's absolved from that promise, because he has made good, and every day he's making better. But if it's the second reason, why then this world is a wicked, dreary place. Poor little Vi — poor little Vi ... only two things in the whole universe that she can't get — the moon, and David — the moon, and David —"

About noon the next day, David requested speech with his chief.

"Well?" said Uriah. The old man looked worn and feeble. He had had a sorrowful night.

"I haven't had a vacation in a year," said David. "Will you give me three weeks, sir?"

"Want to go back East and pay off your obligations?"

David nodded.

"I have the money and interest in hand," said he.

Mr. Grey smiled.

"I suppose you'll come back smoking like a chimney, drinking like a fish, betting like a book-maker, and keeping a whole chorus in picture-hats."

"I think I'll not even smoke," said David. "About a month ago the last traces of hankering left me, and I feel like a free man at last."

"But you'll be making love right and left," said Mr. Grey cheerfully, but with a shrewd eye upon the young man's expression of face.

David looked grave and troubled. He appeared to be turning over difficult matters in his mind. Then he smiled gayly.

"At least I shall be free to make love if I want to."

"Nonsense," said Mr. Grey. "People don't make love because they want to. They do it because they have to."

Again David looked troubled, and a little sad, perhaps.

"True," said he. And he walked meditatively back to his own desk, took up a pen, meditated for a long time, and then wrote:

Best friend that any man ever had in the world! I shall be in Aiken on the twenty-fifth, bringing with me that which I owe, and can pay, and deeply conscious of that deeper debt that I owe, but never can hope to pay. But I will do what I can. I will not now take back the promises I gave, unless you wish; I will not do anything that you do not wish. And if all the service and devotion that is in me for the rest of time seem worth having to you, they are yours. But you know that.

David.

This, looking white, tired, and austere, he reread, folded, enveloped, stamped, sealed, and addressed to Miss Tennant.

Neither the hand which Miss Tennant laid on his, nor the cigarette which she lighted for him, completely mollified Mr. Billy McAllen. He was no longer young enough to dance with pleasure to a maiden's whims. The experience of dancing from New York to Newport and back, and over the deep ocean and back, and up and down Europe and back with the late Mrs. McAllen — now Mrs. Jimmie Greenleaf — had sufficed. He would walk to the altar any day with Miss Tennant, but he would not dance.

"You have so many secrets with yourself," he complained, "and I'm so very reasonable."

"True, Billy," said Miss Tennant. "But if I put up with your secrets, you should put up with mine."

"I have none," said he, "unless you are rudely referring to the fact that I gave my wife such grounds for divorce as every gentleman must be prepared to give to a lady who has tired of him. I might have contracted a pleasant liaison; but I didn't. I merely drove up and down Piccadilly with a notorious woman until the courts were sufficiently scandalized. You know that."

"But is it nothing," she said, "to have me feel this way toward you?" And she leaned and rested her lovely cheek against his.

"At least, Dolly," said he, more gently, "announce our engagement, and marry me inside of six months. I've been patient for eighteen. It would have been easy if you had given a good reason. . . ."

"My reason," said she, "will be in Aiken tomorrow."

"You speak with such assurance," said he, smiling, "that I feel sure your reason is not travelling by the Southern. And you'll tell me the reason tomorrow?"

She shook her head.

"Not tomorrow, Billy — now."

He made no comment, fearing that she might seize upon any as a pretext for putting him off. But he slipped an arm around her waist.

"Tighter if you like," she said. "I don't mind. My reason, Billy, is a young man. Don't let your arm slacken that way. I don't see any one or anything beyond you in any direction in this world. You know that. There is nothing in the expression 'a young man' to turn you suddenly cold toward me. Don't be a goose. . . . Not so tight." They laughed happily. "I will even tell you his name," she resumed — "David Larkin; and I was a little gone on him, and he was over ears with me. You weren't in Aiken the year he was. Well, he misbehaved something dreadful, Billy; betted himself into a deep, deep hole, and tried to float himself out. I took him in hand, loaned him money, and took his solemn word that he would not even make love until he had paid me back. There was no real understanding between us, only —"

"Only?" McAllen was troubled.

"Only I think he couldn't have changed suddenly from a little fool into a man if *he* hadn't felt that there was an understanding. And his letters, one every week, confirm that; though he's very careful, because of his promise, not to make love in them. . . . You see, he's been working his head off — there's no way out of it, Billy — for me. . . . If you hadn't crossed my humble path I think I should have possessed enough sentiment for David to have been — the reward."

"But there *was* no understanding."

"No. Not in so many words. But at the last talk we had together he was humble and pathetic and rather manly, and I did a very foolish thing."

"What?"

"Oh," she said with a blush, "I sat still."

"Let me blot it out," said McAllen, drawing her very close.

"But I can only remember up to seven," said she, "and I am afraid that nothing can blot them out as far as David is concerned. He will come tomorrow as sure that I have been faithful to him as that he has been faithful to me. . . . It's all very dreadful. . . . He will pay me back the money, and the interest; and then I shall give him back the promises that he gave, and then he will make love to me. . . ."

She sighed, and said that the thought of the pickle she had got herself into made her temples ache. McAllen kissed them for her.

"But why," he said, "when you got to care for me, didn't you let this young man learn gradually in your letters to him that — that it was all off?"

"I was afraid, don't you see," said she, "that if the incentive was suddenly taken away from him — he might go to pieces. And I was fond of him, and I am proud to think that he has made good for my sake, and the letters. . . . Oh, Billy, it's a dreadful mess. My letters to him have been rather warm, I am afraid."

"Damn!" said McAllen.

"Damn!" said Miss Tennant.

"If he would have gone to pieces before this," said McAllen, "why not now? — after you tell him, I mean."

"Why not?" said she dismally. "But if he does, Billy, I can only be dreadfully sorry. I'm certainly not going to wreck our happiness just to keep him on the war-path."

"But you'll not be weak, Dolly?"

"How! — weak?"

"He'll be very sad and miserable — you won't be carried away? You won't, upon the impulse of the moment, feel that it is your duty to go on saving him?... If that should happen, Dolly, *I* should go to pieces."

"Must I tell him," she said, "that I never really cared? He will think me such a — a liar. And I'm not a liar, Billy, am I? I'm just unlucky."

"I don't believe," said he tenderly, "that you ever told a story in your whole sweet life."

"Oh," she cried, "I *do* love you when you say things like that to me. . . . Let's not talk about horrid things any more, and mistakes, and bugbears. . . . If we're going to show up at the golf club tea. . . . It's Mrs. Carrol's today and we promised her to come."

"Oh," said McAllen, "we need not start for ten minutes. . . . When will you marry me?"

"In May," she said.

"*Good* girl," said he.

"Billy," she said presently, "it was *all* the first Mrs. Billy's fault — wasn't it?"

"No, dear," said he, "it wasn't. It's never all of anybody's fault. Do you care?"

"No."

"Are you afraid?"

"No."

"Do you love me?"

"Yes."

"How much?"

"So much," and she made the gesture that a baby makes when you ask, "How big's the baby?"

"What's your name?"

"Dolly."

"Whose girl are you?"

"I'm Billy McAllen's girl."

"All of you?"

She grew very serious in a moment.

"All of me, Billy — all that is straight in me, all that is crooked, all that is white, all that is black. . . ."

But he would not be serious.

"How about this hand? Is that mine?"

"Yours."

He kissed it.

"This cheek?"

"Yours."

"And this?"

"Yours."

"These eyes?"

"Both yours."

He closed them, first one, then the other.

Then a kind of trembling seized him, so that it was evident in his speech.

"This mouth, Dolly?"

"Mumm."

And so, as the romantic school has it, "the long day dragged slowly on."

David may have thought it pure chance that he should find Dolly Tennant alone. But it was not. She had given the matter not a little strategy and arrangement. Why, however, in view of her relations with McAllen, she should have made herself as attractive as possible to the eye is for other women to say.

It was to be April in a few days, and March was going out like a fiery dragon. The long, broad shadow of the terrace awning helped to darken the Tennants' drawing-room, and Venetian blinds, half-drawn, made a kind of cool dusk, in which it came natural to speak in a lowered voice, and to move quietly, as if some one were sick in the house. Miss Tennant sat very low, with her hands clasped over her knees; a brocade and Irish lace work-bag spilled its contents at her feet. She wore a twig of tea olive in her dress so that the whole room smelled of ripe peaches. She had never looked lovelier or more desirable.

"David!" she exclaimed. Her tone at once expressed delight at seeing him, and was an apology for remaining languidly seated. And she looked him over in a critical, maternal way.

"If you hadn't sent in your name," she said, "I should never have known you. You stand taller and broader, David. You filled the door-way. But you're not really much bigger, now that I look at you. It's your character that has grown. . . . I'm *so* proud of you."

David was very pale. It may have been from his long journey. But he at least did not know, because he said that he didn't when she asked him.

"And now," she said, "you must tell me all that you haven't

written."

"Not quite yet," said David. "There is first a little matter of business...."

"Oh —" she protested.

But David counted out his debt to her methodically, with the accrued interest.

"Put it in my work-bag," she said.

"Did you ever expect to see it again?"

"Yes, David."

"Thank you," he said.

"But I," she said, "I, too, have things of yours to return."

"Of mine?" He lifted his eyebrows expectantly.

She waved a hand, white and clean as a cherry blossom, toward a claw-footed table on which stood decanters, ice, soda, cigarettes, cigars, and matches.

"Your collateral," she said.

"Oh," said David. "But I have decided not to be a backslider."

"I know," she said. "But in business — as a matter of form."

"Oh," said David, "if it's a matter of form, it must be complied with."

He stepped to the table, smiling charmingly, and poured from the nearest decanter into a glass, added ice and soda, and lifting the mixture touched it to his lips, and murmured, "To you."

Then he put a cigarette in his mouth, and, after drawing the one breath that served to light it, flicked it, with perfect accuracy, half across the room and into the fireplace.

Still smiling, he walked slowly toward Miss Tennant, who was really excited to know what he would do next.

"Betcher two cents it snows tomorrow," said he.

"Done with you, David," she took him up merrily. And after that a painful silence came over them. David set his jaws.

"I gave you one more promise," he said. "Is that, too, returned?"

"Of course," she said, "all the promises you gave are herewith returned."

"Then I may make love?" he asked very gently.

She did not answer for some moments, and then, steeling herself, for she thought that she must hurt him:

"Yes, David," she said slowly, "you may — as a matter of form."

"Only in that way?"

"In that way only, David — to me."

"I thought — I thought," said the young man in confusion.

"I made you think so," she said generously. "Let all of the punishment, that can, be heaped on me ... David. . . ." There was a deep appeal in her voice as for mercy and forgiveness.

"Then," said he, "you never did care — at all."

But even at this juncture Miss Tennant could not speak the truth.

"Never, David — never at all — at least not in *that* way," she said. "If I let you think so it was because I thought it would help you to be strong and to succeed. . . . God knows I think I was wrong to let you think so. . . ."

But she broke off suddenly a stream of extenuation that was welling in her mind; for David did not look like a man about to be cut off in the heyday of his youth by despair.

She had the tenderest heart; and in a moment the truth blossomed therein — a truth that brought her pleasure, bewilderment, and was not unmixed with mortification.

"The man," she said gently, "has found him another girl!"

The man bowed his head and blushed.

"But I have kept my promise, Dolly."

"Of course you have, you poor, dear, long-suffering soul. Oh, David, when I think what I have been taking for granted I am humiliated, and ashamed — but I am glad, too. I cannot tell you how glad."

A pair of white gloves, still showing the shape of her hands, lay in the chair where Miss Tennant had tossed them. David brought her one of these gloves.

"Put it on," he said.

When she had done so, he took her gloved hand in his and kissed it.

"As a matter of form," he said.

She laughed easily, though the blush of humiliation had not yet left her cheeks.

"Tell me," she said, "what you would have done, David, if — if I *did* care."

"God punish me," he said gravely, "oh, best friend that ever a man had in the world, if I should not then have made you a good husband."

Not long after McAllen was with her.

"Well?" he said.

"Well," said she, "there was a train that he could catch. And I suppose he caught it."

"How did he — er, behave?"

"Considering the circumstances," said she, "he behaved very well."

"Is he hard hit?"

She considered a while; but the strict truth was not in that young lady.

"I think," she said, "that you may say that he is hard hit — very hard hit."

"Poor soul," said Billy tenderly.

"Oh, Billy!" she exclaimed, "I feel so false and so old."

"Old!" he cried. "You! You at twenty-five say that to me at —"

"It isn't as if I was *just* twenty-five, Billy," and she burst out laughing. "The terrible part of it is that I'm still twenty-five."

But he only smiled and smiled. She seemed like a little child to him, all innocence, and inexperience, and candor.

Then as her laughter merged into tears he knelt and caught her in his arms.

"Dolly — Dolly!" he said in a choking voice. "What is your name?"

"Dolly." The tears came slowly.

"Whose girl are you?"

"I'm Billy McAllen's girl." The tears ceased.

"All of you?"

"All of me. . . . Oh, Billy — love me always — only love me. . . ."

And for these two the afternoon dragged slowly on, and very much as usual.

"You are two days ahead of schedule, David. I'm glad to see you."

Though Uriah Grey's smile was bland and simple, beneath it lay a complicated maze of speculation; and the old man endeavored to read in the young man's face the answers to those questions which so greatly concerned him. Uriah Grey's eyesight was famous for two things: for its miraculous, almost chemical ability to detect the metals in ore and the gold in men. He sighed; but not so that David could hear. The magnate detected happiness where less than two weeks before he had read doubt, hesitation, and a kind of dumb misery.

"You have had a pleasant holiday?"

"A happy one, Mr. Grey." David's eyes twinkled and sparkled.

"Tell me about it."

"Well, sir, I paid my debts and got back my collateral."

"Well, sir?"

"I tasted whiskey," said David. "I lighted a cigarette, I registered a bet of two cents upon the weather, and I made love."

Uriah Grey with difficulty suppressed a moan.

"Did you!" he said dully.

"Yes," said David. "I kissed the glove upon a lady's hand." He laughed. "It smelled of gasoline," he said.

Mr. Grey grunted.

"And what are your plans?"

"What!" cried David offendedly. "Are you through with me?"

"No, my boy — no."

David hesitated.

"Mr. Grey," he began, and paused.

"Well, sir?"

"It is now lawful for me to make love," said David; "but I should do so with a better grace if I had your permission and approval."

Mr. Grey was puzzled.

"What have I to do with it?"

"You have a granddaughter. . . ."

"What!" thundered the old man. "You want to make love to my granddaughter!"

"Yes," said David boldly, "and I wonder what you are going to say."

"I have only one word to say — Hurry!"

"David!"

Spools of silk rattled from her lap to the floor. She was frankly and childishly delighted to see him again, and she hurried to him and gave him both her hands. But he looked so happy that her heart misgave her for a moment, and then she read his eyes aright, just as long since he must have read the confession in hers. At this juncture in their lives there could not have been detected in either of them the least show of hesitation or embarrassment. It was as if two travellers in the desert, dying of thirst, should meet, and each conceive in hallucination that the other was a spring of sweet water.

Presently David was looking into the lovely face that he held between his hands. He had by this time squeezed her shoulders, patted her back, kissed her feet, her dress, her hands, her eyes, and pawed her hair. They were both very short of breath.

"Violet," he gasped, "what is your name?"

"Violet."

"Whose girl are you?"

"I'm David Larkin's girl."

"All of you?"

"All — all — all —"

It was the beginning of another of those long, tedious afternoons. But to the young people concerned it seemed that never until then had such words as they spoke to each other been spoken, or such feelings of almost insupportable tenderness and adoration been experienced.

Yet back there in Aiken, Sapphira was experiencing the same feelings, and thinking the same thoughts about them; and so was Billy McAllen. And when you think that he had already been divorced once, and that Sapphira, as she herself (for once truthfully) confessed, was still twenty-five, it gives you as high an opinion of the little bare god — as he deserves.

THE BRIDE'S DEAD

I

Only Farallone's face was untroubled. His big, bold eyes held a kind of grim humor, and he rolled them unblinkingly from the groom to the bride, and back again. His duck trousers, drenched and stained with sea-water, clung to the great muscles of his legs, particles of damp sand glistened upon his naked feet, and the hairless bronze of his chest and columnar throat glowed through the openings of his torn and buttonless shirt. Except for the life and vitality that literally sparkled from him, he was more like a statue of a shipwrecked sailor than the real article itself. Yet he had not the proper attributes of a shipwrecked sailor. There was neither despair upon his countenance nor hunger; instead a kind of enjoyment, and the expression of one who has been set free. Indeed, he must have secured a kind of liberty, for after the years of serving one master and another, he had, in our recent struggle with the sea, but served himself. His was the mind and his the hand that had brought us at length to that desert coast. He it was that had extended to us the ghost of a chance. He who so recently had been but one of forty in the groom's luxurious employ; a polisher of brass, a holy-stoner of decks, a wage-earning paragon who was not permitted to think, was now a thinker and a strategist, a wage-taker from no man, and the obvious master of us three.

The bride slept on the sand where Farallone had laid her. Her stained and draggled clothes were beginning to dry and her hair to blaze in the pulsing rays of the sun. Her breath came and went with the long-drawn placidity of deep sleep. One shoe had been torn from her by the surf, and through a tear in her left stocking blinked a pink and tiny toe. Her face lay upon her arm and was hidden by it, and by her blazing hair. In the loose-jointed abandon of exhaustion and sleep she had the effect of a flower that has wilted; the color and the fabric were still lovely, but the robust erectness and crispness were gone. The groom, almost unmanned and wholly forlorn, sat beside her in a kind of huddled attitude, as if he was very cold. He had drawn his knees close to his chest, and held them in that position with thin, clasped fingers. His hair, which he wore rather long, was in a wild tangle, and his neat eye-glasses with their black cord looked absurdly out of keeping with his general dishevelment. The groom, never strong or robust, looked as if he had shrunk. The bride, too, looked as if she had shrunk, and I certainly felt as if I had.

But, however strong the contrast between us three small humans and the vast stretches of empty ocean and desert coast, there was no diminution about Farallone, but the contrary. I have never seen the presence of a man loom so strongly and so large. He sat upon his rock with a kind of vastness, so bold and strong he seemed, so utterly unperturbed.

Suddenly the groom, a kind of querulous shiver in his voice, spoke.

"The brandy, Farallone, the brandy."

The big sailor rolled his bold eyes from the groom to the bride, but returned no answer.

The groom's voice rose to a note of vexation.

"I said I wanted the brandy," he said.

Farallone's voice was large and free like a fresh breeze.

"I heard you," said he.

"Well," snapped the groom, "get it."

"Get it yourself," said Farallone quickly, and he fell to whistling in a major key.

The groom, born and accustomed to command, was on his feet shaking with fury.

"You damned insolent loafer —" he shouted.

"Cut it out — cut it out," said the big sailor, "you'll wake her."

The groom's voice sank to an angry whisper.

"Are you going to do what I tell you or not?"

"Not," said Farallone.

"I'll" — the groom's voice loudened — his eye sought an ally in mine. But I turned my face away and pretended that I had not seen or heard. There had been born in my breast suddenly a cold unreasoning fear of Farallone and of what he might do to us weaklings. I heard no more words and, venturing a look, saw that the groom was seating himself once more by the bride.

"If you sit on the other side of her," said Farallone, "you'll keep the sun off her head."

He turned his bold eyes on me and winked one of them. And I was so taken by surprise that I winked back and could have kicked myself for doing so.

II

Farallone helped the bride to her feet. "That's right," he said with a kind of nursely playfulness, and he turned to the groom.

"Because I told you to help yourself," he said, "doesn't mean that I'm not going to do the lion's share of everything. I am. I'm fit.

You and the writer man aren't. But you must do just a little more than you're able, and that's all we'll ask of you. Everybody works this voyage except the woman."

"I can work," said the bride.

"Rot!" said Farallone. "We'll ask you to walk ahead, like a kind of north star. Only we'll tell you which way to turn. Do you see that sugar-loaf? You head for that. Vamoose! We'll overhaul you."

The bride moved upon the desert alone, her face toward an easterly hill that had given Farallone his figure of the sugar-loaf. She had no longer the effect of a wilted flower, but walked with quick, considered steps. What the groom carried and what I carried is of little moment. Our packs united would not have made the half of the lumbersome weight that Farallone swung upon his giant shoulders.

"Follow the woman," said he, and we began to march upon the shoe-and-stocking track of the bride. Farallone, rolling like a ship (I had many a look at him over my shoulder) brought up the rear. From time to time he flung forward a phrase to us in explanation of his rebellious attitude.

"I take command because I'm fit; you're not. I give the orders because I can get 'em obeyed; you can't." And, again: "You don't know east from west; I do."

All the morning he kept firing disagreeable and very personal remarks at us. His proposition that we were not in any way fit for anything he enlarged upon and illustrated. He flung the groom's unemployed ancestry at him; he likened the groom to Rome at the time of the fall, which he attributed to luxury; he informed me that only men who were unable to work, or in any way help themselves, wrote books. "The woman's worth the two of you," he said. "Her people were workers. See it in her stride. She could milk a cow if she had one. If anything happens to me she'll give the orders. Mark my words. She's got a head on her shoulders, she has."

The bride halted suddenly in her tracks and, turning, faced the groom.

"Are you going to allow this man's insolence to run on forever?" she said.

The groom frowned at her and shook his head covertly.

"Pooh," said the bride, and I think I heard her call him "*my champion*," in a bitter whisper. She walked straight back to Farallone and looked him fearlessly in the face.

"The bigger a man is, Mr. Farallone," she said, "and the stronger, the more he ought to mind his manners. We are grateful to you for all you have done, but if you cannot keep a civil tongue in your head, then the sooner we part company the better."

For a full minute the fearless eyes snapped at Farallone, then, suddenly abashed, softened, and turned away.

"There mustn't be any more mutiny," said Farallone. "But you've got sand, you have. I could love a woman like you. How did you come to hitch your wagon to little Nicodemus there? He's no star. You deserved a man. You've got sand, and when your poor feet go back on you, as they will in this swill (here he kicked the burning sand), I'll carry you. But if you hadn't spoken up so pert, I wouldn't. Now you walk ahead and pretend you're Christopher Columbus De Soto Peary leading a flock of sheep to the Fountain of Eternal Youth. . . . Bear to the left of the sage-brush, there's a tarantula under it. . . ."

We went forward a few steps, when suddenly I heard Farallone's voice in my ear. "Isn't she splendid?" he said, and at the same time he thumped me so violently between the shoulders that I stumbled and fell. For a moment all fear of the man left me on the wings of rage, and I was for attacking him with my fists. But something in his steady eye brought me to my senses.

"Why did you do that?" I meant to speak sharply, but I think I whined.

"Because," said Farallone, "when the woman spoke up to me you began to brindle and act lion-like and bold. For a minute you looked dangerous — for a little feller. So I patted your back, in a friendly way — as a kind of reminder — a feeble reminder."

We had dropped behind the others. The groom had caught up with the bride, and from his nervous, irritable gestures I gathered that the poor soul was trying to explain and to ingratiate himself. But she walked on, steadily averted, you might say, her head very high, her shoulders drawn back. The groom, his eyes intent upon her averted face, kept stumbling with his feet.

"Just look," said Farallone in a friendly voice. "Those whom God hath joined together. What did the press say of it?"

"I don't remember," I said.

"You lie," said Farallone. "The press called it an ideal match. My God!" he cried — and so loudly that the bride and the groom must have heard — "think of being a woman like that and getting hitched to a little bit of a fuss with a few fine feathers"; and with a kind of sing-song he began to misquote and extemporize:

"Just for a handful of silver she left me,
Just for a yacht and a mansion of stone,
Just for a little fool nest of fine feathers
She wed Nicodemus and left me alone."

"But she'd never seen me," he went on, and mused for a moment. "Having seen me — do you guess what she's saying to herself? She's saying: 'Thank God I'm not too old to begin life over again,' or thinking it. Look at him! Even you wouldn't have been such a joke. I've a mind to kick the life out of him. One little kick with bare toes. Life? There's no life in him — nothing but a jenny-wren."

The groom, who must have heard at least the half of Farallone's speech, stopped suddenly and waited for us to come up. His face was red and white — blotchy with rage and vindictiveness. When we were within ten feet of him he suddenly drew a revolver and fired it point-blank at Farallone. He had no time for a second shot. Farallone caught his wrist and shook it till the revolver spun through the air and fell at a distance. Then Farallone seated himself and, drawing the groom across his knee, spanked him. Since the beginning of the world children have been punished by spankings, and the event is memorable, if at all, as a something rather comical and domestic. But to see a grown man spanked for the crime of attempted murder is horrible. Farallone's fury got the better of him, and the blows resounded in the desert. I grappled his arm, and the recoil of it flung me head over heels. When Farallone had finished, the groom could not stand. He rolled in the sands, moaning and hiding his face.

The bride was white as paper; but she had no eye for the groom.

"Did he miss you?" she said.

"No," said Farallone, "he hit me — Nicodemus hit me."

"Where?" said the bride.

"In the arm."

Indeed, the left sleeve of Farallone's shirt was glittering with blood.

"I will bandage it for you," she said, "if you will tell me how."

Farallone ripped open the sleeve of his shirt.

"What shall I bandage it with?" asked the bride.

"Anything," said Farallone.

The bride turned her back on us, stooped, and we heard a sound of tearing. When she had bandaged Farallone's wound (it was in the flesh and the bullet had been extracted by its own impetus) she looked him gravely in the face.

"What's the use of goading him?" she said gently.

"Look," said Farallone.

The groom was reaching for the fallen revolver.

"Drop it," bellowed Farallone.

The groom's hand, which had been on the point of grasping the revolver's stock, jerked away. The bride walked to the revolver and picked it up. She handed it to Farallone.

"Now," she said, "that all the power is with you, you will not go on abusing it."

"*You* carry it," said Farallone, "and any time *you* think I ought to be shot, why, you just shoot me. I won't say a word."

"Do you mean it?" said the bride.

"I cross my heart," said Farallone.

"I sha'n't forget," said the bride. She took the revolver and dropped it into the pocket of her jacket.

"Vamoose!" said Farallone. And we resumed our march.

III

The line between the desert and the blossoming hills was as distinctly drawn as that between a lake and its shore. The sage-brush, closer massed than any through which we had yet passed, seemed to have gathered itself for a serried assault upon the lovely verdure beyond. Outposts of the sage-brush, its unsung heroes, perhaps, showed here and there among ferns and wild roses — leafless, gaunt, and dead; one knotted specimen even had planted its banner of desolation in the shade of a wild lilac and there died. A twittering of birds gladdened our dusty ears, and from afar there came a splashing of water. Our feet, burned by the desert sands, torn by yucca and cactus, trod now upon a cool and delicious moss, above which nodded the delicate blossoms of the shooting-star, swung at the ends of strong and delicate stems. In the shadows the chocolate lilies and trilliums dully glinted, and flag flowers trooped in the sunlight. The resinous paradisiacal smell of tarweed and bay-tree refreshed us, and the wonder of life was a something strong and tangible like bread and wine.

The wine of it rushed in particular to Farallone's head; his brain became flooded with it; his feet cavorted upon the moss; his bellowed singing awoke the echoes, and the whole heavenly choir of the birds answered him.

"You, Nicodemus," he cried gayly, "thought that man was given a nose to be a tripod for his eye-glasses — but now — oh, smell — smell!"

His great bulk under its mighty pack tripped lightly, dancingly at the bride's elbow. Now his agile fingers nipped some tiny, scarce perceivable flower to delight her eye, and now his great hand scooped up whole sheaves of strong-growing columbine, and flung them where her feet must tread. He made her see great beauties and minute, and whatever had a look of smelling sweet he crushed in his hands for her to smell.

He was no longer that limb of Satan, that sardonic bully of the desert days, but a gay wood-god intent upon the gentle ways of wooing. At first the bride turned away her senses from his offerings to eye and nostril; for a time she made shift to turn aside from the flowers that he cast for her feet to tread. But after a time, like one in a trance, she began to yield up her indifference and aloofness. The magic of the riotous spring began to intoxicate her. I saw her turn to the sailor and smile a gracious smile. And after awhile she began to talk with him.

We came at length to a bright stream, from whose guileless superabundance Farallone, with a bent pin and a speck of red cloth, jerked a string of gaudy rainbow-trout. He made a fire and began to broil them; the bride searched the vicinal woods for dried branches to feed the fire. The groom knelt by the brook and washed the dust from his face and ears, snuffing the cool water into his dusty nose and blowing it out.

And I lay in the shade and wondered by what courses the brook found its way to what sea or lake; whether it touched in its wanderings only the virginal wilderness, or flowed at length among the habitations of men.

Farallone, of a sudden, jerked up his head from the broiling and answered my unspoken questions.

"A man," he said, "who followed this brook could come in a few days to the river Maria Cleofas, and following that, to the town of that name, in a matter of ten days more. I tell you," he went on, "because some day some of you may be going that voyage; no ill-found voyage either — spring-water and trout all the way to the river; and all the rest of the way river-water and trout; and at this season birds' eggs in the reeds and a turtlelike terrapin, and Brodeia roots and wild onion, and young sassafras — a child could do it. Eat that. . . ." he tossed me with his fingers a split, sputtering, piping hot trout. . . .

We spent the rest of that day and the night following by the stream. Farallone was in a riotous good-humor, and the fear of him grew less in us until we felt at ease and could take an unmixed pleasure in the loafing.

Early the next morning he was astir, and began to prepare himself for further marching, but for the rest of us he said there would be one day more of rest.

"Who knows," he said, "but this is Sunday?"

"Where are you going?" asked the bride politely.

"Me?" said Farallone, and he laughed. "I'm going house-hunting — not for a house, of course, but for a site. It's not so easy to pick out just the place where you want to spend the balance of your days. The neighborhood's easy, but the exact spot's hard." He spoke now directly to the bride, and as if her opinion was law to him. "There must be sun and shade, mustn't there? Spring-water? — running water? A hill handy to take the view from? An easterly slope to be out of the trades? A big tree or two. . . . I'll find 'em all before dark. I'll be back by dark or at late moonrise, and you rest yourselves, because tomorrow or the next day we go at house-raising."

Had he left us then and there, I think that we would have waited for him. He had us, so to speak, abjectly under his thumbs. His word had come to be our law, since it was but child's play for him to enforce it. But it so happened that he now took a step which was to call into life and action that last vestige of manhood and independence that flickered in the groom and me. For suddenly, and not till after a moment of consideration, he took a step toward the bride, caught her around the waist, crushed her to his breast, and kissed her on the mouth.

But she must have bitten him, for the tender passion changed in him to an unmanly fury.

"You damned cat!" he cried; and he struck her heavily upon the face with his open palm. Not once only, but twice, three, four times, till she fell at his feet.

By that the groom and I, poor, helpless atoms, had made shift to grapple with him. I heard his giant laugh. I had one glimpse of the groom's face rushing at mine — and then it was as if showers of stars fell about me. What little strength I had was loosened from my joints, and more than half-senseless I fell full length upon my back. Farallone had foiled our attack by the simple method of catching us by the hair and knocking our heads together.

I could hear his great mocking laugh resounding through the forest.

"Let him go," I heard the groom moan.

The bride laughed. It was a very curious laugh. I could not make it out. There seemed to be no anger in it, and yet how, I wondered, could there be anything else?

IV

When distance had blotted from our ears the sound of Farallone's laughter, and when we had humbled ourselves to the bride for allowing her to be maltreated, I told the groom what Farallone had said about a man who should follow the stream by which we were encamped.

"See," I said, "we have a whole day's start of him. Even he can't make that up. We must go at once, and there mustn't be any letting up till we get somewhere."

The groom was all for running away, and the bride, silent and white, acquiesced with a nod. We made three light packs, and started — *bolted* is the better word.

For a mile or more, so thick was the underwood, we walked in the bed of the stream; now freely, where it was smooth-spread sand, and now where it narrowed and deepened among rocks, scramblingly and with many a splashing stumble. The bride met her various mishaps with a kind of silent disdain; she made no complaints, not even comments. She made me think of a sleep-walker. There was a set, far-off, cold expression upon her usually gentle and vivacious face, and once or twice it occurred to me that she went with us unwillingly. But when I remembered the humiliation that Farallone had put upon her and the blows that he had struck her, I could not well credit the recurrent doubt of her willingness. The groom, on the other hand, recovered his long-lost spirits with immeasurable rapidity. He talked gayly and bravely, and you would have said that he was a man who had never had occasion to be ashamed of himself. He went ahead, the bride following next, and he kept giving a constant string of advices and imperatives. "That stone's loose"; "keep to the left, there's a hole." "Splash — dash — damn, look out for that one." Branches that hung low across our course he bent and held back until the bride had passed. Now he turned and smiled in her face, and now he offered her the helping hand. But she met his courtesies, and the whole punctilious fabric of his behavior, with the utmost absence and nonchalance. He had, it seemed, been too long in contempt to recover soon his former position of husband and beloved. For long days she had contemplated his naked soul, limited, weak, incapable. He had shown a certain capacity for sudden, explosive temper, but not for courage of any kind, or force. Nor had he played the gentleman in his helplessness. Nor had I. We had not in us the stuff of heroes; at first sight of instruments of torture we were of those who would confess to anything, abjure, swear falsely, beg for mercy, change our so-called religions — anything. The bride had learned to despise us from the bottom of her heart. She despised us still. And I would have staked my last dollar, or, better, my hopes of escaping from Farallone, that as man and wife she and the groom would never live together again. I felt terribly sorry for the groom. He had, as had I, been utterly inefficient, helpless, babyish, and cowardly — yet the odds against us had seemed overwhelming. But now as we journeyed down the river, and the distance between us and Farallone grew more, I kept thinking of men whom I had known; men physically weaker than the groom and I, who, had Farallone offered to bully them, would have fought him and endured his torture till they died. In my immediate past, then, there was nothing of which I was not burningly ashamed, and in the not-too-distant future I hoped to separate from the bride and the groom, and never see them or hear of them in this world again. At that, I had a real affection for the bride, a real admiration. On the yacht, before trouble showed me up, we had bid fair to become fast and enduring friends. But that was all over — a bud, nipped by the frost of conduct and circumstance, or ever the fruit could so much as set. For many days now I had avoided her eye; I had avoided addressing her; I had exerted my ingenuity to keep out of her sight. It is a terrible thing for a man to be thrown daily into the society of a woman who has found him out, and who despises him, mind, soul, marrow, and bone.

The stream broke at length from the forest and, swelled by a sizable tributary, flowed broad and deep into a rolling, park-like landscape. Grass spread over the country's undulations and looked in the distance like well-kept lawns; and at wide intervals splendidly grown live-oaks lent an effect of calculated planting. Here our flight, for our muscles were hardened to walking, became easy and swift. I think there were hours when we must have covered our four miles, and even on long, upward slopes we must have made better than three. There is in swift walking, when the muscles are hard, the wind long, and the atmosphere exhilarating, a buoyant rhythm that more, perhaps, than merited success, or valorous conduct, smoothes out the creases in a man's soul. And so quick is a man to recover from his own baseness, and to ape outwardly his transient inner feelings, that I found myself presently, walking with a high head and a mind full of martial thoughts.

All that day, except for a short halt at noon, we followed the river across the great natural park; now paralleling its convolutions, and now cutting diagonals. Late in the afternoon we came to the end of the park land. A more or less precipitous formation of glistening quartz marked its boundary, and into a fissure of this the stream, now a small river, plunged with accelerated speed. The going became difficult. The walls of the fissure through which the river rushed were smooth and water-worn, impossible to ascend; and between the brink of the river and the base of the walls were congestions of boulders, jammed drift-wood, and tangled alder bushes. There were times when we had to crawl upon our hands and knees, under one log and over the next. To add to our difficulties darkness was swiftly falling, and we were glad, indeed, when the wall of the fissure leaned at length so far from the perpendicular that we were able to scramble up it. We found ourselves upon a levelish little meadow of grass. In the centre of it there grew a monstrous and gigantic live-oak, between two of whose roots there glittered a spring. On all sides of the meadow, except on that toward the river, were superimpending cliffs of quartz. Along the base of these was a dense growth of bushes.

"We'll rest here," said the groom. "What a place. It's a natural fortress. Only one way into it." He stood looking down at the noisy river and considering the steep slope we had just climbed. "See this boulder?" he said. "It's wobbly. If that damned longshoreman tries to get us here, all we've got to do is to choose the psychological moment and push it over on him."

The groom looked quite bellicose and daring. Suddenly he flung his fragment of a cap high into the air and at the very top of his lungs cried: "Liberty!"

The echoes answered him, and the glorious, abused word was tossed from cliff to cliff, across the river and back, and presently died away.

At that, from the very branches of the great oak that stood in the centre of the meadow there burst a titanic clap of laughter, and Farallone, literally bursting with merriment, dropped lightly into our midst.

I can only speak for myself. I was frightened — I say it deliberately and truthfully — *almost* into a fit. And for fully five minutes I could not command either of my legs. The groom, I believe, screamed. The bride became whiter than paper — then suddenly the color rushed into her cheeks, and she laughed. She laughed until she had to sit down, until the tears literally gushed from her eyes. It was not hysterics either — could it have been amusement? After a while, and many prolonged gasps and relapses, she stopped.

"This," said Farallone, "is my building site. Do you like it?"

"Oh, oh," said the bride, "I think it's the m — most am — ma — musing site I ever saw," and she went into another uncontrollable burst of laughter.

"Oh — oh," she said at length, and her shining eyes were turned from the groom to me, and back and forth between us, "if you *could* have seen your faces!"

V

It seemed strange to us, an alteration in the logical and natural, but neither the groom nor I received corporal punishment for our attempt at escape. Farallone had read our minds like an open book; he had, as it were, put us up to the escapade in order to have the pure joy of thwarting us. That we should have been drawn to his exact waiting-place like needles to the magnet had a smack of the supernatural, but was in reality a simple and explicable happening. For if we had not ascended to the little meadow, Farallone, alertly watching, would have descended from it, and surprised us at some further point. That we should have caught no glimpse of his great bulk anywhere ahead of us in the day-long stretch of open, park-like country was also easily explained. For Farallone had made the most of the journey in the stream itself, drifting with a log.

And although, as I have said, we were not to receive corporal punishment, Farallone visited his power upon us in other ways. He would not at first admit that we had intended to escape, but kept praising us for having followed him so loyally and devotedly, for saving him the trouble of a return journey, and for thinking to bring along the bulk of our worldly possessions. Tiring at length of this, he switched to the opposite point of view. He goaded us nearly to madness with his criticisms of our inefficiency, and he mocked repeatedly the groom's ill-timed cry of Liberty.

"Liberty!" he said, "you never knew, you never will know, what that is — you miserable little pin-head. Liberty is for great natures.

> 'Stone walls do not a prison make,
> Nor iron bars a cage.'

But the woman shall know what liberty is. If she had wanted to leave me there was nothing to stop her. Do you think she'd have followed the river, leaving a broad trail? Do you think she'd have walked right into this meadow — unless she hadn't cared? Not she. Did you ask her advice, you self-sufficiencies? Not you. You were the men-folk, you thought, and you were to have the ordering of everything. You make me sick, the pair of you. . . ."

He kept us awake until far into the night with his jibes and his laughter.

"Well," he said lastly, "good-night, girls. I'm about sick of you, and in the morning we part company. . . ."

At the break of dawn he waked us from heavy sleep — me with a cuff, the groom with a kick, the bride with a feline touch upon the hair.

"And now," said he, "be off."

He caught the bride by the shoulder.

"Not *you*," he said.

"I am to stay?" she asked, as if to settle some trivial and unimportant point.

"Do you ask?" said he; "Was man meant to live alone? This will be enough home for us." And he turned to the groom. "Get," he said savagely.

"Mr. Farallone," said the bride — she was very white, but calm, apparently, and collected — "you have had your joke. Let us go now, or better, come with us. We will forget our former differences, and you will never regret your future kindnesses."

"Don't you *want* to stay?" exclaimed Farallone in a tone of astonishment.

"If I did," said the bride gently, "I could not, and I would not."

"What's to stop you?" asked Farallone.

"My place is with my husband," said the bride, "whom I have sworn to love, and to honor, and to obey."

"Woman," said Farallone, "do you love him, do you honor him?"

She pondered a moment, then held her head high.

"I do," she said.

"God bless you," cried the groom.

"Rats," said Farallone, and he laughed bitterly. "But you'll get over it," he went on. "Let's have no more words." He turned to the groom and to me.

"Will you climb down the cliff or shall I throw you?"

"Let us all go," said the bride, and she caught at his trembling arm, "and I will bless you, and wish you all good things — and kiss you good-by."

"If you go," said Farallone, and his great voice trembled, "I die. You are everything. You know that. Would I have hit you if I hadn't loved you so — poor little cheek!" His voice became a kind of mumble.

"Let us go," said the bride, "if you love me."

"Not *you*," said Farallone, "while I live. I would not be such a fool. Don't you know that in a little while you'll be glad?"

"Is that your final word?" said the bride.

"It must be," said Farallone. "Are you not a gift to me from God?"

"I think you must be mad," said the bride.

"I am unalterable," said Farallone, "as God made me — I *am*.

And you are mine to take."

"Do you remember," said the bride, "what you said when you gave me the revolver? You said that if ever I thought it best to shoot you — you would let me do it."

"I remember," said Farallone, and he smiled.

"That was just talk, of course?" said the bride.

"It was not," said Farallone; "shoot me."

"Let us go," said the bride. Her voice faltered.

"Not you," said Farallone, "while I live."

His voice, low and gentle, had in it a kind of far-off sadness. He turned his eyes from the bride and looked the rising sun in the face. He turned back to her and smiled.

"You haven't the heart to shoot me," he said. "My darling."

"Let us go."

"Let — you — go!" He laughed. "Send — away — my — mate!"

His eyes clouded and became vacant. He blinked them rapidly and raised his hand to his brow. It seemed to me that in that instant, suddenly come and suddenly gone, I perceived a look of insanity in his face. The bride, too, perhaps, saw something of the kind, for like a flash she had the revolver out and cocked it.

"Splendid," cried Farallone, and his eyes blazed with a tremendous love and admiration. "This is something like," he cried. "Two forces face to face — a man and a bullet — love behind them both. Ah, you do love me — don't you?"

"Let us go," said the bride. Her voice shook violently.

"Not you," said Farallone, "while I live."

He took a step toward her, his eyes dancing and smiling. "Do you know," he said, "I don't know if you'll do it or not. By my soul, I don't know. This is living, this is. This is gambling. I'll do nothing violent," he said, "until my hands are touching you. I'll move toward you slowly one slow step at a time — with my arms open — like this — you'll have plenty of chance to shoot me — we'll see if you'll do it."

"We shall see," said the bride.

They faced each other motionless. Then Farallone, his eyes glorious with excitement and passion, his arms open, moved toward her one slow, deliberate step.

"Wait," he cried suddenly. "This is too good for *them*." He jerked his thumb toward the groom and me. "This is a sight for gods — not jackasses. Go down to the river," he said to us. "If you hear a shot come back. If you hear a scream — then as you value your miserable hides — get!"

We did not move.

The bride, her voice tense and high-pitched, turned to us.

"Do as you're told," she cried, "or I shall ask this man to throw you over the cliff." She stamped her foot.

"And this man," said Farallone, "will do as he's told."

There was nothing for it. We left them alone in the meadow and descended the cliff to the river. And there we stood for what seemed the ages of ages, listening and trembling.

A faint, far-off detonation, followed swiftly by louder and fainter echoes, broke suddenly upon the rushing noises of the river. We commenced feverishly to scramble back up the cliff. Half-way to the top we heard another shot, a second later a third, and after a longer interval, as if to put a quietus upon some final show of life — a fourth.

A nebulous drift of smoke hung above the meadow.

Farallone lay upon his face at the bride's feet. The groom sprang to her side and threw a trembling arm about her.

"Come away," he cried, "come away."

But the bride freed herself gently from his encircling arm, and her eyes still bent upon Farallone —

"Not till I have buried my dead," she said.

HOLDING HANDS

At first nobody knew him; then the Hotchkisses knew him, and then it seemed as if everybody had always known him. He had run the gauntlet of gossip and come through without a scratch. He was first noticed sitting in the warm corner made by Willcox's annex and the covered passage that leads to the main building. Pairs or trios of people, bareheaded, their tennis clothes (it was a tennis year) mostly covered from view by clumsy coonskin coats, passing Willcox's in dilapidated runabouts drawn by uncurried horses, a nigger boy sitting in the back of each, his thin legs dangling, had glimpses of him through the driveway gap in the tall Amor privet hedge that is between Willcox's and the road. These pairs or trios having seen would break in upon whatever else they may have been saying to make such remarks as: "He can't be, or he wouldn't be at Willcox's"; or, contradictorily: "He must be, or he'd do something besides sit in the sun"; or, "Don't they always have to drink lots of milk?" or, "Anyway, they're quite positive that it's not catching"; or, "Poor boy, what nice hair he's got."

With the old-timers the new-comer, whose case was otherwise so doubtful, had one thing in common: a coonskin coat. It was handsome of its kind, unusually long, voluminous, and black. The upturned collar came above his ears, and in the opening his face showed thin and white, and his eyes, always intent upon the book in his lap, had a look of being closed. Two things distinguished him from other men: his great length of limb and the color and close-cropped, almost moulded, effect of his hair. It was the color of old Domingo mahogany, and showed off the contour of his fine round head with excellent effect.

The suspicion that this interesting young man was a consumptive was set aside by Willcox himself. He told Mrs. Bainbridge, who asked (on account of her little children who, et cetera, et cetera), that Mr. Masters was recuperating from a very stubborn attack of typhoid. But was Mr. Willcox quite sure? Yes, Mr. Willcox had to be sure of just such things. So Mrs. Bainbridge drove out to Miss Langrais' tea at the golf club, and passed on the glad tidings with an addition of circumstantial detail. Mister Masters (people found that it was quite good fun to say this, with assorted intonations) had been sick for many months at — she thought — the New York Hospital. Sometimes his temperature had touched a hundred and fifteen degrees and sometimes he had not had any temperature at all. There was quite a romance involved, "his trained nurse, my dear, not one of the ordinary creatures, but a born lady in impoverished circumstances," et cetera, et cetera. And later, when even Mister Masters himself had contradicted these brightly colored statements, Mrs. Bainbridge continued to believe them. Even among wealthy and idle women she was remarkable for the number of impossible things she could believe before breakfast, and after. But she never made these things seem even half plausible to others, and so she wasn't dangerous.

Mister Masters never remembered to have passed so lonely and dreary a February. The sunny South was a medicine that had been prescribed and that had to be swallowed. Aiken on the label had looked inviting enough, but he found the contents of the bottle distasteful in the extreme. "The South is sunny," he wrote to his mother, "but oh, my great jumping grandmother, how seldom! And it's cold, mummy, like being beaten with whips. And it rains — well, if it rained cats and dogs a fellow wouldn't mind. Maybe they'd speak to him, but it rains solid cold water, and it hits the windows the way waves hit the port-holes at sea; and the only thing that stops the rain is a wind that comes all the way from Alaska for the purpose. In protected corners the sun has a certain warmth. But the other morning the waiter put my milk on the wrong side of my chair, in the shade, namely, and when I went to drink it it was frozen solid. You were right about the people here all being kind; they are all the same kind. I know them all now — by sight; but not by name, except, of course, some who are stopping at Willcox's. We have had three ice storms — 'Kennst du das Land wo die Citronen blühen?' I am getting to kennst it very well. But Willcox, who keeps a record of such things, says that this is the coldest winter Aiken has known since last winter!

"But in spite of all this there is a truth that must be spoken. I feel a thousand times better and stronger than when I came. And yesterday, exercising in the privacy of my room, I discovered that there are once more calves upon my legs. This is truth, too. I have no one to talk to but your letters. So don't stint me. Stint me with money if you can (here I defy you), but for the love of Heaven keep me posted. If you will promise to write every day I will tell you the name of the prettiest girl in Aiken. She goes by eight times every day, and she looks my way out of the corner of her eye. And I pretend to be reading and try very hard to look handsome and interesting. . . . Mother! ... just now I rested my hand on the arm of my chair and the wood felt hot to the touch! It's high noon and the sun's been on it since eight o'clock, but still it seems very wonderful. Willcox says that the winter is practically over; but I begged him not to hurry. . . ."

Such was the usual trend of his letters. But that one dated March 7 began with the following astonishing statement:

"I love Aiken ..." and went on to explain why.

But Mister Masters was not allowed to love Aiken until he had come through the whole gauntlet of gossip. It had first been suggested that he was a consumptive and a menace ("though of course one feels terribly sorry for them, my dear"). This had been disproved. Then it was spread about that he belonged to a wealthy family of Masters from the upper West Side ("very well in their way, no doubt, and the backbone of the country, my dear, but one doesn't seem to get on with them, and I shouldn't think they'd come to Aiken of all places"). But a gentleman who knew the West Side Masters, root and branch, shook his head to this, and went so far as to say, "Not much, he isn't"; and went further and shuddered. Then it got about that Mister Masters was poor (and that made people suspicious of him). Then it got about that he was rich (and that made them even more so). Then that he wrote for a living (and that was nearly as bad as to say that he cheated at cards — or at least it was the kind of thing that *they* didn't do). And then, finally, the real truth about him, or something like it, got out; and the hatchet of suspicion was buried, and there was peace in Aiken. In that Aiken of whose peace the judge, referring to a pock-marked mulatto girl, had thundered that it should not be disturbed for any woman — "no — not even were she Helen of Troy."

This was the truth that got out about Mister Masters. He was a nephew of the late Bishop Masters. His mother, on whom he was dependent, was very rich; she had once been prominent in society. He was thirty, and was good at games. He did not work at anything.

So he was something that Aiken could understand and appreciate: a young man who was well-born, who didn't have to work — and who didn't *want* to.

But old Mrs. Hotchkiss did not know of these things when, one bright day in passing Willcox's (she was on one good foot, one rheumatic foot, and a long black cane with a gold handle), she noticed the young man pale and rather sad-looking in his fur coat and steamer-rug, his eyes on his book, and stopped abruptly and spoke to him through the gap in the hedge.

"I hope you'll forgive an old woman for scraping an acquaintance," she piped in her brisk, cheerful voice, "but I want to know if you're getting better, and I thought the best way to find out was to stop and ask."

Mister Masters's steamer-rug fell from about his long legs and his face became rosy, for he was very shy.

"Indeed I am," he said, "ever so much. And thank you for asking."

"I'm tired," said the old lady, "of seeing you always sitting by yourself, dead tired of it. I shall come for you this afternoon at four in my carriage, and take you for a drive. . . ."

"It was abrupt," Mister Masters wrote to his mother, "but it was kind. When I had done blushing and scraping with my feet and pulling my forelock, we had the nicest little talk. And she remembered you in the old days at Lenox, and said why hadn't I told her before. And then she asked if I liked Aiken, and, seeing how the land lay, I lied and said I loved it. And she said that that was her nice, sensible young fellow, or words to that effect. And then she asked me why, and I said because it has such a fine climate; and then she laughed in my face, and said that I was without reverence for her age — not a man — a scalawag.

"And do you know, Mrs. Hotchkiss is like one of those magic keys in fairy stories? All doors open to her. Between you and me I have been thinking Aiken's floating population snobbish, purse-proud, and generally absurd. And instead, the place seems to exist so that kindness and hospitality may not fail on earth. Of course I'm not up to genuine sprees, such as dining out and sitting up till half-past ten or eleven. But I can go to luncheons, and watch other people play tennis, and poke about gardens with old ladies, and guess when particular flowers will be out, and learn the names of birds and of hostile bushes that prick and of friendly bushes that don't.

"All the cold weather has gone to glory; and it's really spring because the roosters crow all night. Mrs. Hotchkiss says it's because they are roosters and immoral. But I think they're crowing because they've survived the winter. I am. . . ."

Aiken took a great fancy to Mister Masters. First because Aiken was giving him a good time; and second because he was really good company when you got him well cornered and his habitual fright had worn off. He was the shyest, most frightened six-footer in the memory of Aiken. If you spoke to him suddenly he blushed, and if you prepared him by first clearing your throat he blushed just the same. And he had a crooked, embarrassed smile that was a delight to see.

But gradually he became almost at ease with nearly everybody; and in the shyest, gentlest way enjoyed himself hugely. But the prettiest girl in Aiken had very hard work with him.

As a stag fights when brought to bay, so Mister Masters when driven into a corner could talk as well and as freely as the next man;

but on his own initiative there was, as we Americans say, "nothing doing." Whether or not the prettiest girl in Aiken ever rolled off a log is unknown; but such an act would have been no more difficult for her than to corner Mister Masters. The man courted cornering, especially by her. But given the desired situation, neither could make anything of it. Mister Masters's tongue became forthwith as helpless as a man tied hand and foot and gagged. He had nothing with which to pay for the delight of being cornered but his rosiest, steadiest blush and his crookedest and most embarrassed smile. But he retained a certain activity of mind and within himself was positively voluble with what he would say if he only could.

I don't mean that the pair sat or stood or walked in absolute silence. Indeed, little Miss Blythe could never be silent for a long period nor permit it in others, but I mean that with the lines and the machinery of a North Atlantic liner, their craft of propinquity made about as much progress as a scow. Nevertheless, though neither was really aware of this, each kept saying things, that cannot be put into words, to the other; otherwise the very first cornering of Mister Masters by little Miss Blythe must have been the last. But even as it was way back at the beginning of things, and always will be, Beauty spoke to Handsome and Handsome up and spoke back.

"No," said little Miss Blythe, upon being sharply cross-questioned by Mrs. Hotchkiss, "he practically never does say anything."

Mrs. Hotchkiss dug a little round hole in the sand with her long black cane, and made an insulting face at little Miss Blythe.

"Some men," said she, "can't say 'Boo' to a goose."

If other countries produce girls like little Miss Blythe, I have never met a specimen; and I feel very sure that foreign young ladies do not become personages at the age of seventeen. When she met Mister Masters she had been a personage for six years, and it was time for her to yield her high place to another; to marry, to bear children, and to prove that all the little matters for which she was celebrated were merely passing phases and glitterings of a character which fundamentally was composed of simple and noble traits.

Little Miss Blythe had many brothers and sisters; no money, as we reckon money; and only such prospects as she herself might choose from innumerable offers. She was little; her figure looked best in athletic clothes (low neck didn't do well with her, because her face was tanned so brown) and she was strong and quick as a pony. All the year round she kept herself in the pink of condition ("overkept herself" some said) dancing, walking, running, swimming, playing all games and eating to match. She had a beautiful, clean-cut face, not delicate and to be hidden and coaxed by veils and soft things, but a face that looked beautiful above a severe Eton collar, and at any distance. She had the bright, wide eyes of a collected athlete, unbelievably blue, and the whites of them were only matched for whiteness by her teeth (the deep tan of her skin heightened this effect, perhaps); and it was said by one admirer that if she were to be in a dark room and were to press the button of a kodak and to smile at one and the same instant, there would be a picture taken.

She had friends in almost every country-clubbed city in America. Whenever, and almost wherever, a horse show was held she was there to show the horses of some magnate or other to the best advantage. Between times she won tennis tournaments and swimming matches, or tried her hand at hunting or polo (these things in secret because her father had forbidden them), and the people who continually pressed hospitality upon her said that they were repaid a thousand-fold. In the first place, it was a distinction to have her. "Who are the Ebers?" "Why, don't you know? They are the people Miss Blythe is stopping with."

She was always good-natured; she never kept anybody waiting; and she must have known five thousand people well enough to call them by their first names. But what really distinguished her most from other young women was that her success in inspiring others with admiration and affection was not confined to men; she had the same effect upon all women, old and young, and all children.

Foolish people said that she had no heart, merely because no one had as yet touched it. Wise people said that when she did fall in love sparks would fly. Hitherto her friendships with men, whatever the men in question may have wished, had existed upon a basis of good-natured banter and prowess in games. Men were absolutely necessary to Miss Blythe to play games with, because women who could "give her a game" were rare as ivory-billed woodpeckers. It was even thought by some, as an instance, that little Miss Blythe could beat the famous Miss May Sutton once out of three times at lawn-tennis. But Miss Sutton, with the good-natured and indomitable aggression of her genius, set this supposition at rest. Little Miss Blythe could not beat Miss Sutton once out of three or three hundred times. But for all that, little Miss Blythe was a splendid player and a master of strokes and strategy.

Nothing would have astonished her world more than to learn that little Miss Blythe had a secret, darkly hidden quality of which she was dreadfully ashamed. At heart she was nothing if not sentimental and romantic. And often when she was thought to be sleeping the dreamless sleep of the trained athlete who stores up energy for the morrow's contest, she was sitting at the windows in her night-gown, looking at the moon (in hers) and weaving all sorts of absurd adventures about herself and her particular fancy of the moment.

It would be a surprise and pleasure to some men, a tragedy perhaps to others, if they should learn that little Miss Blythe had fancied them all at different times, almost to the boiling point, and that in her own deeply concealed imagination Jim had rescued her from pirates and Jack from a burning hotel, or that just as her family were selling her to a rich widower, John had appeared on his favorite hunter and carried her off. The truth is that little Miss Blythe had engaged in a hundred love affairs concerning which no one but herself was the wiser.

And at twenty-three it was high time for her to marry and settle down. First because she couldn't go on playing games and showing horses forever, and second because she wanted to. But with whom she wanted to marry and settle down she could not for the life of her have said. Sometimes she thought that it would be with Mr. Blagdon. He *was* rich and he *was* a widower; but wherever she went he managed to go, and he had some of the finest horses in the world, and he wouldn't take no for an answer. Sometimes she said to the moon:

"I'll give myself a year, and if at the end of that time I don't like anybody better than Bob, why. . . ." Or, in a different mood, "I'm tired of everything I do; if he happens to ask me tomorrow I'll say yes." Or, "I've ridden his horses, and broken his golf clubs, and borrowed his guns (and he won't lend them to anybody else), and I suppose I've got to pay him back." Or, "I really *do* like him a lot," or "I really don't like him at all."

Then there came into this young woman's life Mister Masters. And he blushed his blush and smiled his crooked smile and looked at her when she wasn't looking at him (and she knew that he was looking) and was unable to say as much as "Boo" to her; and in the hidden springs of her nature that which she had always longed for happened, and became, and was. And one night she said to the moon: "I know it isn't proper for me to be so attentive to him, and I know everybody is talking about it, but —" and she rested her beautiful brown chin on her shapely, strong, brown hands, and a tear like a diamond stood in each of her unbelievably blue eyes, and she looked at the moon, and said: "But it's Harry Masters or — *bust!*"

Mr. Bob Blagdon, the rich widower, had been content to play a waiting game; for he knew very well that beneath her good-nature little Miss Blythe had a proud temper and was to be won rather by the man who should make himself indispensable to her than by him who should be forever pestering her with speaking and pleading his cause. She is an honest girl, he told himself, and without thinking of consequences she is always putting herself under obligations to me. Let her ride down lover's lane with young Blank or young Dash, she will not be able to forget that she is on my favorite mare. In his soul he felt a certain proprietorship in little Miss Blythe; but to this his ruddy, dark-mustached face and slow-moving eyes were a screen.

Mr. Blagdon had always gone after what he wanted in a kind of slow, indifferent way that begot confidence in himself and in the beholder; and (in the case of Miss Blythe) a kind of panic in the object sought. She liked him because she was used to him, and because he could and would talk sense upon subjects which interested her. But she was afraid of him because she knew that he expected her to marry him some day, and because she knew that other people, including her own family, expected this of her. Sometimes she felt ready to take unto herself all the horses and country places and automobiles and yachts, and in a life lived regardless of expense to bury and forget her better self. But more often, like a fly caught in a spider's web, she wished by one desperate effort (even should it cost her a wing, to carry out the figure) to free herself once and forever from the entanglement.

It was pleasant enough in the web. The strands were soft and silky; they held rather by persuasion than by force. And had it not been for the spider she could have lived out her life in the web without any very desperate regrets. But it was never quite possible to forget the spider; and that in his own time he would approach slowly and deliberately, sure of himself and of little Miss Fly. . . .

But, after all, the spider in the case was not such a terrible fellow. Just because a man wants a girl that doesn't want him, and means to have her, he hasn't necessarily earned a hard name. Such a man as often as not becomes one-half of a very happy marriage. And Mr. Bob Blagdon was considered an exceptionally good fellow. In his heart, though I have never heard him say so openly, I think he actually looked down on people who gambled and drank to excess, and who were uneducated and had acquired (whatever they may have been born with) perfectly empty heads. I think that he had a sound and sensible virtue; one ear for one side of an argument, and one for the other.

There is no reason to doubt that he was a good husband to his first wife, and wished to replace her with little Miss Blythe, not to supplant her. To his three young children he was more of a grandfather than a father; though strong-willed and even stubborn, he was unable half the time to say no to them. And I have seen him going on all-fours with the youngest child perched on his back kicking him in the ribs and urging him to canter. So if he intended by the strength of his will and of his riches to compel little Miss Blythe to marry (and to be happy with him; he thought he could manage that, too), it is only one blot on a decent and upright character. And it is unjust to have called him spider.

But when Mister Masters entered (so timidly to the eye, but really so masterfully) into little Miss Blythe's life, she could no longer tolerate the idea of marrying Mr. Blagdon. All in a twinkle she knew that horses and yachts and great riches could never make up to her for the loss of a long, bashful youth with a crooked smile. You can't be really happy if you are shivering with cold; you can't be really happy if you are dripping with heat. And she knew that without Mister Masters she must always be one thing or the other — too cold or too hot, never quite comfortable.

Her own mind was made up from the first; even to going through any number of awful scenes with Blagdon. But as time passed and her attentions (I shall have to call it that) to Mister Masters made no visible progress, there were times when she was obliged to think that she would never marry anybody at all. But in her heart she knew that Masters was attracted by her, and to this strand of knowledge she clung so as not to be drowned in a sea of despair.

Her position was one of extreme difficulty and delicacy. Sometimes Mister Masters came near her of his own accord, and remained in bashful silence; but more often she was obliged to have recourse to "accidents" in order to bring about propinquity. And even when propinquity had been established there was never any progress made that could be favorably noted. Behind her back, for instance, when she was playing tennis and he was looking on, he was quite bold in his admiration of her. And whereas most people's eyes when they are watching tennis follow the flight of the ball, Mister Masters's faithful eyes never left the person of his favorite player.

One reason for his awful bashfulness and silence was that certain people, who seemed to know, had told him in the very beginning that it was only a question of time before little Miss Blythe would become Mrs. Bob Blagdon. "She's always been fond of him," they said, "and of course he can give her everything worth having." So when he was with her he felt as if he was with an engaged girl, and his real feelings not being proper to express in any way under such circumstances, and his nature being single and without deceit, he was put in a quandary that defied solution.

But what was hidden from Mister Masters was presently obvious to Mr. Blagdon and to others. So the spider, sleepily watching the automatic enmeshment of the fly, may spring into alert and formidable action at seeing a powerful beetle blunder into the web and threaten by his stupid, aimless struggles to set the fly at liberty and to destroy the whole fabric spun with care and toil.

To a man in love there is no redder danger signal than a sight of the object of his affections standing or sitting contentedly with another man and neither of them saying as much as "Boo" to the other. He may, with more equanimity, regard and countenance a genuine flirtation, full of laughter and eye-making. The first time Mr. Blagdon saw them together he thought; the second time he felt; the third time he came forward graciously smiling. The web might be in danger from the beetle; the fly at the point of kicking up her heels and flying gayly away; but it may be in the power of the spider to spin enough fresh threads on the spur of the moment to rebind the fly, and even to make prisoner the doughty beetle.

"Don't you ride, Mister Masters?" said Mr. Blagdon.

"Of course," said the shy one, blushing. "But I'm not to do anything violent before June."

"Sorry," said Mr. Blagdon, "because I've a string of ponies that are eating their heads off. I'd be delighted to mount you."

But Mister Masters smiled with unusual crookedness and stammered his thanks and his regrets. And so that thread came to nothing.

The spider attempted three more threads; but little Miss Blythe looked serenely up.

"I never saw such a fellow as you, Bob," said she, "for putting other people under obligations. When I think of the weight of my personal ones I shudder." She smiled innocently and looked up into his face. "When people can't pay their debts they have to go through bankruptcy, don't they? And then their debts all have to be forgiven."

Mr. Blagdon felt as if an icy cold hand had been suddenly laid upon the most sensitive part of his back; but his expression underwent no change. His slow eyes continued to look into the beautiful, brightly colored face that was turned up to him.

"Very honorable bankrupts," said he carelessly, "always pay what they can on the dollar."

Presently he strolled away, easy and nonchalant; but inwardly he carried a load of dread and he saw clearly that he must learn where he stood with little Miss Blythe, or not know the feeling of easiness from one day to the next. Better, he thought, to be the recipient of a painful and undeserved ultimatum, than to breakfast, lunch, and dine with uncertainty.

The next day, there being some dozens of people almost in ear-shot, Mr. Blagdon had an opportunity to speak to little Miss Blythe. Under the circumstances, the last thing she expected was a declaration; they were in full view of everybody; anybody might stroll up and interrupt. So what Mr. Blagdon had to say came to her with something the effect of sudden thunder from a clear sky.

"Phyllis," said he, "you have been looking about you since you were seventeen. Will I do?"

"Oh, Bob!" she protested.

"I have tried to do," said he, not without a fine ring of manliness. "Have I made good?"

She smiled bravely and looked as nonchalant as possible; but her heart was beating heavily.

"I've liked being good friends — *so* much," she said. "Don't spoil it."

"I tell her," said he, "that in all the world there is only the one girl — only the one. And she says — Don't spoil it.'"

"Bob —"

"I will *make* you happy," he said. . . . "Has it never entered your dear head that some time you must give me an answer?"

She nodded her dear head, for she was very honest.

"I suppose so," she said.

"Well," said he.

"In my mind," she said, "I have never been able to give you the same answer twice. . . ."

"A decision is expected from us," said he. "People are growing tired of our long backing and filling."

"People! Do they matter?"

"They matter a great deal. And you know it."

"Yes. I suppose they do. Let me off for now, Bob. People are looking at us. . . ."

"I want an answer."

But she would not be coerced.

"You shall have one, but not now. I'm not sure what it will be."

"If you can't be sure now, can you ever be sure?"

"Yes. Give me two weeks. I shall think about nothing else."

"Thank you," he said. "Two weeks. . . . That will be full moon. . . . I shall ask all Aiken to a picnic in the woods, weather permitting ... and — and if your answer is to be my happiness, why, you shall come up to me, and say, 'Bob — drive me home, will you?'"

"And if it's the other answer, Bob?"

He smiled in his usual bantering way.

"If it's the other, Phyllis — why — you — you can walk home."

She laughed joyously, and he laughed, just as if nothing but what was light and amusing was in question between them.

Along the Whiskey Road nearly the whole floating population of Aiken moved on horseback or on wheels. Every fourth or fifth runabout carried a lantern; but the presence in the long, wide-gapped procession of other vehicles or equestrians was denoted only by the sounds of voices. Half a dozen family squabbles, half a dozen flirtations (which would result in family squabbles), and half a dozen genuine romances were moving through the sweet-smelling dark to Mr. Bob Blagdon's picnic in Red Oak Hollow. Only three of the guests knew where Red Oak Hollow was, and two of these were sure that they could only find it by daylight; but the third, a noted hunter and pigeon shot, rode at the head of the procession, and pretended (he was forty-five with the heart of a child) that he was Buffalo Bill leading a lost wagon-train to water. And though nobody could see him for the darkness, he played his part with minute attention to detail, listening, pulling up short, scowling to right and left, wetting a finger and holding it up to see from which direction the air was moving. He was so intent upon bringing his convoy safely through a hostile country that the sounds of laughter or of people in one runabout calling gayly to people in another were a genuine annoyance to him.

Mr. Bob Blagdon had preceded his guests by half an hour, and was already at the scene of the picnic. Fate, or perhaps the weather bureau at Washington, had favored him with just the conditions he would have wished for. The night was hot without heaviness; in the forenoon of that day there had been a shower, just wet enough to keep the surfaces of roads from rising in dust. It was now clear and bestarred, and perhaps a shade less dark than when he had started. Furthermore, it was so still that candles burned without flickering. He surveyed his preparations with satisfaction. And because he was fastidious in entertainment this meant a great deal.

A table thirty feet long, and low to the ground so that people sitting on rugs or cushions could eat from it with comfort, stood beneath the giant red oak that gave a name to the hollow. The white damask with which it was laid and the silver and cut glass gleamed in the light of dozens of candles. The flowers were Maréchal Niel roses in a long bank of molten gold.

Except for the lanterns at the serving tables, dimly to be seen through a dense hedgelike growth of Kalmia latifolia, there were no other lights in the hollow; so that the dinner-table had the effect of standing in a cave; for where the gleam of the candles ended, the surrounding darkness appeared solid like a wall.

It might have been a secret meeting of smugglers or pirates, the Georgian silver on the table representing years of daring theft; it seemed as if blood must have been spilled for the wonderful glass and linen and porcelain. Even those guests most hardened in luxury and extravagance looked twice at Mr. Bob Blagdon's picnic preparations before they could find words with which to compliment him upon them; and the less experienced were beside themselves with enthusiasm and delight. But Mr. Bob Blagdon was wondering what little Miss Blythe would think and say, and he thought it unkind of her, under the circumstances, to be the last to arrive. Unkind, because her doing so was either a good omen or an evil one, and he could not make up his mind which.

The guests were not homogeneously dressed. Some of the men were in dinner clothes; some were in full evening dress; some wore dinner coats above riding breeches and boots; some had come bare-headed, some with hats which they did not propose to remove. Half the women were in low neck and short sleeves; one with short curly hair was breeched and booted like a man; others wore what I suppose may be called theatre gowns; and a few who were pretty enough to stand it wore clothes suited to the hazards of a picnic in the woods.

Mr. Blagdon's servants wore his racing colors, blue and silver, knee-breeches, black silk stockings, pumps with silver buckles, and powdered hair. They were men picked for their height, wooden faces, and well-turned calves. They moved and behaved as if utterly untouched and uninterested in their unusual and romantic surroundings; they were like jinns summoned for the occasion by the rubbing of a magic lamp.

At the last moment, when to have been any later would have been either rude or accidental, little Miss Blythe's voice was heard calling from the darkness and asking which of two roads she should take. Half a dozen men rushed off to guide her, and presently she came blinking into the circle of light, followed by Mister Masters, who smiled his crookedest smile and stumbled on a root so that he was cruelly embarrassed.

Little Miss Blythe blinked at the lights and looked very beautiful. She was all in white and wore no hat. She had a red rose at her throat. She was grave for her — and silent.

The truth was that she had during the last ten minutes made up her mind to ask Mr. Bob Blagdon to drive her home when the picnic should be over. She had asked Mister Masters to drive out with her; and how much that had delighted him nobody knew (alas!) except Mister Masters himself. She had during the last few weeks given him every opportunity which her somewhat unconventional soul could sanction. In a hundred ways she had showed him that she liked him immensely; and well — if he liked her in the same way, he would have managed to show it, in spite of his shyness. The drive out had been a failure. They had gotten no further in conversation than the beauty and the sweet smells of the night. And finally, but God alone knows with what reluctance, she had given him up as a bad job.

The long table with its dozens of candles looked like a huge altar, and she was Iphigenia come to the sacrifice. She had never heard of Iphigenia, but that doesn't matter. At Mister Masters, now seated near the other end of the table, she lifted shy eyes; but he was looking at his plate and crumbling a piece of bread. It was like saying good-by. She was silent for a moment; then, smiling with a kind of reckless gayety, she lifted her glass of champagne and turned to the host.

"To you!" she said.

Delight swelled in the breast of Mr. Bob Blagdon. He raised his hand, and from a neighboring thicket there rose abruptly the music of banjos and guitars and the loud, sweet singing of negroes.

Aiken will always remember that dinner in the woods for its beauty and for its gayety. Two or three men, funny by gift and habit, were at their very best; and fortune adapted the wits of others to the occasion. So that the most unexpected persons became humorous for once in their lives, and said things worth remembering. People gather together for one of three reasons: to make laws, to break them, or to laugh. The first sort of gathering is nearly always funny, and if the last isn't, why then, to be sure, it is a failure. Mr. Bob Blagdon's picnic was an uproarious success. Now and then somebody's whole soul seemed to go into a laugh, in which others could not help joining, until uncontrollable snorts resounded in the hollow and eyes became blinded with tears.

And then suddenly, toward dessert, laughter died away and nothing was to be heard but such exclamations as: "For Heaven's sake, look at the moon!" "Did you ever see anything like it?"

Mr. Blagdon had paid money to the owner of Red Oak Hollow for permission to remove certain trees and thickets that would otherwise have obstructed his guests' view of the moonrise. At the end of the vista thus obtained the upper rim of the moon now appeared, as in a frame. And, watching in silence, Mr. Blagdon's guests saw the amazing luminary emerge, as it were, from the earth like a bright and blameless soul from the grave, and sail clear, presently, and upward into untroubled space; a glory, serene, smiling, and unanswerable.

No one remembered to have seen the moon so large or so bright. Atomized silver poured like tides of light into the surrounding woods; and at the same time heavenly odors of flowers began to move hither and thither, to change places, to return, and pass, like disembodied spirits engaged in some tranquil and celestial dance.

And it became cooler, so that women called for light wraps and men tied sweaters round their necks by the arms. Then at a long distance from the dinner-table a bonfire began to flicker, and then grow bright and red. And it was discovered that rugs and cushions had been placed (not too near the fire) for people to sit on while they drank their coffee and liquors, and that there were logs to lean against, and boxes of cigars and cigarettes where they could most easily be reached.

It was only a question now of how long the guests would care to stay. As a gathering the picnic was over. Some did not use the rugs and cushions that had been provided for them, but strolled away into the woods. A number of slightly intoxicated gentlemen felt it their duty to gather about their host and entertain him. Two married couples brought candles from the dinner-table and began a best two out of three at bridge. Sometimes two men and one woman would sit together with their backs against a log; but always after a few minutes one of the men would go away "to get something" and would not return.

It was not wholly by accident that Mister Masters found himself alone with little Miss Blythe. Emboldened by the gayety of the dinner, and then by the wonder of the moon, he had had the courage to hurry to her side; and though there his courage had failed utterly, his action had been such as to deter others from joining her. So, for there was nothing else to do, they found a thick rug and sat upon it, and leaned their backs against a log.

Little Miss Blythe had not yet asked Mr. Blagdon to drive her home. Though she had made up her mind to do so, it would only be at the last possible moment of the twelfth hour. It was now that eleventh hour in which heroines are rescued by bold lovers. But Mister Masters was no bolder than a mouse. And the moon sailed higher and higher in the heavens.

"Isn't it wonderful?" said little Miss Blythe.

"Wonderful!"

"Just smell it!"

"Umm."

Her sad, rather frightened eyes wandered over to the noisy group of which Mr. Bob Blagdon was the grave and silent centre. He knew that little Miss Blythe would keep her promise. He believed in his heart that her decision would be favorable to him; but he was watching her where she sat with Masters and knew that his belief in what she would decide was not strong enough to make him altogether happy.

"*And* he was old enough to be her father!" repeated the gentleman in the Scotch deer-stalker who had been gossiping. Mr. Blagdon smiled, but the words hurt — "old enough to be her father." "My God," he thought, "*I* am old enough — just!" But then he comforted himself with "Why not? It's how old a man feels, not how old he is."

Then his eyes caught little Miss Blythe's, but she turned hers instantly away.

"This will be the end of the season," she said.

Mister Masters assented. He wanted to tell her how beautiful she looked.

"Do you see old Mr. Black over there?" she said. "He's pretending not to watch us, but he's watching us like a lynx. . . . Did you ever start a piece of news?"

"Never," said Mister Masters.

"It would be rather fun," said little Miss Blythe. "For instance, if we held hands for a moment Mr. Black would see it, and five minutes later everybody would know about it."

Mister Masters screwed his courage up to the sticking point, and took her hand in his. Both looked toward Mr. Black as if inviting him to notice them. Mr. Black was seen almost instantly to whisper to the nearest gentleman.

"There," said little Miss Blythe, and was for withdrawing her hand. But Masters's fingers tightened upon it, and she could feel the pulses beating in their tips. She knew that people were looking, but she felt brazen, unabashed, and happy. Mister Masters's grip tightened; it said: "My master has a dozen hearts, and they are all beating — for *you*." To return that pressure was not an act of little Miss Blythe's will. She could not help herself. Her hand said to Masters: "With the heart — with the soul." Then she was frightened and ashamed, and had a rush of color to the face.

"Let go," she whispered.

But Masters leaned toward her, and though he was trembling with fear and awe and wonder, he found a certain courage and his voice was wonderfully gentle and tender, and he smiled and he whispered: "Boo!"

Only then did he set her hand free. For one reason there was no need now of so slight a bondage; for another, Mr. Bob Blagdon was approaching them, a little pale but smiling. He held out his hand to little Miss Blythe, and she took it.

"Phyllis," said he, "I know your face so well that there is no need for me to ask, and for you — to deny." He smiled upon her gently, though it cost him an effort. "I wanted her for myself," he turned to Masters with charming frankness, "but even an old man's selfish desires are not proof against the eloquence of youth, and I find a certain happiness in saying from the bottom of my heart — bless you, my children. . . ."

The two young people stood before him with bowed heads.

"I am going to send you the silver and glass from the table," said he, "for a wedding present to remind you of my picnic. . . ." He looked upward at the moon. "If I could," said he, "I would give you that."

Then the three stood in silence and looked upward at the moon.

THE CLAWS OF THE TIGER

What her given name was in the old country has never reached me; but when her family had learned a little English, and had begun to affect the manners and characteristics of their more Americanized acquaintances, they called her Daisy. She was the only daughter; her age was less than that of two brothers, and she was older than three. The family consisted of these six, Mr. and Mrs. Obloski, the parents, Grandfather Pinnievitch, and Great-grandmother Brenda — a woman so old, so shrunken, so bearded, and so eager to live that her like was not to be found in the city.

Upon settling in America two chief problems seemed to confront the family: to make a living and to educate the five boys. The first problem was solved for a time by The Organization. Obloski was told by an interpreter that he would be taken care of if he and his father-in-law voted as directed and as often as is decent under a wise and paternal system of government. To Obloski, who had about as much idea what the franchise stands for as The Organization had, this seemed an agreeable arrangement. Work was found for him, at a wage. He worked with immense vigor, for the wage seemed good. Soon, however, he perceived that older Americans (of his own nationality) were laughing at him. Then he did not work so hard; but the wage, froth of the city treasury, came to him just the same. He ceased working, and pottered. Still he received pay. He ceased pottering. He joined a saloon. And he became the right-hand man of a right-hand man of a right-hand man who was a right-hand man of a very important man who was — left-handed.

The two older boys were at school in a school; the three others were at school in the street. Mrs. Obloski was occupied with a seventh child, whose sex was not yet determined. Grandfather Pinnievitch was learning to smoke three cigars for five cents; and Great-grandmother Brenda sat in the sun, stroking her beard and clinging to life. Nose and chin almost obstructed the direct passage to Mrs. Brenda's mouth. She looked as if she had gone far in an attempt to smell her own chin, and would soon succeed.

But for Daisy there was neither school, nor play in the street, nor sitting in the sun. She cooked, and she washed the dishes, and she did the mending, and she made the beds, and she slept in one of the beds with her three younger brothers. In spite of the great wage so easily won the Obloskis were very poor, for New York. All would be well when the two older boys had finished school and begun to vote. They were thirteen and fourteen, but the school records had them as fifteen and sixteen, for the interpreter had explained to their father that a man cannot vote until he is twenty-one.

Daisy was twelve, but she had room in her heart for all her family, and for a doll besides. This was of rags; and on the way from Castle Garden to the tenement she had found it, neglected, forsaken — starving, perhaps — in a gutter. In its single garment, in its woollen hair, and upon its maculate body the doll carried, perhaps, the germs of typhoid, of pneumonia, of tetanus, and of consumption; but all night it lay in the arms of its little mother, and was not permitted to harm her or hers.

The Obloskis, with the exception of Mrs. Brenda, were a handsome family — the grandfather, indeed, was an old beauty in his way, with streaming white hair and beard, and eyes that reminded you of locomotive headlights seen far off down a dark tunnel; but their good features were marred by an expression of hardness, of greed, of unsatisfied desire. And Mr. Obloski's face was beginning to bloat with drink. It was only natural that Daisy, upon whom all the work was put, should have been too busy to look hard or greedy. She had no time to brood upon life or to think upon unattainable things. She had only time to cook, time to wash the dishes, to mend the clothes, to make the beds, and to play the mother to her little brothers and to her doll. And so, and naturally, as the skin upon her little hands thickened and grew rough and red, the expression in her great eyes became more and more luminous, translucent, and joyous.

Even to a class of people whose standards of beauty differ, perhaps, from ours, she promised to be very beautiful. She was a brown-and-crimson beauty, with ocean-blue eyes and teeth dazzling white, like the snow on mountains when the sun shines. And though she was only twelve, her name, underlined, was in the notebook of many an ambitious young man. I knew a young man who was a missionary in that quarter of the city (indeed, it was through him that this story reached me), an earnest, Christian, upstanding, and, I am afraid, futile young man, who, for a while, thought he had fallen in love with her, and talked of having his aunt adopt her, sending her to school, ladyizing her. He had a very pretty little romance mapped out. She would develop into an ornament to any society, he said. Her beauty — he snapped his fingers — had nothing to do with his infatuation. She had a soul, a great soul. This it was that had so moved him. "You should see her," he said, "with her kid brother, and the whole family shooting-match. I know; lots of little girls have the instinct of mothering things — but it's more in her case, it amounts to genius — and she's so clever, and so quick, and in spite of all the wicked hard work they put upon her she sings a little, and laughs a little, and mothers them all the time — the selfish beasts!"

My friend's pipe-dreams came to nothing. He drifted out of missionizing, through a sudden hobby for chemistry, into orchids; sickened of having them turn black just when they ought to have bloomed; ran for Congress and was defeated; decided that the country was going to the dogs, went to live in England, and is now spending his time in a vigorous and, I am afraid, vain attempt to get himself elected to a first-class London club. He is quite a charming man — and quite unnecessary. I mention all this, being myself enough of a pipe-dreamer to think that, if he had not been frightened out of his ideas about Daisy, life might have dealt more handsomely with them both.

As Obloski became more useful to the great organization that owned him he received proportionately larger pay; but as he drank proportionately more, his family remained in much its usual straits. Presently Obloski fell off in utility, allowing choice newly landed men of his nationality to miss the polls. Then strange things happened. The great man (who was left-handed) spoke an order mingled with the awful names of gods. Then certain shares, underwritten by his right-hand man, clamored for promised cash. A blue pallor appeared in the cheeks of the right-hand man, and he spoke an order, so that a contract for leaving the pavement of a certain city street exactly as it was went elsewhere. The defrauded contractor swore very bitterly, and reduced the salary of his right-hand man. This one caused a raid of police to ascend into the disorderly house of his. This one in turn punished his right-hand man; until finally the lowest of all in the scale, save only Mr. Obloski, remarked to the latter, pressing for his wage, that money was "heap scarce." And Mr. Obloski, upon opening his envelope, discovered that it contained but the half of that to which he had accustomed his appetite. Than Obloski there was none lower. Therefore, to pass on the shiver of pain that had descended to him from the throne, he worked upon his feelings with raw whiskey, then went home to his family and broke its workings to bits. Daisy should go sit in an employment agency until she was employed and earning money. The youngest boy and the next youngest should sell newspapers upon the street. Mrs. Obloski should stop mourning for the baby which she had rolled into a better world three years before, and do the housework. The better to fit her for this, for she was lazy and not strong, he kicked her in the ribs until she fainted, and removed thereby any possibility of her making good the loss for which her proneness to luxurious rolling had been directly responsible.

So Daisy, who was now nearly sixteen, went to sit with other young women in a row: some were older than she, one or two younger; but no one of the others was lovely to look at or had a joyous face.

II

After about an hour's waiting in an atmosphere of sour garments disguised by cheap perfumery, employment came to Daisy in the stout form of a middle aged, showily dressed woman, decisive in speech, and rich, apparently, who desired a waitress.

"I want something cheap and green," she explained to the manager. "I form 'em then to suit myself." Her eyes, small, quick, and decided, flashed along the row of candidates, and selected Daisy without so much as one glance at the next girl beyond. "There's my article, Mrs. Goldsmith," she said.

Mrs. Goldsmith shook her head and whispered something.

The wealthy lady frowned. "Seventy-five?" she said. "That's ridiculous."

"My Gott!" exclaimed Mrs. Goldsmith. "Ain't she fresh? Loog at her. Ain't she a fresh, sweet liddle-thing?"

"Well, she looks fresh enough," said the lady, "but I don't go on looks. But I'll soon find out if what you say is true. And then I'll pay you seventy-five. Meanwhile" — as Mrs. Goldsmith began to protest — "there's nothing in it — nothing in it."

"But I haf your bromice — to pay up."

The lady bowed grandly.

"You are sugh an old customer —" Thus Mrs. Goldsmith explained her weakness in yielding.

Daisy, carrying her few possessions in a newspaper bundle, walked lightly at the side of her new employer.

"My name is Mrs. Holt, Daisy," said the lady. "And I think we'll hit things off, if you always try to do just what I tell you."

Daisy was in high spirits. It was wonderful to have found work so easily and so soon. She was to receive three dollars a week. She could not understand her good fortune. Again and again Mrs. Holt's hard eyes flicked over the joyous, brightly colored young face. Less often an expression not altogether hard accompanied such surveys. For although Mrs. Holt knew that she had found a pearl among swine, her feelings of elation were not altogether free from a curious and most unaccustomed tinge of regret.

"But I must get you a better dress than that," she said. "I want my help to look cared for and smart. I don't mean you're not neat and clean looking; but maybe you've something newer and nicer in your bundle?"

"Oh, yes," said Daisy. "I have my Sunday dress. That is almost new."

"Well," said Mrs. Holt, "I'll have a look at it. This is where I live."

She opened the front door with a latch-key; and to Daisy it seemed as if paradise had been opened — from the carved walnut rack, upon which entering angels might hang their hats and coats, to the carpet upon the stair and the curtains of purple plush that, slightly parted, disclosed glimpses of an inner and more sumptuous paradise upon the right — a grand crayon of Mrs. Holt herself, life-size, upon an easel of bamboo; chairs and sofas with tremendously stuffed seats and backs and arms, a tapestry-work fire-screen — a purple puppy against a pink-and-yellow ground.

"I'll take you up to your room right off," said Mrs. Holt, "and you can show me your other dress, and I'll tell you if it's nice enough."

So up they went three flights. But it was in no garret that Daisy was to sleep. Mrs. Holt conducted her into a large, high-ceilinged, old-fashioned room. To be sure, it was ill lighted and ill ventilated — giving on a court; but its furniture, from the marble-topped wash-stand to the great double bed, was very grand and overpowering. Daisy could only gape with wonder and delight. To call such a room her own, to earn three dollars a week — with a golden promise of more later on if she proved a good girl — it was all very much too wonderful to be true.

"Now, Daisy, let me see your Sunday dress — open the bundle on the bed there."

Daisy, obedient and swift (but blushing, for she knew that her dress would look very humble in such surroundings), untied the string and opened the parcel. But it was not the Sunday dress that caught Mrs. Holt's eye. She spoke in the voice of one the most of whose breath has suddenly been snatched away.

"And what," she exclaimed, "for mercy sake, is *that*?"

"That," said Daisy, already in an anguish lest it be taken from her, "is my doll."

Mrs. Holt took the doll in her hands and turned it over and back. She looked at it, her head bent, for quite a long time. Then, all of a sudden, she made a curious sound in the back of her throat that sounded like a cross between a choke and a sob. Then she spoke swiftly — and like one ashamed:

"You won't suit me, girlie — I can see that. Wrap up those things again, and — No, you mustn't go back to Goldsmith's — she's a bad woman — you wouldn't understand. Can't you go back home? No?... They need what you can earn. . . . Here, you go to Hauptman's employment agency and tell him I sent you. No. . . . You're too blazing innocent. I'll go with you. I've got some influence. I'll see to it that he gets a job for you from some one who — who'll let you alone."

"But," said Daisy, gone quite white with disappointment, "I would have tried so hard to please you, Mrs. Holt. I —"

"You don't know what you're saying, child," exclaimed Mrs. Holt. "I — I don't need you. I've got trouble here." She touched what appeared to be an ample bosom. "One-half's the real thing and one-half's just padding. I'm not long for this world, and you've cost me a pretty penny, my dear; but it's all right. I don't need *you!*"

So Mrs. Holt took Daisy to Hauptman's agency. And he, standing in fear of Mrs. Holt, found employment for her as waitress in a Polish restaurant. Here the work was cruel and hard, and the management thunderous and savage; but the dangers of the place were not machine made, and Daisy could sleep at home.

III

Daisy had not been at work in the restaurant many weeks before the proprietor perceived that business was increasing. The four tables to which Daisy attended were nearly always full, and the other waitresses were beginning to show symptoms of jealousy and nerves. More dishes were smashed; more orders went wrong; and Daisy, a smooth, quick, eager worker, was frequently delayed and thrown out of her stride, so to speak, by malicious stratagems and tricks. But Linnevitch, the proprietor, had a clear mind and an excellent knowledge of human nature. He got rid of his cash-girl, and put Daisy in her place; and this in face of the fact that Daisy had had the scantiest practice with figures and was at first dismally slow in the making of change. But Linnevitch bore with her, and encouraged her. If now and then she made too much change, he forgave her. He had only to look at the full tables to forget. For every nickel that she lost for him, she brought a new customer. And soon, too, she became at ease with money, and sure of her subtraction. Linnevitch advanced her sufficient funds to buy a neat black dress; he insisted that she wear a white turnover collar and white cuffs. The plain severity of this costume set off the bright coloring of her face and hair to wonderful advantage. In the dingy, ill-lighted restaurant she was like that serene, golden, glowing light that Rembrandt alone has known how to place among shadows. And her temper was so sweet, and her disposition so childlike and gentle, that one by one the waitresses who hated her for her popularity and her quick success forgave her and began to like her. They discussed her a great deal among themselves, and wondered what would become of her. Something good, they prophesied; for under all the guilelessness and simplicity she was able. And you had to look but once into those eyes to know that she was string-straight. Among the waitresses was no very potent or instructed imagination. They could not formulate the steps upon which Daisy should rise, nor name the happy height to which she should ascend. They knew that she was exceptional; no common pottery like themselves, but of that fine clay of which even porcelain is made. It was common talk among them that Linnevitch was in love with her; and, recalling what had been the event in the case of the Barnhelm girl, and of Lotta Gorski, they knew that Linnevitch sometimes put pleasure ahead of business. Yet it was their common belief that the more he pined after Daisy the less she had to fear from him.

A new look had come into the man's protruding eyes. Either prosperity or Daisy, or both, had changed him for the better. The place no longer echoed with thunderous assaults upon slight faults. The words, "If you will, please, Helena"; "Well, well, pick it up," fell now from his lips, or the even more reassuring and courteous, "Never mind; I say, never mind."

Meanwhile, if her position and work in the restaurant were pleasant enough, Daisy's evenings and nights at home were hard to bear. Her mother, sick, bitter, and made to work against her will, had no tolerant words for her. Grandfather Pinnievitch, deprived of even pipe tobacco by his bibulous son-in-law, whined and complained by the hour. Old Mrs. Brenda declared that she was being starved to death, and she reviled whomever came near her. The oldest boy had left school in disgrace, together with a classmate of the opposite sex, whom he abandoned shortly at a profit. The family had turned him off at first; had then seen that he had in spite of this an air of prosperity; invited him to live at home once more, and were told that he was done with them. His first venture in the business of pandering had been a success; a company, always on the lookout for bright young men, offered him good pay, work intricate but interesting, and that protection without which crime would not be profitable.

Yes, in the secure shadow of The Organization's secret dark wings, there was room even for this obscure young Pole, fatherless, now, and motherless. For The Organization stands at the gates of the young Republic to welcome in the unfortunate of all nations, to find work for them, and security. Let your bent be what it will, if only you will serve the master, young immigrant, you may safely follow that bent to the uttermost dregs in which it ends. Whatever you wish to be, that you may become, provided only that your ambition is sordid, criminal, and unchaste.

Mr. Obloski was now an incorrigible drunkard. He could no longer be relied on to cast even his own vote once, should the occasion for voting arise. So The Great Organization spat Obloski aside. He threatened certain reprisals and tale-bearings. He was promptly arrested for a theft which not only he had not committed, but which had never been committed at all. The Organization spared itself the expense of actually putting him in jail; but he had felt the power of the claws. He would threaten no more.

To support the family on Daisy's earnings and the younger boys' newspaper sellings, and at the same time to keep drunk from morning to night, taxed his talents to the utmost. There were times when he had to give blows instead of bread. But he did his best, and was as patient and long-suffering as possible with those who sapped his income and kept him down.

One night, in a peculiarly speculative mood, he addressed his business instincts to Daisy. "Fourteen dollars a month!" he said. "And there are girls without half your looks — right here in this city — that earn as much in a night. What good are you?"

I cannot say that Daisy was so innocent as not to gather his meaning. She sat and looked at him, a terrible pathos in her great eyes, and said nothing.

"Well," said her father, "what good are you?"

"No good," said Daisy gently.

That night she hugged her old doll to her breast and wept bitterly, but very quietly, so as not to waken her brothers. The next morning, very early, she made a parcel of her belongings, and carried it with her to the restaurant. The glass door with its dingy gilt lettering was being unlocked for the day by Mr. Linnevitch. He was surprised to see her a full half-hour before opening time.

"Mr. Linnevitch," said Daisy, "things are so that I can't stay at home any more. I will send them the money, but I have to find another place to live."

"We got a little room," he said; "you can have if Mrs. Linnevitch says so. I was going to give you more pay. We give you that room instead — eh?"

Mrs. Linnevitch gave her consent. She was a dreary, weary

woman of American birth. When she was alone with her husband she never upbraided him for his infidelities, or referred to them. But later, on this particular day, having a chance to speak, she said:

"I hope you ain't going to bother this one, Linne?"

He patted his wife's bony back and shook his head. "The better as I know that girl, Minnie," he said, "the sorrier I am for what I used to be doing sometimes. You and her is going to have a square deal."

"I bin up to put her room straight," said Mrs. Linnevitch. "She's got a doll."

She delivered this for what it was worth, in an uninterested, emotionless voice.

"I tell you what she ought to have got," said her husband. "She ought to have got now a good husband, and some live dolls — eh?"

IV

New customers were not uncommon in the restaurant, but the young man who dropped in for noon dinner upon the following Friday was of a plumage gayer than any to which the waitresses and habitués of the place were accustomed. To Daisy, sitting at her high cashier's desk, like a young queen enthroned, he seemed to have something of the nature of a prince from a far country. She watched him eat. She saw in his cuffs the glint of gold; she noted with what elegance he held his little fingers aloof from his hands. She noted the polish and cleanliness of his nails, the shortness of his recent hair-cut, the great breadth of his shoulders (they were his coat's shoulders, but she did not know this), the narrowness of his waist, the interesting pallor of his face.

Not until the restaurant was well filled did any one have the audacity to sit at the stranger's table. His elegance and refinement were as a barrier between him and all that was rude and coarse. If he glanced about the place, taking notes in his turn of this and that, it was covertly and quietly and without offence. His eyes passed across Daisy's without resting or any show of interest. Once or twice he spoke quietly to the girl who waited on him, his eyebrows slightly raised, as if he were finding fault but without anger. For the first time in her life Daisy had a sensation of jealousy; but in the pale nostalgic form, rather than the yellow corrosive.

Though the interesting stranger had been one of the earliest arrivals, he ate slowly, busied himself with important-looking papers out of his coat-pockets, and was the last to go. He paid his bill, and if he looked at Daisy while she made change it was in an absent-minded, uninterested way.

She had an access of boldness. "I hope you liked your dinner," she said.

"I?" The young man came out of the clouds. "Oh, yes. Very nice." He thanked her as courteously for his change as if his receiving any at all was purely a matter for her discretion to decide, wished her good afternoon, and went out.

The waitresses were gathered about the one who had served the stranger. It seemed that he had made her a present of a dime. It was vaguely known that up-town, in more favored restaurants, a system of tipping prevailed; but in Linnevitch's this was the first instance in a long history. The stranger's stock, as they say, went up by leaps and bounds. Then, on removing the cloth from the table at which he had dined, there was discovered a heart-shaped locket that resembled gold. The girls were for opening it, and at least one ill-kept thumb-nail was painfully broken over backward in the attempt. Daisy joined the group. She was authoritative for the first time in her life.

"He wouldn't like us to open it," she said.

A dispute arose, presently a clamor; Linnevitch came in. There was a silence.

Linnevitch examined the locket. "Trible-plate," he said judicially. "Maybe there's a name and address inside." As the locket opened for his strong thumb-nail, Daisy gave out a little sound as of pain. Linnevitch stood looking into the locket, smiling.

"Only hair," he said presently, and closed the thing with a snap, "Put that in the cash-drawer," he said, "until it is called for."

Daisy turned the key on the locket and wondered what color the hair was. The stranger, of course, had a sweetheart, and of course the hair was hers. Was it brown, chestnut, red, blond, black? Beneath each of these colors in turn she imagined a face.

Long before the first habitués had arrived for supper Daisy was at her place. All the afternoon her imagination had been so fed, and her curiosity thereby so aroused, that she was prepared, in the face of what she knew at heart was proper, to open the locket and see, at least, the color of the magic hair. But she still hesitated, and for a long time. Finally, however, overmastered, she drew out the cash-drawer a little way and managed, without taking it out, to open the locket. The lock of hair which it contained was white as snow.

Daisy rested, chin on hands, looking into space. She had almost always been happy in a negative way, or, better, contented. Now she was positively happy. But she could not have explained why. She had closed the locket gently and tenderly, revering the white hairs and the filial piety that had enshrined them in gold ("triple-plated gold, at that!"). And when presently the stranger entered to recover his property, Daisy felt as if she had always known him, and that there was nothing to know of him but good.

He was greatly and gravely concerned for his loss, but when Daisy, without speaking, opened the cash-drawer and handed him his property, he gave her a brilliant smile of gratitude.

"One of the girls found it under your table," she said.

"Is she here now?" he asked. "But never mind; you'll thank her for me, won't you? And —" A hand that seemed wonderfully ready for financial emergencies slipped into a trousers pocket and pulled from a great roll of various denominations a dollar bill. "Thank her and give her that," he said. Then, and thus belittling the transaction, "I have to be in this part of the city quite often on business," he said, "and I don't mind saying that I like to take my meals among honest people. You can tell the boss that I intend to patronize this place."

He turned to go, but the fact that she had been included as being one of honest people troubled Daisy.

"Excuse me," she said. He turned back. "It was wrong for me to do it," she said, blushing deeply, and looking him full in the face with her great, honest eyes. "I opened your locket. And looked in."

"Did you?" said the young man. He did not seem to mind in the least. "I do, often. That lock of hair," he said, rather solemn now, and a little sad, perhaps, "was my mother's."

He now allowed his eyes to rest on Daisy's beautiful face for, perhaps, the first time.

"In a city like this," he said, "there's always temptations to do wrong, but I think having this" (he touched his breast pocket where the locket was) "helps me to do what mother would have liked me to."

He brushed the corner of one eye with the back of his hand. Perhaps there was a tear in it. Perhaps a cinder.

V

It came to be known in the restaurant that the stranger's name was Barstow, and very soon he had ceased to be a stranger. His business in that quarter of the city, whatever it may have been, was at first intermittent; he would take, perhaps, three meals in a week at Linnevitch's; latterly he often came twice in one day. Always orderly and quiet, Barstow gradually, however, established pleasant and even joking terms with the waitresses. But with Daisy he never joked. He called the other girls by their first names, as became a social superior, but Daisy was always Miss Obloski to him. With Linnevitch alone he made no headway. Linnevitch maintained a pointedly surly and repellent attitude, as if he really wished to turn away a profitable patronage. And Barstow learned to leave the proprietor severely alone.

One night, after Barstow had received his change, he remained for a few minutes talking with Daisy. "What do you find to do with yourself evenings, Miss Obloski?" he asked.

"I generally sit with Mr. and Mrs. Linnevitch and sew," she answered.

"That's not a very exciting life for a young lady. Don't you ever take in a show, or go to a dance?"

She shook her head.

"Don't you like to dance?"

"I know I'd like it," she said with enthusiasm; "but I never had a chance to try."

"You haven't!" exclaimed Barstow. "What a shame! Some night, if you like, I'll take you to an academy — a nice quiet one, mostly for beginners — where they give lessons. If you'd like, I'll teach you myself."

Delight showed in Daisy's face.

"Good!" said Barstow. "It's a go. How about to-n —" He broke off short. Linnevitch, very surly and very big, was within hearing, although his attention appeared elsewhere.

"Some time soon, then," said Barstow in a lower voice, and aloud, "Well, good-night, Miss Obloski."

Her eyes were upon the glass door and the darkness beyond into which Barstow had disappeared. She was returned to earth by Linnevitch's voice close to her ear. It was gentle and understanding.

"You like dot feller — eh?"

Daisy blushed very crimson, but her great eyes were steadfast and without guile. "I like him very much, Mr. Linnevitch."

"Not too much — eh?"

Daisy did not answer. She did not know the answer.

"Liddle girl," said Linnevitch kindly, "you don't know noddings. What was he saying to you, just now?"

"He said some evening he'd take me to an academy and learn me dancing," said Daisy.

"He said dot, did he?" said Linnevitch. "I say don't have nodding to do with them academies. You ask Mrs. Linnevitch to tell you some stories — eh?"

"But he didn't mean a regular dance-hall," said Daisy. "He said a place for beginners."

"For beginners!" said Linnevitch with infinite sarcasm. And then with a really tender paternalism, "If I am your father, I beat you sometimes for a liddle fool — eh?"

Mrs. Linnevitch was more explicit. "I've knowed hundreds of girls that was taught to dance," she said. "First they go to the hall, and then they go to hell."

Daisy defended her favorite character. "Any man," she said, "that carries a lock of his mother's white hair with him to help keep him straight is good enough for me, I guess."

"How do you know it is not hair of some old man's beard to fool you? Or some goat — eh? How do you know it make him keep straight — eh?"

Linnevitch began to mimic the quiet voice and elegant manner of Barstow: "Good-morning, Miss Obloski, I have just given one dollar to a poor cribble. . . . Oh, how do you do today, Miss Obloski? My mouth is full of butter, but it don't seem to melt. . . . Oh, Miss Obloski, I am ready to faint with disgust. I have just seen a man drink one stein of beer. I am a temptation this evening — let me just look in dot locket and save myself."

Daisy was not amused. She was even angry with Linnevitch, but too gentle to show it. Presently she said good-night and went to bed.

"*Now*," said Mrs. Linnevitch, "she'll go with that young feller sure. The way you mocked him made her mad. I've got eyes in my head. Whatever she used to think, now she thinks he's a live saint."

"I wonder, now?" said Linnevitch. A few minutes' wondering must have brought him into agreement with his wife, for presently he toiled up three flights of stairs and knocked at Daisy's door.

"Daisy," he said.

"What is it, Mr. Linnevitch?" If her voice had not been tearful it would have been cold.

The man winced. "Mebbe that young feller is O. K.," he said. "I have come just to say that. Mebbe he is. But you just let me look him up a liddle bit — eh?"

He did not catch her answer.

"You promise me that — eh? Mrs. Linnevitch and me, we want to do what is right and best. We don't want our liddle Daisy to make no mistakes."

He had no answer but the sounds that go with tears. He knew by this that his mockings and insinuations had been forgiven.

"Good-night, liddle girl," he said. "Sleep tight." His own voice broke. "I be your popper — eh?" he said.

To Barstow's surprise and disappointment, when he named a time for her first lesson in dancing Daisy refused to go.

"Mrs. Linnevitch thinks I better not be going out nights, Mr. Barstow," she said. "But thank you ever so much, all the same."

"Well," said Barstow, "I'm disappointed. But that's nothing, if you're not."

Daisy blushed. "But I am," she said.

"Then," said he, "never mind what *they* say. Come on!"

Daisy shook her head. "I promised."

"Look here, Miss Obloski, what's wrong? Let's be honest, whatever else we are. Is it because they *know* something against me, because they *think* they do, or because they *know* that they don't?"

"It's that," said Daisy. "Mr. Linnevitch don't want me to be going out with any one he don't know about."

Barstow was obviously relieved. "Thank you," he said. "That's all square now. It isn't Mrs. Linnevitch; it's the boss. It isn't going out in general; it's going out with me!"

Then he surprised her. "The boss is absolutely right," he said. "I'm for him, and, Miss Obloski, I won't ask you to trust me until I've proved to Linnevitch that I'm a proper guardian —"

"It's only Mr. Linnevitch," said Daisy, smiling very sweetly. "It's not me. *I* trust you." Her eyes were like two serene stars.

Barstow leaned closer and spoke lower. "Miss Obloski," he said, "Daisy" — and he lingered on the name — "there's only one thing you could say that I'd rather hear."

Daisy wanted to ask what that was. But there was no natural coquetry in the girl. She did not dare.

She did not see him again for three whole days; but she fed upon his last words to her until she was ready, and even eager, to say that other thing which alone he would rather hear than that she trusted him.

Between breakfast and dinner on the fourth day a tremendous great man, thick in the chest and stomach, wearing a frock coat and a glossy silk hat, entered the restaurant. The man's face, a miracle of close shaving, had the same descending look of heaviness as his body. But it was a strong, commanding face in spite of the pouched eyes and the drooping flesh about the jaws and chin. Daisy, busy with her book-keeping, looked up and smiled, with her strong instinct for friendliness.

The gentleman removed his hat. Most of his head was bald. "You'll be Miss Obloski," he said. "The top o' the mornin' to you, miss. My boy has often spoken of you. I call him my boy bekase he's been like a son to me — like a son. Is Linnevitch in? Never mind, I know the way."

He opened, without knocking upon it, the door which led from the restaurant into the Linnevitches' parlor. Evidently a great man. And how beautifully and touchingly he had spoken of Barstow! Daisy returned to her addition. Two and three are six and seven are twelve and four are nineteen. Then she frowned and tried again.

The great man was a long time closeted with Linnevitch. She could hear their voices, now loud and angry, now subdued. But she could not gather what they were talking about.

At length the two emerged from the parlor — Linnevitch flushed, red, sullen, and browbeaten; the stranger grandly at ease, an unlighted cigar in his mouth. He took off his hat to Daisy, bent his brows upon her with an admiring glance, and passed out into the sunlight.

"Who was it?" said Daisy.

"That," said Linnevitch, "is Cullinan, the boss — Bull Cullinan. Once he was a policeman, and now he is a millionaire."

There was a curious mixture of contempt, of fear, and of adulation in Linnevitch's voice.

"He is come here," he said, "to tell me about that young feller."

"Oh!" exclaimed Daisy. "Mr. Barstow?"

Linnevitch did not meet her eye. "I am wrong," he said, "and that young feller is O. K."

When Daisy came back from her first dancing lesson, Mr. and Mrs. Linnevitch were sitting up for her. Her gayety and high spirits seemed to move the couple, especially Linnevitch, deeply. He insisted that she eat some crackers and drink a glass of milk. He was wonderfully gentle, almost tender, in his manner; but whenever she looked at him he looked away.

VI

It was as if heaven had opened before Daisy. The blood in her veins moved to the rhythm of dance music; her vision was being fed upon color and light. And, for she was still a child, she was taken great wonders to behold: dogs that rode upon bicycles, men who played upon fifty instruments, clowns that caused whole theatres to roar with laughter, ladies that dove from dizzy heights, bears that drank beer, Apollos that seemed to have been born turning wonderful somersaults. And always at her side was her man, her well-beloved, to explain and to protect. He was careful of her, careful as a man is careful who carries a glass of water filled to overflowing without losing a drop. And if little by little he explained what he called "life" to her, it was with delicacy, with gravity — even, as it seemed, with sorrow.

His kisses filled her at first with a wonderful tenderness; at last with desire, so that her eyes narrowed and she breathed quickly. At this point in their relations Barstow put off his pleading, cajoling manner, and began, little by little, to play the master. In the matter of dress and deportment he issued orders now instead of suggestions; and she only worshipped him the more.

When he knew in his heart that she could refuse him nothing he proposed marriage. Or rather, he issued a mandate. He had led her to a seat after a romping dance. She was highly flushed with the exercise and the contact, a little in disarray, breathing fast, a wonderful look of exaltation and promise in her face. He was white, as always, methodic, and cool — the man who arranges, who makes light of difficulties, who gives orders; the man who has money in his pocket.

"Kid," he whispered, "when the restaurant closes tomorrow night I am going to take you to see a friend of mine — an alderman."

She smiled brightly, lips parted in expectation. She knew by experience that he would presently tell her why.

"You're to quit Linnevitch for good," he said. "So have your things ready."

Although the place was so crowded that whirling couples occasionally bumped into their knees or stumbled over their feet, Barstow took her hand with the naïve and easy manner of those East Siders whom he affected to despise.

"You didn't guess we were going to be married so soon, did you?" he said.

She pressed his hand. Her eyes were round with wonder.

"At first," he went on, "we'll look about before we go to housekeeping. I've taken nice rooms for us — a parlor and bedroom suite. Then we can take our time looking until we find just the right house-keeping flat."

"Oh," she said, "are you sure you want me?"

He teased her. He said, "Oh, I don't know" and "I wouldn't wonder," and pursed up his lips in scorn; but at the same time he regarded her out of the corners of roguish eyes. "Say, kid," he said presently — and his gravity betokened the importance of the matter — "Cullinan's dead for it. He's going to be a witness, and afterward he's going to blow us to supper — just us two. How's that?"

"Oh," she exclaimed, "that's fine!"

The next morning Daisy told Mr. and Mrs. Linnevitch that she was to be married as soon as the restaurant closed. But they had schooled themselves by now to expect this event, and said very little.

Linnevitch, however, was very quiet all day. Every now and then an expression little short of murderous came into his face, to be followed by a vacant, dazed look, and this in turn by sudden uncontrollable starts of horror. At these times he might have stood for "Judas beginning to realize what he has done."

Barstow, carrying Daisy's parcel, went out first. He was always tactful. Daisy flung herself into Mrs. Linnevitch's arms. The undemonstrative woman shed tears and kissed her. Linnevitch could not speak. And when Daisy had gone at last, the couple stood and looked at the floor between them. So I have seen a father and mother stand and look into the coffin of their only child.

If the reader's suspicions have been aroused, let me set them at rest. The marriage was genuine. It was performed in good faith by a genuine alderman. The groom and the great Mr. Cullinan even went so far as to disport genuine and generous white boutonnières. Daisy cried a little; the words that she had to say seemed so wonderful to her, a new revelation, as it were, of the kingdom and glory of love. But when she was promising to cleave to Barstow in sickness and peril till death parted them, her heart beat with a great, valiant fierceness. So the heart of the female tiger beats in tenderness for her young.

Barstow was excited and nervous, as became a groom. Even the great Mr. Cullinan shook a little under the paternal jocoseness with which he came forward to kiss the bride.

There was a supper waiting in the parlor of the rooms which Barstow had hired: cold meats, salad, fruit, and a bottle of champagne. While the gentlemen divested themselves of their hats and overcoats, Daisy carried her parcel into the bedroom and opened it on the bureau. Then she took off her hat and tidied her hair. She hardly recognized the face that looked out of the mirror. She had never, before that moment, realized that she was beautiful, that she had something to give to the man she loved that was worth giving. Her eyes fell upon her old doll, the companion of so many years. She laughed a happy little laugh. She had grown up. The doll was only a doll now. But she kissed it, because she loved it still. And she put it carefully away in a drawer, lest the sight of a childishness offend the lord and master.

As she passed the great double bed, with its two snow-white pillows, her knees weakened. It was like a hint to perform a neglected duty. She knelt, and prayed God to let her make Barstow happy forever and ever. Then, beautiful and abashed, she joined the gentlemen.

As she seated herself with dignity, as became a good housewife presiding at her own table, the two gentlemen lifted their glasses of champagne. There was a full glass beside Daisy's plate. Her fingers closed lightly about the stem; but she looked to Barstow for orders. "Ought I?" she said.

"Sure," said he, "a little champagne — won't hurt you."

No, Daisy; only what was in the champagne. She had her little moment of exhilaration, of self-delighting ease and vivacity — then dizziness, then awful nausea, and awful fear, and oblivion.

The great Mr. Cullinan — Bull Cullinan — caught her as she was falling. He regarded the bridegroom with eyes in which there was no expression whatever.

"Get out!" he said.

And then he was alone with her, and safe, in the dark shadow of the wings.

GROWING UP

The children were all down in the salt-marsh playing at marriage-by-capture. It was a very good play. You ran just as fast after the ugly girls as the pretty ones, and you didn't have to abide by the result. One little girl got so excited that she fell into the river, and it was Andramark who pulled her out, and beat her on the back till she stopped choking. It may be well to remember that she was named Tassel Top, a figure taken from the Indian-corn ear when it is in silk.

Andramark was the name of the boy. He was the seventh son of Squirrel Eyes, and all his six brothers were dead, because they had been born in hard times, or had fallen out of trees, or had been drowned. To grow up in an Indian village, especially when it is travelling, is very difficult. Sometimes a boy's mother has to work so hard that she runs plumb out of milk; and sometimes he gets playing too roughly with the other boys, and gets wounded, and blood-poisoning sets in; or he finds a dead fish and cooks it and eats it, and ptomaine poisoning sets in; or he catches too much cold on a full stomach, or too much malaria on an empty one. Or he tries to win glory by stealing a bear cub when its mother isn't looking, or a neighboring tribe drops in between days for an unfriendly visit, and some big painted devil knocks him over the head and takes his scalp home to his own little boy to play with.

Contrariwise, if he does manage to grow up and reach man's estate he's got something to brag of. Only he doesn't do it; because the first thing that people learn who have to live very intimately together is that bore and boaster are synonymous terms. So he never brags of what he has accomplished in the way of deeds and experiences until he is married. And then only in the privacy of his own lodge, when that big hickory stick which he keeps for the purpose assures him of the beloved one's best ears and most flattering attention.

Andramark's father was worse than dead. He had been tried in the council-lodge by the elders, and had been found guilty of something which need not be gone into here, and driven forth into the wilderness which surrounded the summer village to shift for himself. By the same judgment the culprit's wife, Squirrel Eyes, was pronounced a widow. Most women in her position would have been ambitious to marry again, but Squirrel Eyes's only ambition was to raise her seventh son to be the pride and support of her old age. She had had quite enough of marriage, she would have thanked you.

So, when Andramark was thirteen years old, and very swift and husky for his age, Squirrel Eyes went to the Wisest Medicine-man, and begged him to take her boy in hand and make a man of him.

"Woman," the Wisest Medicine-man had said, "fifteen is the very greenest age at which boys are made men, but seeing that you are a widow, and without support, it may be that something can be done. We will look into the matter."

That was why Owl Eyes, the Wisest Medicine-man, invited two of his cronies to sit with him on the bluff overlooking the salt-marsh and watch the children playing at marriage-by-capture.

Those old men were among the best judges of sports and form living. They could remember three generations of hunters and fighters. They had all the records for jumping, swimming under water, spear-throwing, axe-throwing, and bow-shooting at their tongues' ends. And they knew the pedigree for many, many generations of every child at that moment playing in the meadow, and into just what sort of man or woman that child should grow, with good luck and proper training.

Owl Eyes did not call his two cronies' attention to Andramark. If there was any precocity in the lad it would show of itself, and nothing would escape their black, jewel-like, inscrutable eyes. When Tassel Top fell into the river the aged pair laughed heartily, and when Andramark, without changing his stride, followed her in and fished her out, one of them said, "That's a quick boy," and the other said, "Why hasn't that girl been taught to swim?" Owl Eyes said, "That's a big boy for only thirteen — that Andramark."

In the next event Andramark from scratch ran through a field — some of the boys were older and taller than himself — and captured yet another wife, who, because she expected and longed to be caught by some other boy, promptly boxed — the air where his ears had been. Andramark, smiling, caught both her hands in one of his, tripped her over a neatly placed foot, threw her, face down, and seated himself quietly on the small of her back and rubbed her nose in the mud.

The other children, laughing and shouting, rushed to the rescue. Simultaneously Andramark, also laughing, was on his feet, running and dodging. Twice he passed through the whole mob of his pursuers without, so it seemed to the aged watchers on the bluff, being touched. Then, having won some ten yards clear of them, he wheeled about and stood with folded arms. A great lad foremost in the pursuit reached for him, was caught instead by the outstretched hand and jerked forward on his face. Some of the children laughed so hard that they had to stop running. Others redoubled their efforts to close with the once more darting, dodging, and squirming

Andramark, who, however, threading through them for the third and last time in the most mocking and insulting manner, headed straight for the bluff a little to the right of where his elders and betters were seated with their legs hanging over, leaped at a dangling wild grape-vine, squirmed to the top, turned, and prepared to defend his position against any one insolent enough to assail it.

The children, crowded at the base of the little bluff, looked up. Andramark looked down. With one hand and the tip of his nose he made the insulting gesture which is older than antiquity.

Meanwhile, Owl Eyes had left his front-row seat, and not even a waving of the grasses showed that he was crawling upon Andramark from behind.

Owl Eyes's idea was to push the boy over the bluff as a lesson to him never to concentrate himself too much on one thing at a time. But just at the crucial moment Andramark leaped to one side, and it was a completely flabbergasted old gentleman who descended through the air in his stead upon a scattering flock of children. Owl Eyes, still agile at eighty, gathered himself into a ball, jerked violently with his head and arms, and managed to land on his feet. But he was very much shaken, and nobody laughed. He turned and looked up at Andramark, and Andramark looked down.

"I couldn't help it," said Andramark. "I knew you were there all the time."

Owl Eyes's two cronies grinned behind their hands.

"Come down," said Owl Eyes sternly.

Andramark leaped and landed lightly, and stood with folded arms and looked straight into the eyes of the Wisest Medicine-man. Everybody made sure that there was going to be one heap big beating, and there were not wanting those who would have volunteered to fetch a stick, even from a great distance. But Owl Eyes was not called the Wisest Medicine-man for nothing. His first thought had been, "I will beat the life out of this boy." But then (it was a strict rule that he always followed) he recited to himself the first three stanzas of the Rain-Maker's song, and had a new and wiser thought. This he spoke aloud.

"Boy," he said, "beginning tomorrow I myself shall take you in hand and make a man of you. You will be at the medicine-lodge at noon. Meanwhile go to your mother's lodge and tell her from me to give you a sound beating."

The children marvelled, the boys envied, and Andramark, his head very high, his heart thumping, passed among them and went home to his mother and repeated what the Wisest Medicine-man had said.

"And you are to give me a sound beating, mother," said Andramark, "because after today they will begin making a man of me, and when I am a man it will be the other way around, and I shall have to beat you."

His back was bare, and he bent forward so that his mother could beat him. And she took down from the lodge-pole a heavy whip of raw buckskin. It was not so heavy as her heart.

Then she raised the whip and said:

"A blow for the carrying," and she struck; "a blow for the bearing," and she struck; "a blow for the milking," and she struck; "a blow for lies spoken," and she did *not* strike; "a blow for food stolen," and she did *not* strike.

And she went through the whole litany of the beating ceremonial and struck such blows as the law demanded, and spared those she honestly could spare, and when in doubt she quibbled — struck, but struck lightly.

When the beating was over they sat down facing each other and talked. And Squirrel Eyes said: "What must be, must. The next few days will soon be over."

And Andramark shuddered (he was alone with his mother) and said, "If I show that they hurt me they will never let me be a man."

And Squirrel Eyes did her best to comfort him and put courage in his heart, just as modern mothers do for sons who are about to have a tooth pulled or a tonsil taken out.

The next day at noon sharp Andramark stood before the entrance of the medicine-lodge with his arms folded; and all his boy and girl friends watched him from a distance. And all the boys envied him, and all the girls wished that they were boys. Andramark stood very still, almost without swaying, for the better part of an hour. His body was nicely greased, and he resembled a wet terracotta statue. A few mosquitoes were fattening themselves on him, and a bite in the small of his back itched so that he wanted very much to squirm and wriggle. But that would have been almost as bad an offence against ceremonial as complaining of hunger during the fast or shedding tears under the torture.

Andramark had never seen the inside of the medicine-lodge; but it was well known to be very dark, and to contain skulls and thigh-bones of famous enemies, and devil-masks, and horns and rattles and other disturbing and ghostly properties. Of what would happen to him when he had passed between the flaps of the lodge and was alone with the medicine-men he did not know. But he reasoned that if they really wanted to make a man of him they would not really try to kill him or maim him. And he was strong in the determination, no matter what should happen, to show neither surprise, fear, nor pain.

A quiet voice spoke suddenly, just within the flaps of the lodge:

"Who is standing without?"

"The boy Andramark."

"What do you wish of us?"

"To be made a man."

"Then say farewell to your companions of childhood."

Andramark turned toward the boys and girls who were watching him. Their faces swam a little before his eyes, and he felt a big lump coming slowly up in his throat. He raised his right arm to its full length, palm forward, and said:

"Farewell, O children; I shall never play with you any more."

Then the children set up a great howl of lamentation, which was all part of the ceremonial, and Andramark turned and found that the flaps of the lodge had been drawn aside, and that within there was thick darkness and the sound of men breathing.

"Come in, Andramark."

The flaps of the lodge fell together behind him. Fingers touched his shoulder and guided him in the dark, and then a voice told him to sit down. His quick eyes, already accustomed to the darkness, recognized one after another the eleven medicine-men of his tribe. They were seated cross-legged in a semicircle, and one of them was thumbing tobacco into the bowl of a poppy-red pipe. Some of the medicine-men had rattles handy in their laps, others devil-horns. They were all smiling and looking kindly at the little boy who sat all alone by himself facing them. Then old Owl Eyes, who was the central medicine-man of the eleven, spoke.

"In this lodge," he said, "no harm will befall you. But lest the women and children grow to think lightly of manhood there will be from time to time much din and devil-noises."

At that the eleven medicine-men began to rock their bodies and groan like lost souls (they groaned louder and louder, with a kind of awful rhythm), and to shake the devil-rattles, which were dried gourds, brightly painted, and containing teeth of famous enemies, and one of the medicine-men tossed a devil-horn to Andramark, and the boy put it to his lips and blew for all he was worth. It was quite obvious that the medicine-men were just having fun, not with him, but with all the women and children of the village who were outside listening — at a safe distance, of course — and imagining that the medicine-lodge was at that moment a scene of the most awful visitations and terrors. And all that afternoon, at intervals, the ghastly uproar was repeated, until Andramark's lips were chapped with blowing the devil-horn and his insides felt very shaky. But between times the business of the medicine-men with Andramark was very serious, and they talked to him like so many fathers, and he listened with both ears and pulled at the poppy-red medicine-pipe whenever it was passed to him.

They lectured him upon anatomy and hygiene; upon tribal laws and intertribal laws; and always they explained "why" as well as they could, and if they didn't know "why" they said it must be right because it's always been done that way. Sometimes they said things that made him feel very self-conscious and uncomfortable. And sometimes they became so interesting that it was the other way round.

"The gulf," said Owl Eyes, "between the race of men and the races of women and children is knowledge. For, whereas many squaws and little children possess courage, knowledge is kept from them, even as the first-run shad of the spring. The duty of the child is to acquire strength and skill, of the woman to bear children, to labor in the corn-field, and to keep the lodge. But the duty of man is to hunt, and to fight, and to make medicine, to know, and to keep knowledge to himself. Hence the saying that whatever man betrays the secrets of the council-lodge to a squaw is a squaw himself. Hitherto, Andramark, you have been a talkative child, but henceforth you will watch your tongue as a warrior watches the prisoner that he is bringing to his village for torture. When a man ceases to be a mystery to the women and children he ceases to be a man. Do not tell them what has passed in the medicine-lodge, but let it appear that you could discourse of ghostly mysteries and devilish visitations and other dread wonders — if you would; so that even to the mother that bore you you will be henceforward and forever a thing apart, a thing above, a thing beyond."

And the old medicine-man who sat on Owl Eyes's left cleared his throat and said:

"When a man's wife is in torment, it is as well for him to nod his head and let her believe that she does not know what suffering is."

Another said:

"Should a man's child ask what the moon is made of, let that man answer that it is made of foolish questions, but at the same time let him smile, as much as to say that he could give the truthful answer — if he would."

Another said:

"When you lie to women and children, lie foolishly, so that they may know that you are making sport of them and may be ashamed. In this way a man may keep the whole of his knowledge to himself, like a basket of corn hidden in a place of his own secret choosing."

Still another pulled one flap of the lodge a little so that a ray of light entered. He held his hand in the ray and said:

"The palm of my hand is in darkness, the back is in light. It is the same with all acts and happenings — there is a bright side and a dark side. Never be so foolish as to look on the dark side of things; there may be somewhat there worth discovering, but it is in vain to look because it cannot be seen."

And Owl Eyes said:

"It will be well now to rest ourselves from seriousness with more din and devil-noises. And after that we shall lead the man-boy Andramark to the Lodge of Nettles, there to sit alone for a space and to turn over in his mind all that we have said to him."

"One thing more." This from a very little medicine-man who had done very little talking. "When you run the gauntlet of the women and children from the Hot Lodge to the river, watch neither their eyes nor their whips; watch only their feet, lest you be tripped and thrown at the very threshold of manhood."

Nettles, thistles, and last year's burdocks and sandspurs strewed the floor of the lodge to which Andramark was now taken. And he was told that he must not thrust these to one side and make himself comfortable upon the bare ground. He might sit, or stand, or lie down; he might walk about; but he mustn't think of going to sleep, or, indeed, of anything but the knowledge and mysteries which had been revealed to him in the medicine-lodge.

All that night, all the next day, and all the next night he meditated. For the first six hours he meditated on knowledge, mystery, and the whole duty of man, just as he had been told to do. And he only stopped once to listen to a flute-player who had stolen into the forest back of the lodge and was trying to tell some young squaw how much he loved her and how lonely he was without her. The flute had only four notes and one of them was out of order; but Andramark had been brought up on that sort of music and it sounded very beautiful to him. Still, he only listened with one ear, Indian fashion. The other was busy taking in all the other noises of the night and the village. Somebody passed by the Lodge of Nettles, walking very slowly and softly. "A man," thought Andramark, "would not make any noise at all. A child would be in bed."

The slow, soft steps were nearing the forest back of the lodge, quickening a little. Contrariwise, the flute was being played more and more slowly. Each of its three good notes was a stab at the feelings, and so, for that matter, was the note that had gone wrong. An owl hooted. Andramark smiled. If he had been born enough hundreds of years later he might have said, "You can't fool me!"

The flute-playing stopped abruptly. Andramark forgot all about the nettles and sat down. Then he stood up.

He meditated on war and women, just as he had been told to do. Then, because he was thirsty, he meditated upon suffering. And he finished the night meditating — upon an empty stomach.

Light filtered under the skirts of the lodge. He heard the early women going to their work in the fields. The young leaves were on the oaks, and it was corn-planting time. Even very old corn, however, tastes very good prepared in any number of different ways. Andramark agreed with himself that when he gave himself in marriage it would be to a woman who was a thoroughly good cook. But quite raw food is acceptable at times. It is pleasant to crack quail eggs between the teeth, or to rip the roe out of a fresh-caught shad with your forefinger and just let it melt in your mouth.

The light brightened. It was a fine day. It grew warm in the lodge, hot, intolerably hot. The skins of which it was made exhaled a smoky, meaty smell. Andramark was tempted to see if he couldn't suck a little nourishment out of them. A shadow lapped the skirts of the lodge and crawled upward. It became cool, cold. The boy, almost naked, began to shiver and shake. He swung his arms as cab-drivers do, and tried very hard to meditate upon the art of being a man.

During the second night one of his former companions crept up to the lodge and spoke to him under its skirts. "Sst! Heh! What does it feel like to be a man?" — chuckled and withdrew.

Andramark said to himself the Indian for "I'll lay for that boy." He was very angry. He had been gratuitously insulted in the midst of his new dignities.

Suddenly the flaps of the lodge were opened and some one leaned in and set something upon the floor. Andramark did not move. His nostrils dilated, and he said to himself, "Venison — broiled to the second."

In the morning he saw that there was not only venison, but a bowl of water, and a soft bearskin upon which he might stretch himself and sleep. His lips curled with a great scorn. And he remained standing and aloof from the temptations. And meditated upon the privileges of being a man.

About noon he began to have visitors. At first they were vague, dark spots that hopped and ziddied in the overheated air. But these became, with careful looking, all sorts of devils and evil spirits, and beasts the like of which were not in the experience of any living man. There were creatures made like men, only that they were covered with long, silky hair and had cry-baby faces and long tails. And there was a vague, yellowish beast, very terrible, something like a huge cat, only that it had curling tusks like a very big wild pig. And there were other things that looked like men, only that they were quite white, as if they had been most awfully frightened. And suddenly Andramark imagined that he was hanging to a tree, but not by his hands or his feet, and the limb to which he was hanging broke, and, after falling for two or three days, he landed on his feet among burs and nettles that were spread over the floor of a lodge.

The child had slept standing up, and had evolved from his subconsciousness, as children will, beasts and conditions that had existed when the whole human race was a frightened cry-baby in its cradle. He had never heard of a monkey or a sabre-tooth tiger; but he had managed to see a sort of vision of them both, and had dreamed that he was a monkey hanging by his tail.

He was very faint and sick when the medicine-men came for him. But it did not show in his face, and he walked firmly among them to the great Torture Lodge, his head very high and the ghost of a smile hovering about his mouth.

It was a grim business that waited him in the Torture Lodge. He was strung up by his thumbs to a peg high up the great lodge pole, and drawn taut by thongs from his big toes to another peg in the base of the pole, and then, without any unnecessary delays, for every step in the proceeding was according to a ceremonial that was almost as old as suffering, they gave him, what with blunt flint-knives and lighted slivers of pitch-pine, a very good working idea of hell. They told him, without words, which are the very tenderest and most nervous places in all the human anatomy, and showed him how simple it is to give a little boy all the sensations of major operations without actually removing his arms and legs. And they talked to him. They told him that because he came of a somewhat timorous family they were letting him off very easily; that they weren't really hurting him, because it was evident from the look of him that at the first hint of real pain he would scream and cry. And then suddenly, just when the child was passing through the ultimate border-land of endurance, they cut him down, and praised him, and said that he had behaved splendidly, and had taken to torture as a young duck takes to water. And poor little Andramark found that under the circumstances kindness was the very hardest thing of all to bear. One after another great lumps rushed up his throat, and he began to tremble and totter and struggle with the corners of his mouth.

Old Owl Eyes, who had tortured plenty of brave boys in his day, was ready for this phase. He caught up a great bowl of ice-cold spring-water and emptied it with all his strength against Andramark's bloody back. The shock of that sudden icy blow brought the boy's runaway nerves back into hand. He shook himself, drew a long breath, and, without a quiver anywhere, smiled.

And the old men were as glad as he was that the very necessary trial by torture was at an end. And, blowing triumphantly upon devil-horns and shaking devil-rattles, they carried him the whole length of the village to the base of the hill where the Hot Lodge was.

This was a little cave, in the mouth of which was a spring, said to be very full of Big Medicine. The entrance to the cave was closed by a heavy arras of bearskins, three or four thick, and the ground in front was thickly strewn with round and flat stones cracked and blackened by fire. From the cave to the fifteen-foot bluff overhanging a deep pool of the river the ground was level, and worn in a smooth band eight or ten feet wide as by the trampling of many feet.

Andramark, stark naked and still bleeding in many places, sat cross-legged in the cave, at the very rim of the medicine-spring. His head hung forward on his chest. All his muscles were soft and relaxed. After a while the hangings of the cave entrance were drawn a little to one side and a stone plumped into the spring with a savage hiss; another followed — another — and another and another. Steam began to rise from the surface of the spring, little bubbles darted up from the bottom and burst. More hot stones were thrown into the water. Steam, soft and caressing, filled the cave. The temperature rose by leaps and bounds. The roots of Andramark's hair began to tickle — the tickling became unendurable, and ceased suddenly as the sweat burst from every pore of his body. His eyes closed; in his heart it was as if love-music were being played upon a flute. He was no longer conscious of hunger or thirst. He yielded, body and soul, to the sensuous miracle of the steam, and slept.

He was awakened by many shrill voices that laughed and dared him to come out.

"It's only one big beating," he said, rose, stepped over the spring, pushed through the bearskins, and stood gleaming and steaming in the fading light.

The gantlet that he was to run extended from the cave to the bluff overhanging the river. He looked the length of the double row of grinning women and children — the active agents in what was to come. Back of the women and children were warriors and old men, their faces relaxed into holiday expressions. Toward the river end of the gauntlet were stationed the youngest, the most vigorous, the most fun-loving of the women, and the larger boys, with only a negligible sprinkling of really little children. Every woman and child in the two rows was armed with a savage-looking whip of willow, hickory, or even green brier, and the still more savage intention of using these whips to the utmost extent of their speed and accuracy in striking.

Upon a signal Andramark darted forward and was lost in a whistling smother. It was as if an untrimmed hedge had suddenly gone mad. Andramark made the best of a bad business, guarded his face and the top of his head with his arms, ran swiftly, but not too swiftly, and kept his eyes out for feet that were thrust forward to trip him.

A dozen feet ahead he saw a pair of little moccasins that were familiar to him. As he passed them he looked into their owner's face, and wondered why, of all the little girls in the village, Tassel Top alone did not use her whip on him.

At last, half blinded, lurching as he ran, he came to the edge of the bluff, and dived, almost without a splash, into the deep, fresh water. The cold of it stung his overheated, bleeding body like a swarm of wild bees, and it is possible that when he reached the Canoe Beach the water in his eyes was not all fresh. Here, however, smiling chiefs and warriors surrounded the stoic, and welcomed him to their number with kind words and grunts of approval. And then, because he that had been but a moment before a naked child was now a naked man, and no fit spectacle for women and children, they formed a bright-colored moving screen about him and conducted him to the great council-lodge. There they eased his wounds with pleasant greases, and dressed him in softest buckskin, and gave him just as much food as it was safe for him to eat — a couple of quail eggs and a little dish of corn and freshwater mussels baked.

And after that they sent him home armed with a big stick. And there was his mother, squatting on the floor of their lodge, with her back bared in readiness for a good beating. But Andramark closed the lodge-flaps, and dropped his big stick, and began to blubber and sob. And his mother leaped up and caught him in her arms; and then — once a mother, always tactful — she began to howl and yell, just as if she were actually receiving the ceremonial beating which was her due. And the neighbors pricked up their ears and chuckled, and said the Indian for "Squirrel Eyes is getting what was coming to her."

Maybe Andramark didn't sleep that night, and maybe he did. And all the dreams that he dreamed were pleasant, and he got the best of everybody in them, and he woke next morning to a pleasant smell of broiling shad, and lay on his back blinking and yawning, and wondering why of all the little girls in the village Tassel Top alone had not used her whip on him.

THE BATTLE OF AIKEN

At the Palmetto Golf Club one bright, warm day in January they held a tournament which came to be known as the Battle of Aiken. Colonel Bogey, however, was not in command.

Each contestant's caddie was provided with a stick cleft at one end and pointed at the other. In the cleft was stuck a square of white card-board on which was printed the contestant's name, Colonel Bogey's record for the course, the contestant's handicap, and the sum of these two. Thus:

A. B. Smith
78 + 9 = 87

And the winner was to be he who travelled farthest around the links in the number of strokes allotted to him.

Old Major Jennings did not understand, and Jimmy Traquair, the professional, explained.

"Do you know what the bogey for the course is?" said he. "It's seventy-eight. Do you know what your handicap is? It's twenty."

Old Major Jennings winced slightly. His handicap had never seemed quite adequate to him.

"Well?" he said.

"Well," said Jimmie, who ever tempered his speech to his hearer's understanding, "what's twenty added to seventy-eight?"

"Eighty-eight — ninety-eight," said old Major Jennings (but not conceitedly).

"Right," said Jimmie. "Well, you start at the first tee and play ninety-eight strokes. Where the ball lies after the ninety-eighth, you plant the card with your name on it. And that's all."

"Suppose after my ninety-eighth stroke that my ball lies in the pond?" said old Major Jennings with a certain timid conviction. The pond hole is only the twelfth, and Jimmie wanted to laugh, but did not.

"If that happens," he said, "you'll have to report it, I'm afraid, to the Green Committee. Who are you going around with?"

"I haven't got anybody to go around with," said the major. "I didn't know there was going to be a tournament till it was too late to ask any one to play with me."

This conversation took place in the new shop, a place all windows, sunshine, labels, varnishes, vises, files, grips, and clubs of exquisite workmanship. At one of the benches a grave-eyed young negro, aproned and concentrated, was enamelling the head of a driver with shellac. Sudden cannon fire would not have shaken his hand. In one corner a rosy lad with curly yellow hair dangled his legs from the height of a packing-case and chewed gum. He had been born with a golden spoon in his mouth, and was learning golf from the inside. Sometimes he winked with one eye. But these silent comments were hidden from the major.

"I don't care about the tournament," said the latter, his loose lip trembling slightly. "I'll just practice a little."

"Don't be in a hurry, sir," said Jimmie sympathetically; "General Bullwigg hasn't any one to go around with either. And if you don't mind —"

"Bullwigg," said the major vaguely; "I used to know a Bullwigg."

"He's a very fine gentleman indeed, sir," said Jimmie. "Same handicap as yourself, sir, and if you don't mind —"

"Where is he from?" asked the major.

"I don't know, sir. Mr. Bowers extended the privileges of the club to him. He's stopping at the Park in the Pines."

"Oh!" said the major, and then with a certain dignity and resolution: "If Mr. Bowers knows him, and if *he* doesn't mind, I'm sure I don't. Is he here?"

"He's waiting at the first tee," said Jimmie, and he averted his face.

At the first tee old Major Jennings found a portly, red-faced gentleman, with fierce, bushy eyebrows, who seemed prepared to play golf under any condition of circumstance and weather. He had two caddies. One carried a monstrous bag, which, in addition to twice the usual number of clubs, contained a crook-handled walking-stick and a crook-handled umbrella; the other carried over his right arm a greatcoat, in case the June-like weather should turn cold, and over his left a mackintosh, in case rain should fall from the cloudless, azure heavens. The gentleman himself was swinging a wooden club, with pudgy vehemence, at an imaginary ball. Upon his countenance was that expression of fortitude which wins battles and championships. Old Major Jennings approached timidly. He was very shy. In the distance he saw two of his intimate friends finishing out the first hole. Except for himself and the well-prepared stranger they had been the last pair to start, and the old major's pale blue eyes clung to them as those of a shipwrecked mariner may cling to ships upon the horizon. Then he pulled himself together and said:

"General Bullwigg, I presume."

"The very man," said the general, and the two gentlemen lifted their plaid golfing caps and bowed to each other. Owing to extreme diffidence, Major Jennings did not volunteer his own name; owing to the fact that he seldom thought of anything but himself, General Bullwigg did not ask it.

Major Jennings was impatient to be off, but it was General Bullwigg's honor, and he could not compel that gentleman to drive until he was quite ready. General Bullwigg apostrophized the weather and the links. He spoke at some length of "*My* game," "*My* swing," "*My* wrist motion," "*My* notion of getting out of a bunker." He told an anecdote which reminded him of another. He touched briefly upon the manufacture of balls, the principle of imparting pure back-spin; the best seed for Northern greens, the best sand for Southern. And then, by way of adding insult to injury, he stepped up to his ball and, with due consideration for his age and stomach, drove it far and straight.

"Fine shot, sir," was Major Jennings's comment.

"I've seen better, sir," said General Bullwigg. "But I won't take it over."

Major Jennings teed up his ball, and addressed it, and waggled, and shifted his feet, and had just received that sudden inner knowledge that the time was come to strike, when General Bullwigg interrupted him.

"My first visit to Aiken," said he, "was in the 60's. But that was no visit of pleasure. No, sir. Along the brow of this hill upon which we are standing was an earthwork. In the pines yonder, back of the first green, was a battery. In those days we did not fight it out with the pacific putter, but with bullets and bayonets."

"Were you in the battle of Aiken?" asked the major, so quietly as to make the question sound purely perfunctory.

General Bullwigg laughed, as strong men laugh, from the stomach, and with a sweeping gesture of his left hand appeared to dismiss a hundred flatterers.

"I have heard men say," said he, "that I *was* the battle of Aiken."

With an involuntary shudder Major Jennings hastily addressed his ball, swung jerkily, and topped it feebly down the hill. Then, smiling a sickly smile, he said:

"We're off."

"Get a good one?" asked General Bullwigg. "I wasn't looking."

"Not a very good one," said Major Jennings, inwardly writhing, "but straight — perfectly straight. A little on top."

They sagged down the hill, the major in a pained silence, the general describing, with sweeping gestures, the positions of the various troops among the surrounding hills at the beginning of the battle of Aiken.

"In those days," he went on, "I was second lieutenant in the gallant Twenty-ninth; but it often happens that a young man has an old head on his shoulders, and as one after the other of my superior officers — superior in rank — bit the dust — That ball is badly cupped. You will hardly get it away with a brassy; if I were you I should play my niblick. Well out, sir! A fine recovery! On this very spot I saw a bomb burst. The air was filled with arms and legs. It seemed as if they would never come down. I shall play my brassy spoon, Purnell, the one with the yellow head. I see you don't carry a spoon. Most invaluable club. There are days when I can do anything with a spoon. I used to own one of which I often said that it could do anything but talk."

Major Jennings shuddered as if he were very cold; while General Bullwigg swung his spoon and made another fine shot. He had a perfect four for the first hole, to Major Jennings's imperfect and doddering seven.

"The enemy," said General Bullwigg, "had a breastwork of pine logs all along this line. I remember the general said to me: 'Bullwigg,' he said, 'to get them out of that timber is like getting rats out of the walls of a house.' And I said: 'General —'"

"It's your honor," the major interrupted mildly.

But General Bullwigg would not drive until he had brought his anecdote to a self-laudatory end. And his ball was not half through its course before he had begun another. The major, compelled to listen, again foozled, and a dull red began to mantle his whole face. And in his peaceful and affable heart there waxed a sullen, feverish rage against his companion.

The battle of Aiken was on.

Sing, O chaste and reluctant Muse, the battle of Aiken! Only don't sing it! State it, as is the fashion of our glorious times, in humble and perishable prose. Fling grammar of which nothing is now known to the demnition bow-wows, and state how in the beginning General Bullwigg had an advantage of many strokes, not wasted, over his self-effacing companion. State how, because of the general's incessant chatter, the gentle and gallant major foozled shot after shot; how once his ball hid in a jasmine bower, once behind the stem of a tree, and once in a sort of cavern over which the broom straw waved. But omit not, O truthful and ecstatic one, to mention that dull rage which grew from small beginnings in the major's breast until it became furious and all-consuming, like a prairie fire. At this stage your narrative becomes heroic, and it might be in order for you, O capable and delectable one, to switch from humble stating to loud singing. Only don't do it. State on. State how the rage into which he had fallen served to lend precision to the major's eye, steel to his wrist, rhythm to his tempo, and fiery ambition to his gentle and retiring soul. He is filled with memories of daring: of other battles in other days. He remembers what times he sought the bubble reputation in the cannon's mouth, and spiked the aforementioned cannon's touch-hole into the bargain. And he remembers the greater war that he fought single-handed for a number of years against the demon rum.

State, too, exquisite Parnassian, and keep stating, how that General Bullwigg did incessantly talk, prattle, jabber, joke, boast, praise himself, stand in the wrong place, and rehearse the noble deeds that he himself had performed in the first battle of Aiken. And state how the major answered him less and less frequently, but more and more loudly and curtly — but I see that you are exhausted, and, thanking you kindly, I shall resume the narrative myself.

They came to the pond hole, which was the twelfth; the general, still upon his interminable reminiscences of his own military glory, stood up to drive, and was visited by his first real disaster. He swung — and he looked up. His ball, beaten downward into the hard clay tee, leaped forward with a sound as of a stone breaking in two and dove swiftly into the centre of the pond. The major spoke never a word. For the first time during the long dreary round his risibles were tickled and he wanted to laugh. Instead he concentrated all his faculties upon his ball and made a fine drive.

Not so the general with his second attempt. Again he found water, and fell into a panic at the sudden losing of so many invaluable strokes (not to mention two brand-new balls at seventy-five cents each).

It was at the pond hole that the major's luck began to ameliorate. For the first time in his life he made it in three — a long approach close to the green; a short mashie shot that trickled into the very cup. And it was at the pond hole that the general, who had hitherto played far above his ordinary form, began to go to pieces. He was a little dashed in spirit, but not in eloquence.

Going to the long fourteenth, they found the first evidence of those who had gone before. In the very midst of the fair green they saw, shining afar, like a white tombstone, stuck in its cleft stick, the card of the first competitor to use up the whole of his allotted strokes. They paused a moment to read:

Sacred to the Memory of
W. H. Lands
78 + 6 = 84
Who Sliced Himself to Pieces

Forty yards beyond, another obituary confronted them:

In Loving Memory of
J. C. Nappin
$78 + 10 = 88$
Died of a Broken Mashie
And of Such is the
Kingdom of Heaven

"Ha!" said General Bullwigg. "He little realizes that here where he has pinned his little joke in the lap of mother earth I have seen the dead men lie as thick as kindlings in a wood-yard. Sir, across this very fair green there were no less than three desperate charges, unremembered and unsung, of which I may say without boasting that Magna Pars Fui. But for the desperation of our last charge the battle must have been lost —"

Damn the memory of
E. Hewett
$78 + 10 = 88$
Couldn't Put

Here Lies
G. Norris
$78 + 10 = 88$
A Fool and His Money Are Soon Parted

The little tombstones came thick and fast now. The fairway to the seventeenth, most excellent of all four-shot holes, was dotted with them, and it actually began to look as if General Bullwigg or Major Jennings (they were now on even terms) might be the winner.

It was that psychological moment when of all things a contestant most desires silence. Major Jennings was determined to triumph over his boastful companion. And he was full of courage and resolve. They had reached the seventeenth green in the same number of strokes from the first tee. That is to say, each had used up ninety-five of his allotted ninety-eight. Neither holed his approach put, and the match, so far as they two were concerned, resolved itself into a driving contest. If General Bullwigg drove the farther with his one remaining stroke he would beat the major, and vice versa. As for the other competitors, there was but one who had reached the eighteenth tee, and he, as his tombstone showed, had played his last stroke neither far nor well.

For the major the suspense was terrible. He had never won a tournament. He had never had so golden an opportunity to down a boaster. But it was General Bullwigg's honor, and it occurred to him that the time was riper for talk than play.

"You may think that I am nervous," he said. "But I am not. During one period of the battle of Aiken the firing between ourselves on this spot and the enemy intrenched where the club-house now stands, and spreading right and left in a half-moon, was fast and furious. Once they charged up to our guns; but we drove them back, and after that charge yonder fair green was one infernal shambles of dead and dying. Among the wounded was one of the enemy's general officers; he whipped and thrashed and squirmed like a newly landed fish and screamed for water. It was terrible; it was unendurable. Next to me in the trench was a young fellow named — named Jennings —"

"Jennings?" said the major breathlessly. "And what did he do?"

"He," said General Bullwigg. "Nothing. He said, however, and he was careful not to show his head above the top of the trench: 'I can't stand this,' he said; 'somebody's got to bring that poor fellow in.' As for me, I only needed the suggestion. I jumped out of the trench and ran forward, exposing myself to the fire of both armies. When, however, I reached the general officer, and my purpose was plain, the firing ceased upon both sides, and the enemy stood up and cheered me."

General Bullwigg teed his ball and drove it far.

Major Jennings bit his lip; it was hardly within his ability to hit so long a ball.

"This — er — Jennings," said he, "seems to have been a coward."

General Bullwigg shrugged his shoulders.

"Have I got it straight?" asked Major Jennings. "It was you who brought in the general officer, and not — er — this — er — Jennings who did it?"

"I thought I had made it clear," said General Bullwigg stiffly. And he repeated the anecdote from the beginning. Major Jennings's comment was simply this:

"So *that* was the way of it, was it?"

A deep crimson suffused him. He looked as if he were going to burst. He teed his ball. He trembled. He addressed. He swung back, and then with all the rage, indignation, and accuracy of which he was capable — forward. It was the longest drive he had ever made. His ball lay a good yard beyond the General's. He had beaten all competitors, but that was nothing. He had beaten his companion, and that was worth more to him than all the wealth of Ormuzd and of Ind. He had won the second battle of Aiken.

In silence he took his tombstone from his caddie's hand, in silence wrote upon it, in silence planted it where his ball had stopped. General Bullwigg bent himself stiffly to see what the fortunate winner had written. And this was what he read:

Sacred to the Memory of
E. O. Jennings
$78 + 20 = 98$
Late Major in the Gallant 29th,
Talked to Death by a Liar

As for the gallant major (still far from mollified), he turned his back upon a foe for the first time in his life and made off — almost running.

AN IDYL OF PELHAM BAY PARK

"It's real country out there," Fannie Davis had said. "Buttercups and daisies. Come on, Lila! I won't go if you won't."

This sudden demonstration of friendship was too much for Lila. She forgot that she had no stylish dress for the occasion, or that her mother could not very well spare her for a whole day, and she promised to be ready at nine o'clock on the following Sunday morning.

"Fannie Davis," she explained to her mother, "has asked me to go out to Pelham Bay Park with her Sunday. And finally I said I would. I feel sometimes as if I'd blow up if I didn't get a breath of fresh air after all this hot spell."

She set her pretty mouth defiantly. She expected an argument. But he mother only shrugged her shoulders and said,

"We could make your blue dress look real nice with a few trimmings."

They discussed ways and means until long after the younger children were in bed and asleep.

By Saturday night the dress was ready, and Lila had turned her week's wages back into the coffers of the department store where she worked in exchange for a pair of near-silk brown stockings and a pair of stylish oxford ties of patent leather.

"You look like a show-girl," was Fannie's enthusiastic comment. "I wouldn't have believed it of you. Why, Lila, you're a regular little peach!"

Lila became crimson with joy.

They boarded the subway for Simpson Street. The atmosphere was hot and rancid. The two girls found standing-room only. Whenever the express curved they were thrown violently from one side of the car to the other. A young man who stood near them made a point on these occasions of laying a hand on Lila's waist to steady her. She didn't know whether it was proper to be angry or grateful.

"Don't pay any attention to him," said Fannie; "he's just trying to be fresh, and he doesn't know how."

She said it loud enough for the young man to hear. Lila was very much frightened.

They left the subway at Simpson Street and boarded a jammed trolley-car for Westchester. Fannie paid all the fares.

"It's my treat," she said; "I'm flush. Gee, ain't it hot! I wish we'd brought our bathing-suits."

Much to Lila's relief the young man who had annoyed her was

no longer visible. Fannie talked all the way to Westchester in so loud a voice that nearly everybody in the car could hear her. Lila was shocked and awed by her friend's showiness and indifference.

From Westchester they were to walk the two hot miles to the park. Already Lila's new shoes had blistered her feet. But she did not mention this. It was her own fault. She had deliberately bought shoes that were half a size too small.

In the main street of Westchester they prinked, smoothing each other's rumpled dresses and straightening each other's peach-basket hats.

"Lila," said Fannie, "everybody's looking at you. I say you're *too* pretty. Lucky for me I've got my young man where I want him, or else you'd take him away from me."

"I would not!" exclaimed Lila, "and it's you they're looking at."

Fannie was delighted. "*Do* I look nice?" she wheedled.

"You look sweet!"

As a matter of fact, Fannie looked bold and handsome. Her clothes were too expensive for her station in life. Her mother suspected how she came by them, but was so afraid of actually knowing that she never brought the point to an issue; only sighed in secret and tried not to see or understand.

Now and then motors passed through the crowds straggling to the park, and in exchange for gratuitous insults from small boys and girls left behind them long trails of thick dust and the choking smell of burnt gasoline. In the sun the mercury was at one hundred and twenty degrees.

"There's a hog for you," exclaimed Fannie. She indicated a stout man in shirt-sleeves. He had his coat over one arm, his collar and necktie protruding from the breast pocket. His wife, a meagre woman, panted at his side. She carried two heavy children, one of them not yet born.

Half the people carried paper parcels or little suitcases made of straw in which were bathing-suits and sandwiches. It would be low tide, but between floating islands of swill and sewage there would be water, salt, wet, and cool.

"My mother," said Fannie, "doesn't like me to come to these places alone. It's a real nice crowd uses Pelham Park, but there's always a sprinkling of freshies."

"Is that why you invited me?" said Lila gayly. Inwardly she flattered herself to think that she had been asked for herself alone. But Fannie's answer had in it something of a slap in the face.

"Well," said this one, "mother forbade me to come alone. But I do want to get better acquainted with you. Honest."

They rested for a while sitting on a stone wall in the shade of a tree.

"My mother," said Fannie grandly, "thinks everybody's rotten, including me. My God!" she went on angrily, "do me and you work six days of the week only to be bossed about on the seventh? I tell you I won't stand it much longer. I'm going to cut loose. Nothing but work, work, work, and scold, scold, scold."

"If I had all the pretty things you've got," said Lila gently, "I don't believe I'd complain."

Fannie blushed. "It's hard work and skimping does it," she said. "Ever think of marrying, kid?"

Lila admitted that she had.

"Got a beau?"

Lila blushed and shook her head.

"You have, too. Own up. What's he like?"

Lila continued to deny and protest. But she enjoyed being teased upon such a subject.

"Well, if you haven't," said Fannie at last, "I have. It's a dead secret, kid. I wouldn't tell a soul but you. He's got heaps of money, and he's been after me — to marry him — for nearly a year."

"Do you like him?"

"I'm just crazy about him."

"Then why don't you marry him?"

"Well," Fannie temporized, "you never want to be in a rush about these things."

Fannie sighed, and was silent. She might have married the young man in question if she had played her cards better. And she knew it, now that it was too late, and there could not be a new deal. He had wanted her, even at the price of marriage. He was still fond of her. And he was very generous with his money. She met him whenever she could. He would be waiting for her now at the entrance to the park.

"He's got a motor-boat," she explained to Lila, "that he wants to show me. She's a cabin launch, almost new. You won't mind?"

"Mind? Are you going out for a sail with him, and leave me?"

"Well, the truth is," said Fannie, "I've just about made up my mind to say yes, and of course if there was a third party around he couldn't bring the matter up, could he? We wouldn't be out long."

"Don't mind me," said Lila. Inwardly she was terribly hurt and disappointed. "I'll just sit in the shade and wish you joy."

"I wouldn't play it so low down on you," said Fannie, "only my whole future's mixed up in it. We'll be back in lots of time to eat."

Lila walked with them to the end of the pier at the bathing-beach. The water was full of people and rubbish. The former seemed to be enjoying themselves immensely and for the most part innocently, though now and then some young girl would shriek aloud in a sort of delighted terror as her best young man, swimming under water, tugged suddenly at her bathing-skirt or pinched the calf of her leg.

Lila watched Fannie and her young man embark in a tiny row-boat and row out to a clumsy cabin catboat from which the mast had been removed and in whose cockpit a low-power, loud-popping motor had been installed. The young man started the motor, and presently his clumsy craft was dragging herself, like a crippled duck, down Pelham Bay toward the more open water of Long Island Sound.

Lila felt herself abandoned. She would have gone straight home but for the long walk to Westchester and the fact that she had no car fare. She could have cried. The heat on the end of the dock and the glare from the water were intolerable. She was already faint with hunger, and her shoes pinched her so that she could hardly walk without whimpering. It seemed to her that she had never seen so many people at once. And in all the crowds she hadn't a single friend or acquaintance. Several men, seeing that she was without male escort, tried to get to know her, but gave up, discouraged by her shy, frightened face. She was pretty, yes. But a doll. No sport in her. Such was their mental attitude.

"She might have left me the sandwiches," thought Lila. "Suppose the motor breaks down!"

Which was just what it was going to do — 'way out there in the sound. It always did sooner or later when Fannie was on board. She seemed to have been born with an influence for evil over men and gas-engines.

At the other side of green lawns on which were a running-track, swings, trapezes, parallel bars, and a ball-field, were woods. The shade, from where she was, looked black and cold. She walked slowly and timidly toward it. She could cool herself and return in time to meet Fannie. But she returned sooner than she had expected.

She found a smooth stone in the woods and sat down. After the sun there was a certain coolness. She fanned herself with some leaves. They were poison-ivy, but she did not know that. The perspiration dried on her face. There were curious whining, humming sounds in the woods. She began to scratch her ankles and wrists. Her ankles especially tickled and itched to the point of anguish. She was the delightful centre of interest to a swarm of hungry mosquitoes. She leaped to her feet and fought them wildly with her branch of poison-ivy. Then she started to run and almost stepped on a man who was lying face up in the underwood, peacefully snoring. She screamed faintly and hurried on. Some of the bolder mosquitoes followed her into the sunlight, but it was too hot even for them, and one by one they dropped behind and returned to the woods. The drunken man continued his comfortable sleep. The mosquitoes did not trouble him. It is unknown why.

Lila returned to the end of the dock and saw far off a white speck that may or may not have been the motor-boat in which Fannie had gone for a "sail."

If there hadn't been so many people about Lila must have sat down and cried. The warmth of affection which she had felt that morning for Fannie had changed into hatred. Three times she returned to the end of the dock.

All over the park were groups of people eating sandwiches and hard-boiled eggs. They shouted and joked. Under certain circumstances, not the least of sports is eating. Lila was so angry and hungry and abused that she forgot her sore feet. She couldn't stay still. She must have walked — coming and going — a good many miles in all.

At last, exhausted as she had never been even after a day at the department store during the Christmas rush, she found a deep niche between two rough rocks on the beach, over which the tide was now gently rising, and sank into it. The rocks and the sand between them gave out coolness; the sun shone on her head and shoulders, but with less than its meridianal fury. She could look down Pelham Bay and see most of the waters between Fort Schuyler and City Island. Boats of all sorts and descriptions came and went. But there was no sign of that in which Fannie had embarked.

Lila fell asleep. It became quiet in the park. The people were dragging themselves wearily home, dishevelled, dirty, sour with sweat. The sun went down, copper-red and sullen. The trunks of trees showed ebony black against it, swarms of infinitesimal gnats rose from the beaches, and made life hideous to the stragglers still in the park.

Lila was awakened by the tide wetting her feet. She rose on stiff, aching legs. There was a kink in her back; one arm, against which she had rested heavily, was asleep.

"Fannie," Lila thought with a kind of falling despair, "must have come back, looked for me, given me up, and gone home."

In the midst of Pelham Bay a fire twinkled, burning low. It looked like a camp-fire deserted and dying in the centre of a great open plain. Lila gave it no more than a somnambulant look. It told her nothing: no story of sudden frenzied terror, of inextinguishable, unescapable flames, of young people in the midst of health and the vain and wicked pursuit of happiness, half-burned to death, half-drowned. It told her no story of guilt providentially punished, or accidentally.

She had slept through all the shouting and screaming. The boats that had attempted rescue had withdrawn; there remained only the hull of a converted catboat, gasoline-soaked, burnt to the water's edge, a cinder — still smouldering.

Somewhere under the placid waters, gathering speed in the tidal currents, slowing down and swinging in the eddies, was all that remained of Fannie Davis, food for crabs, eels, dogfish, lobsters, and all the thousand and one scavengers of Atlantic bays, blackened shreds of garments still clinging to her.

II

Next to Pelham Bay Park toward the south is a handsome private property. On the low boundary wall of this, facing the road and directly under a ragged cherry-tree, Lila seated herself. She was "all in." She must wait until a vehicle of some sort passed and beg for a lift. She was half-starved; her feet could no longer carry her. A motor thrilled by at high speed, a fiery, stinking dragon in the night. Mosquitoes tormented her. She had no strength with which to oppose them. The hand in which she had held the poison-ivy was beginning to itch and swell.

A second motor approached slowly and came to a halt. A young man got out, opened one of the headlights, struck a match, and lighted it. Then he lighted the other. The low stone wall on which Lila sat and Lila herself were embraced by the ring of illumination. It must have been obvious to any one but a fool that Lila was out of place in her surroundings; her peach-basket hat, the oxford ties of which she had been so proud, told a story of city breeding. Her face, innocent and childlike, was very touching.

The young man shut off his motor, so that there was a sudden silence. "Want a lift somewhere?" he asked cheerfully.

Lila could not remember when she had been too young to be warned against the advances of strange men. "They give you a high old time, and then they expect to be paid for it," had been so dinned into her that if she had given the young man a sharp "No" for an answer it would have been almost instinctive. Training and admonition rose strong within her. She felt that she was going to refuse help. The thought was intolerable. Wherefore, instead of answering, she burst into tears.

A moment later the young man was sitting by her side, and she was pouring her tale of a day gone wrong into amused but sympathetic ears.

His voice and choice of words belonged to a world into which she had never looked. She could not help trusting him and believing that he was good — even when he put his arm around her and let her finish her cry on his shoulder.

"And your friend left you — and you've got no car fare, and you've had nothing to eat, and you can't walk any more because your shoes are too tight. And you live —?"

She told him.

"I could take you right home to your mother," he said, "but I won't. That would be a good ending to a day gone wrong, but not the best. Come."

He supported her to his motor, a high-power runabout, and helped her in. Never before had she sat in such reclining comfort. It was better than sitting up in bed.

"We'll send your mother a telegram from New Rochelle so that she won't worry," he said. "Just you let yourself go and try to enjoy everything. Fortunately I know of a shoe store in New Rochelle. It won't be open; but the proprietor has rooms above the store, and he'll be glad to make a sale even if it is Sunday. The first principle to be observed in a pleasant outing is a pair of comfortable feet."

"But I have no money," protested Lila.

"I have," said the young man; "too much, some people think."

Lila had been taught that if she accepted presents from young men she put herself more or less in their power.

They whirled noiselessly across Pelham Bridge. Lila had given up in the matter of accepting a present of shoes. In so doing she feared that she had committed herself definitely to the paths that lead to destruction. And when, having tried in vain to get a table at two inns between New Rochelle and Larchmont, the young man said that he would take her to his own home to dinner, she felt sure of it. But she was too tired to care, and in the padded seat, and the new easy shoes, too blissfully comfortable. They had sent her mother a telegram. The young man had composed it. He had told the mother not to worry. "I'm dining out and won't be home till late."

"We won't say how late," he had explained with an ingenuous smile, "because we don't know, do we?"

They had gone to a drug store, and the clerk had bound a

soothing dressing on Lila's poisoned hand.

They turned from the main road into a long avenue over which trees met in a continuous arch. The place was all a-twinkle with fireflies. Box, roses, and honeysuckle filled the air with delicious odors — then strong, pungent, bracing as wine, the smell of salt-marshes, and coldness off the water. On a point of land among trees many lights glowed.

"That's my place," said the young man.

"We'll have dinner on the terrace — deep water comes right up to it. There's no wind tonight. The candles won't even flicker."

As if the stopping of the automobile had been a signal, the front door swung quietly open and a Chinese butler in white linen appeared against a background of soft coloring and subdued lights.

As Lila entered the house her knees shook a little. She felt that she was definitely committing herself to what she must always regret. She was a fly walking deliberately into a spider's parlor. That the young man hitherto had behaved most circumspectly, she dared not count in his favor. Was it not always so in the beginning? He seemed like a jolly, kindly boy. She had the impulse to scream and to run out of the house, to hide in the shrubbery, to throw herself into the water. Her heart beat like that of a trapped bird. She heard the front door close behind her.

"I think you'd be more comfy," said the young man, "if you took off your hat, don't you? Dinner'll be ready in about ten minutes. Fong will show you where to go."

She followed the Chinaman up a flight of broad low steps. Their feet made no sound on the thick carpeting. He held open the door of a bedroom. It was all white and delicate and blue. Through a door at the farther end she had a glimpse of white porcelain and shining nickel.

Her first act when the Chinaman had gone was to lock the door by which she had entered. Then she looked from each of the windows in turn. The terrace was beneath her, brick with a balustrade of white, with white urns. The young man, bareheaded, paced the terrace like a sentinel. He was smoking a cigarette.

To the left was a round table, set for two. She could see that the chairs were of white wicker, with deep, soft cushions. In the centre of the table was a bowl of red roses. Four candles burned upright in massive silver candlesticks.

She took off her hat mechanically, washed her face and the hand that had not been bandaged, and "did" her hair. She looked wonderfully pretty in the big mirror over the dressing-table. The heavy ivory brushes looked enormous in her delicate hands. Her eyes were great and round like those of a startled deer.

She heard his voice calling to her from the terrace: "Hello, up there! Got everything you want? Dinner's ready when you are."

She hesitated a long time with her hand on the door-key. But what was a locked door in an isolated house to a bad man? She drew a deep breath, turned the key, waited a little longer, and then, as a person steps into a very cold bath, pushed the door open and went out.

He was waiting for her at the foot of the stairs. She went down slowly, her hand on the rail. She had no idea that she was making an exquisite picture. She knew only that she was frightened.

"It's turned cool," said the young man. He caught up a light scarf of Chinese embroidery and laid it lightly about her shoulders. She looked him for the first time squarely in the face. She saw chiefly a pair of rather small, deep-set blue eyes; at the outer corners were multitudinous little wrinkles, dug by smiling. The eyes were clear as a child's, full of compassionate laughter.

A feeling of perfect security came over her. She thanked Heaven that she had not made a ridiculous scene. The chimes of a tall clock broke the silence with music.

He offered her his arm, and she laid her fingers on it.

"I think we are served," he said, and led her to the terrace. He was solicitous about placing cushions to the best advantage for her. He took one from his own chair, and, on one knee, put it under her feet. He smiled at her across the bowl of roses.

"How old are you?" he said. "You look like a man's kid sister."

She told him that she was seventeen and that she had worked for two years in a department store.

"My father was a farmer," she said, "but he lost one arm, and couldn't make it pay. So we had to come to the city."

"Is your father living?"

"Yes. But he says he is dead. He can't find any work to do. Mother works like a horse, though, and so does Bert, and so do I. The others are at school."

"Do you like your work?"

"Only for what it brings in."

"What does it bring in?"

"Six dollars a week."

The young man smiled. "Never mind," he said; "eat your soup."

It did her good, that soup. It was strong and very hot. It put heart into her. When she had finished, he laughed gleefully.

"It's all very well to talk about rice-powder, and cucumber-cream, and beauty-sleeps, but all you needed to make you look perfectly lovely was a cup of soup. That scarf's becoming to you, too."

She blushed happily. She had lost all fear of him.

"What are you pinching yourself for?" he asked.

"To see if I'm awake."

"You are," he said, "wide awake. Take my word for it, and I hope you're having a good time."

The Chinaman poured something light and sparkling into her glass from a bottle dressed in a napkin. Misgivings returned to her. She had heard of girls being drugged.

"You don't have to drink it," said the young man. "I had some served because dinner doesn't look like dinner without champagne. Still, after the thoroughly unhappy day you've put in, I think a mouthful or two would do you good."

She lifted the glass of champagne, smiled, drank, and choked. He laughed at her merrily.

All through dinner he kept lighting cigarettes and throwing them away. Between times he ate with great relish and heartiness.

Lila was in heaven. All her doubts and fears had vanished. She felt thoroughly at home, as if she had always been used to service and linen and silver and courtesy.

They had coffee, and then they strolled about in the moonlight, while the young man smoked a very long cigar.

He looked at his watch, and sighed. "Well, Miss," he said, "if we're to get you safe home to your mother!"

"I won't be a minute," she said.

"You know the way?"

She ran upstairs, and, having put on her hat, decided that it looked cheap and vulgar, and took it off again.

He wrapped her in a soft white polo-coat for the long run to New York. She looked back at the lights of his house. Would she ever see them again, or smell the salt and the box and the roses?

By the time they had reached the Zoological Gardens at Fordham she had fallen blissfully asleep. He ran the car with considerate slowness, and looked at her very often. She waked as they crossed the river. Her eyes shrank from the piled serried buildings of Manhattan. The air was no longer clean and delicious to the lungs.

"Have I been asleep?"

"Yes."

"Oh," she cried, "how could I! How could I! I've missed some of it. And it never happened before, and it will never happen again."

"Not in the same way, perhaps," he said gravely. "But how do you know? I think you are one girl in ten million, and to you all things are possible."

"How many men in ten million are like you?" she asked.

"Men are all pretty much alike," he said. "They have good impulses and bad."

In the stark darkness between the outer and the inner door of the tenement in which she lived, there was an awkward, troubled silence. He wished very much to kiss her, but had made up his mind that he would not. She thought that he might, and had made up her mind that if he attempted to she would resist. She was not in the least afraid of him any more, but of herself.

He kissed her, and she did not resist.

"Good-night," he said, and then with a half-laugh, "Which is your bell?"

She found it and rang it. Presently there was a rusty click, and the inner door opened an inch or so. Neither of them spoke for a full minute. Then she, her face aflame in the darkness:

"When you came I was only a little fool who'd bought a pair of shoes that were too tight for her. I didn't *know* anything. I'm wise now. I know that I'm dreaming, and that if I wake up before the dream is ended I shall die."

She tried to laugh gayly and could not.

"I've made things harder for you instead of easier," he said. "I'm terribly sorry. I meant well."

"Oh, it isn't that," she said. "Thank you a thousand thousand times. And good-night."

"Wait," he said. "Will you play with me again some time? How about Saturday?"

"No," she said. "It wouldn't be fair — to me. Good-night."

She passed through the inner door and up the narrow creaking stair to the dark tenement in which she lived; she could hear the restless breathing of her sleeping family.

"Oh, my God!" she thought, "if it weren't for *them*!"

As for the young man, having lighted a long cigar, he entered his car and drove off, muttering to himself:

"Damnation! Why does a girl like that *have* a family!"

He never saw her again, nor was he ever haunted by the thought that he had perhaps spoiled her whole life as thoroughly as if he had taken advantage of her ignorance and her innocence.

BACK THERE IN THE GRASS

It was spring in the South Seas when, for the first time, I went ashore at Batengo, which is the Polynesian village, and the only one on the big grass island of the same name. There is a cable station just up the beach from the village, and a good-natured young chap named Graves had charge of it. He was an upstanding, clean-cut fellow, as the fact that he had been among the islands for three years without falling into any of their ways proved. The interior of the corrugated iron house in which he lived, for instance, was bachelor from A to Z. And if that wasn't a sufficient alibi, my pointer dog, Don, who dislikes anything Polynesian or Melanesian, took to him at once. And they established a romping friendship. He gave us lunch on the porch, and because he had not seen a white man for two months, or a liver-and-white dog for two years, he told us the entire story of his young life, with reminiscences of early childhood and plans for the future thrown in.

The future was very simple. There was a girl coming out to him from the States by the next steamer but one; the captain of that steamer would join them together in holy wedlock, and after that the Lord would provide.

"My dear fellow," he said, "you think I'm asking her to share a very lonely sort of life, but if you could imagine all the — the affection and gentleness, and thoughtfulness that I've got stored up to pour out at her feet for the rest of our lives, you wouldn't be a bit afraid for her happiness. If a man spends his whole time and imagination thinking up ways to make a girl happy and occupied, he can think up a whole lot. . . . I'd like ever so much to show her to you."

He led the way to his bedroom, and stood in silent rapture before a large photograph that leaned against the wall over his dressing-table.

She didn't look to me like the sort of girl a cable agent would happen to marry. She looked like a swell — the real thing — beautiful and simple and unaffected.

"Yes," he said, "isn't she?"

I hadn't spoken a word. Now I said:

"It's easy to see why you aren't lonely with that wonderful girl to look at. Is she really coming out by the next steamer but one? It's hard to believe because she's so much too good to be true."

"Yes," he said, "isn't she?"

"The usual cable agent," I said, "keeps from going mad by having a dog or a cat or some pet or other to talk to. But I can understand a photograph like this being all-sufficient to any man — even if he had never seen the original. Allow me to shake hands with you."

Then I got him away from the girl, because my time was short and I wanted to find out about some things that were important to *me*.

"You haven't asked me my business in these parts," I said, "but I'll tell you. I'm collecting grasses for the Bronx Botanical Garden."

"Then, by Jove!" said Graves, "you have certainly come to the right place. There used to be a tree on this island, but the last man who saw it died in 1789 — Grass! The place is all grass: there are fifty kinds right around my house here."

"I've noticed only eighteen," I said, "but that isn't the point. The point is: when do the Batengo Island grasses begin to go to seed?" And I smiled.

"You think you've got me stumped, don't you?" he said. "That a mere cable agent wouldn't notice such things. Well, that grass there," and he pointed — "beach nut we call it — is the first to ripen seed, and, as far as I know, it does it just six weeks from now."

"Are you just making things up to impress me?"

"No, sir, I am not. I know to the minute. You see, I'm a victim of hay-fever."

"In that case," I said, "expect me back about the time your nose begins to run."

"Really?" And his whole face lighted up. "I'm delighted. Only six weeks. Why, then, if you'll stay round for only five or six weeks *more* you'll be here for the wedding."

"I'll make it if I possibly can," I said. "I want to see if that girl's really true."

"Anything I can do to help you while you're gone? I've got loads of spare time —"

"If you knew anything about grasses —"

"I don't. But I'll blow back into the interior and look around. I've been meaning to right along, just for fun. But I can never get any of *them* to go with me."

"The natives?"

"Yes. Poor lot. They're committing race suicide as fast as they can. There are more wooden gods than people in Batengo village, and the superstition's so thick you could cut it with a knife. All the manly virtues have perished. . . . Aloiu!"

The boy who did Graves's chores for him came lazily out of the house.

"Aloiu," said Graves, "just run back into the island to the top of that hill — see? — that one over there — and fetch a handful of grass for this gentleman. He'll give you five dollars for it."

Aloiu grinned sheepishly and shook his head.

"Fifty dollars?"

Aloiu shook his head with even more firmness, and I whistled. Fifty dollars would have made him the Rockefeller-Carnegie-Morgan of those parts.

"All right, coward," said Graves cheerfully. "Run away and play with the other children. . . . Now, isn't that curious? Neither love, money, nor insult will drag one of them a mile from the beach. They say that if you go 'back there in the grass' something awful will happen to you."

"As what?" I asked.

"The last man to try it," said Graves, "in the memory of the oldest inhabitant was a woman. When they found her she was all black and swollen — at least that's what they say. Something had bitten her just above the ankle."

"Nonsense," I said, "there are no snakes in the whole Batengo group."

"They didn't say it was a snake," said Graves. "They said the marks of the bite were like those that would be made by the teeth of a very little — child."

Graves rose and stretched himself.

"What's the use of arguing with people that tell yarns like that! All the same, if you're bent on making expeditions back into the grass, you'll make 'em alone, unless the cable breaks and I'm free to make 'em with you."

Five weeks later I was once more coasting along the wavering hills of Batengo Island, with a sharp eye out for a first sight of the cable station and Graves. Five weeks with no company but Kanakas and a pointer dog makes one white man pretty keen for the society of another. Furthermore, at our one meeting I had taken a great shine to Graves and to the charming young lady who was to brave a life in the South Seas for his sake. If I was eager to get ashore, Don was more so. I had a shot-gun across my knees with which to salute the cable station, and the sight of that weapon, coupled with toothsome memories of a recent big hunt down on Forked Peak, had set the dog quivering from stem to stern, to crouching, wagging his tail till it disappeared, and beating sudden tattoos upon the deck with his forepaws. And when at last we rounded on the cable station and I let off both barrels, he began to bark and race about the schooner like a thing possessed.

The salute brought Graves out of his house. He stood on the

porch waving a handkerchief, and I called to him through a mega-phone; hoped that he was well, said how glad I was to see him, and asked him to meet me in Batengo village.

Even at that distance I detected a something irresolute in his manner; and a few minutes later when he had fetched a hat out of the house, locked the door, and headed toward the village, he looked more like a soldier marching to battle than a man walking half a mile to greet a friend.

"That's funny," I said to Don. "He's coming to meet us in spite of the fact that he'd much rather not. Oh, well!"

I left the schooner while she was still under way, and reached the beach before Graves came up. There were too many strange brown men to suit Don, and he kept very close to my legs. When Graves arrived the natives fell away from him as if he had been a leper. He wore a sort of sickly smile, and when he spoke the dog stiffened his legs and growled menacingly.

"Don!" I exclaimed sternly, and the dog cowered, but the spines along his back bristled and he kept a menacing eye upon Graves. The man's face looked drawn and rather angry. The frank boyish-ness was clean out of it. He had been strained by something or other to the breaking-point — so much was evident.

"My dear fellow," I said, "what the devil is the matter?"

Graves looked to right and left, and the islanders shrank still farther away from him.

"You can see for yourself," he said curtly. "I'm taboo." And then, with a little break in his voice: "Even your dog feels it. Don, good boy! Come here, sir!"

Don growled quietly.

"You see!"

"Don," I said sharply, "this man is my friend and yours. Pat him, Graves."

Graves reached forward and patted Don's head and talked to him soothingly.

But although Don did not growl or menace, he shivered under the caress and was unhappy.

"So you're taboo!" I said cheerfully. "That's the result of any-thing, from stringing pink and yellow shells on the same string to murdering your uncle's grandmother-in-law. Which have *you* done?"

"I've been back there in the grass," he said, "and because — because nothing happened to me I'm taboo."

"Is that all?"

"As far as they know — yes."

"Well!" said I, "my business will take me back there for days at a time, so I'll be taboo, too. Then there'll be two of us. Did you find any curious grasses for me?"

"I don't know about grasses," he said, "but I found something very curious that I want to show you and ask your advice about. Are you going to share my house?"

"I think I'll keep head-quarters on the schooner," I said, "but if you'll put me up now and then for a meal or for the night —"

"I'll put you up for lunch right now," he said, "if you'll come. I'm my own cook and bottle-washer since the taboo, but I must say the change isn't for the worse so far as food goes."

He was looking and speaking more cheerfully.

"May I bring Don?"

He hesitated.

"Why — yes — of course."

"If you'd rather not?"

"No, bring him. I want to make friends again if I can."

So we started for Graves's house, Don very close at my heels.

"Graves," I said, "surely a taboo by a lot of fool islanders hasn't upset you. There's something on your mind. Bad news?"

"Oh, no," he said. "She's coming. It's other things. I'll tell you by and by — everything. Don't mind me. I'm all right. Listen to the wind in the grass. That sound day and night is enough to put a man off his feed."

"You say you found something very curious back there in the grass?"

"I found, among other things, a stone monolith. It's fallen down, but it's almost as big as the Flatiron Building in New York. It's ancient as days — all carved — it's a sort of woman, I think. But we'll go back one day and have a look at it. Then, of course, I saw all the different kinds of grasses in the world — they'd interest you more — but I'm such a punk botanist that I gave up trying to tell 'em apart. I like the flowers best — there's millions of 'em — down among the grass. . . . I tell you, old man, this island is the greatest curiosity-shop in the whole world."

He unlocked the door of his house and stood aside for me to go in first.

"Shut up, Don!"

The dog growled savagely, but I banged him with my open hand across the snout, and he quieted down and followed into the house, all tense and watchful.

On the shelf where Graves kept his books, with its legs hanging over, was what I took to be an idol of some light brownish wood —

say sandalwood, with a touch of pink. But it was the most lifelike and astounding piece of carving I ever saw in the islands or out of them. It was about a foot high, and represented a Polynesian woman in the prime of life, say, fifteen or sixteen years old, only the features were finer and cleaner carved. It was a nude, in an attitude of easy repose — the legs hanging, the toes dangling — the hands resting, palms downward, on the blotter, the trunk relaxed. The eyes, which were a kind of steely blue, seemed to have been made, depth upon depth, of some wonderful translucent enamel, and to make his work still more realistic the artist had planted the statuette's eyebrows, eyelashes, and scalp with real hair, very soft and silky, brown on the head and black for the lashes and eyebrows. The thing was so lifelike that it frightened me. And when Don began to growl like distant thunder I didn't blame him. But I leaned over and caught him by the collar, because it was evident that he wanted to get at that statuette and destroy it.

When I looked up the statuette's eyes had moved. They were turned downward upon the dog, with cool curiosity and indifference. A kind of shudder went through me. And then, lo and behold, the statuette's tiny brown breasts rose and fell slowly, and a long breath came out of its nostrils.

I backed violently into Graves, dragging Don with me and half-choking him. "My God Almighty!" I said. "It's alive!"

"Isn't she!" said he. "I caught her back there in the grass — the little minx. And when I heard your signal I put her up there to keep her out of mischief. It's too high for her to jump — and she's very sore about it."

"You found her in the grass," I said. "For God's sake! — are there more of them?"

"Thick as quail," said he, "but it's hard to get a sight of 'em. But *you* were overcome by curiosity, weren't you, old girl? You came out to have a look at the big white giant and he caught you with his thumb and forefinger by the scruff of the neck — so you couldn't bite him — and here you are."

The womankin's lips parted and I saw a flash of white teeth. She looked up into Graves's face and the steely eyes softened. It was evident that she was very fond of him.

"Rum sort of a pet," said Graves. "What?"

"Rum?" I said. "It's horrible — it isn't decent — it — it ought to be taboo. Don's got it sized up right. He — he wants to kill it."

"Please don't keep calling her It," said Graves. "She wouldn't like it — if she understood." Then he whispered words that were Greek to me, and the womankin laughed aloud. Her laugh was sweet and tinkly, like the upper notes of a spinet.

"You can speak her language?"

"A few words — Tog ma Lao?"

"Na!"

"Aba Ton sug ato."

"Nan Tane dom ud lon anea!"

It sounded like that — only all whispered and very soft. It sounded a little like the wind in the grass.

"She says she isn't afraid of the dog," said Graves, "and that he'd better let her alone."

"I almost hope he won't," said I. "Come outside. I don't like her. I think I've got a touch of the horrors."

Graves remained behind a moment to lift the womankin down from the shelf, and when he rejoined me I had made up my mind to talk to him like a father.

"Graves," I said, "although that creature in there is only a foot high, it isn't a pig or a monkey, it's a woman, and you're guilty of what's considered a pretty ugly crime at home — abduction. You've stolen this woman away from kith and kin, and the least you can do is to carry her back where you found her and turn her loose. Let me ask you one thing — what would Miss Chester think?"

"Oh, that doesn't worry me," said Graves. "But I *am* worried — worried sick. It's early — shall we talk now, or wait till after lunch?"

"Now," I said.

"Well," said he, "you left me pretty well enthused on the subject of botany — so I went back there twice to look up grasses for you. The second time I went I got to a deep sort of valley where the grass is waist-high — that, by the way, is where the big monolith is — and that place was alive with things that were frightened and ran. I could see the directions they took by the way the grass tops acted. There were lots of loose stones about and I began to throw 'em to see if I could knock one of the things over. Suddenly all at once I saw a pair of bright little eyes peering out of a bunch of grass — I let fly at them, and something gave a sort of moan and thrashed about in the grass — and then lay still. I went to look, and found that I'd stunned — *her*. She came to and tried to bite me, but I had her by the scruff of the neck and she couldn't. Further, she was sick with being hit in the chest with the stone, and first thing I knew she keeled over in the palm of my hand in a dead faint. I couldn't find any water or anything — and I didn't want her to die — so I brought her home. She was sick for a week — and I took care of her — as I would a sick pup — and she began to get well and want to play and romp and poke into everything. She'd get the lower drawer of my desk open and hide in it — or crawl into a rubber boot and play house. And she got to be right good company — same as any pet does — a cat or a dog — or a monkey — and naturally, she being so small, I couldn't think of her as anything but a sort of little beast that I'd caught and tamed. . . . You see how it all happened, don't you? Might have happened to anybody."

"Why, yes," I said. "If she didn't give a man the horrors right at the start — I can understand making a sort of pet of her — but, man, there's only one thing to do. Be persuaded. Take her back where you found her, and turn her loose."

"Well and good," said Graves. "I tried that, and next morning I found her at my door, sobbing — horrible, dry sobs — no tears. . . . You've said one thing that's full of sense: she isn't a pig — or a monkey — she's a woman."

"You don't mean to say," said I, "that that mite of a thing is in love with you?"

"I don't know what else you'd call it."

"Graves," I said, "Miss Chester arrives by the next steamer. In the meanwhile something has got to be done."

"What?" said he hopelessly.

"I don't know," I said. "Let me think."

The dog Don laid his head heavily on my knee, as if he wished to offer a solution of the difficulty.

A week before Miss Chester's steamer was due the situation had not changed. Graves's pet was as much a fixture of Graves's house as the front door. And a man was never confronted with a more serious problem. Twice he carried her back into the grass and deserted her, and each time she returned and was found sobbing — horrible, dry sobs — on the porch. And a number of times we took her, or Graves did, in the pocket of his jacket, upon systematic searches for her people. Doubtless she could have helped us to find them, but she wouldn't. She was very sullen on these expeditions and frightened. When Graves tried to put her down she would cling to him, and it took real force to pry her loose.

In the open she could run like a rat; and in open country it would have been impossible to desert her; she would have followed at Graves's heels as fast as he could move them. But forcing through the thick grass tired her after a few hundred yards, and she would gradually drop farther and farther behind — sobbing. There was a pathetic side to it.

She hated me; and made no bones about it; but there was an armed truce between us. She feared my influence over Graves, and I feared her — well, just as some people fear rats or snakes. Things utterly out of the normal always do worry me, and Bo, which was the name Graves had learned for her, was, so far as I know, unique in human experience. In appearance she was like an unusually good-looking island girl observed through the wrong end of an opera-glass, but in habit and action she was different. She would catch flies and little grasshoppers and eat them all alive and kicking, and if you teased her more than she liked her ears would flatten the way a cat's do, and she would hiss like a snapping-turtle, and show her teeth.

But one got accustomed to her. Even poor Don learned that it was not his duty to punish her with one bound and a snap. But he would never let her touch him, believing that in her case discretion was the better part of valor. If she approached him he withdrew, always with dignity, but equally with determination. He knew in his heart that something about her was horribly wrong and against nature. I knew it, too, and I think Graves began to suspect it.

Well, a day came when Graves, who had been up since dawn, saw the smoke of a steamer along the horizon, and began to fire off his revolver so that I, too, might wake and participate in his joy. I made tea and went ashore.

"It's *her* steamer," he said.

"Yes," said I, "and we've got to decide something."

"About Bo?"

"Suppose I take her off your hands — for a week or so — till you and Miss Chester have settled down and put your house in order. Then Miss Chester — Mrs. Graves, that is — can decide what is to be done. I admit that I'd rather wash my hands of the business — but I'm the only white man available, and I propose to stand by my race. Don't say a word to Bo — just bring her out to the schooner and leave her."

In the upshot Graves accepted my offer, and while Bo, fairly bristling with excitement and curiosity, was exploring the farther corners of my cabin, we slipped out and locked the door on her. The minute she knew what had happened she began to tear around and raise Cain. It sounded a little like a cat having a fit.

Graves was white and unhappy. "Let's get away quick," he said; "I feel like a skunk."

But Miss Chester was everything that her photograph said about her, and more too, so that the trick he had played Bo was very soon a negligible weight on Graves's mind.

If the wedding was quick and business-like, it was also jolly and romantic. The oldest passenger gave the bride away. All the crew came aft and sang "The Voice That Breathed O'er E-den That Earliest Wedding-Day" — to the tune called "Blairgowrie." They had worked it up in secret for a surprise. And the bride's dove-brown eyes got a little teary. I was best man. The captain read the service, and choked occasionally. As for Graves — I had never thought him handsome — well, with his brown face and white linen suit, he made me think, and I'm sure I don't know why, of St. Michael — that time he overcame Lucifer. The captain blew us to breakfast, with champagne and a cake, and then the happy pair went ashore in a boat full of the bride's trousseau, and the crew manned the bulwarks and gave three cheers, and then something like twenty-seven more, and last thing of all the brass cannon was fired, and the little square flags that spell G-o-o-d L-u-c-k were run up on the signal halyards.

As for me, I went back to my schooner feeling blue and lonely. I knew little about women and less about love. It didn't seem quite fair. For once I hated my profession — seed-gatherer to a body of scientific gentlemen whom I had never seen. Well, there's nothing so good for the blues as putting things in order.

I cleaned my rifle and revolver. I wrote up my note-book. I developed some plates; I studied a brand-new book on South Sea grasses that had been sent out to me, and I found some mistakes. I went ashore with Don, and had a long walk on the beach — in the opposite direction from Graves's house, of course — and I sent Don into the water after sticks, and he seemed to enjoy it, and so I stripped and went in with him. Then I dried in the sun, and had a match with my hands to see which could find the tiniest shell. Toward dusk we returned to the schooner and had dinner, and after that I went into my cabin to see how Bo was getting on.

She flew at me like a cat, and if I hadn't jerked my foot back she must have bitten me. As it was, her teeth tore a piece out of my trousers. I'm afraid I kicked her. Anyway, I heard her land with a crash in a far corner. I struck a match and lighted candles — they are cooler than lamps — very warily — one eye on Bo. She had retreated under a chair and looked out — very sullen and angry. I sat down and began to talk to her. "It's no use," I said, "you're trying to bite and scratch, because you're only as big as a minute. So come out here and make friends. I don't like you and you don't like me; but we're going to be thrown together for quite some time, so we'd better make the best of it. You come out here and behave pretty and I'll give you a bit of gingersnap."

The last word was intelligible to her, and she came a little way out from under the chair. I had a bit of gingersnap in my pocket, left over from treating Don, and I tossed it on the floor midway between us. She darted forward and ate it with quick bites.

Well, then, she looked up, and her eyes asked — just as plain as day: "Why are things thus? Why have I come to live with you? I don't like you. I want to go back to Graves."

I couldn't explain very well, and just shook my head and then went on trying to make friends — it was no use. She hated me, and after a time I got bored. I threw a pillow on the floor for her to sleep on, and left her. Well, the minute the door was shut and locked she began to sob. You could hear her for quite a distance, and I couldn't stand it. So I went back — and talked to her as nicely and soothingly as I could. But she wouldn't even look at me — just lay face down — heaving and sobbing.

Now I don't like little creatures that snap — so when I picked her up it was by the scruff of the neck. She had to face me then, and I saw that in spite of all the sobbing her eyes were perfectly dry. That struck me as curious. I examined them through a pocket magnifying-glass, and discovered that they had no tear-ducts. Of course she couldn't cry. Perhaps I squeezed the back of her neck harder than I meant to — anyway, her lips began to draw back and her teeth to show.

It was exactly at that second that I recalled the legend Graves had told me about the island woman being found dead, and all black and swollen, back there in the grass, with teeth marks on her that looked as if they had been made by a very little child.

I forced Bo's mouth wide open and looked in. Then I reached for a candle and held it steadily between her face and mine. She struggled furiously so that I had to put down the candle and catch her legs together in my free hand. But I had seen enough. I felt wet and cold all over. For if the swollen glands at the base of the deeply grooved canines meant anything, that which I held between my hands was not a woman — but a snake.

I put her in a wooden box that had contained soap and nailed slats over the top. And, personally, I was quite willing to put scrap-iron in the box with her and fling it overboard. But I did not feel quite justified without consulting Graves.

As an extra precaution in case of accidents, I overhauled my medicine-chest and made up a little package for the breast pocket — a lancet, a rubber bandage, and a pill-box full of permanganate crystals. I had still much collecting to do, "back there in the grass," and I did not propose to step on any of Bo's cousins or her sisters or her aunts — without having some of the elementary first-aids to the snake-bitten handy.

It was a lovely starry night, and I determined to sleep on deck.

Before turning in I went to have a look at Bo. Having nailed her in a box securely, as I thought, I must have left my cabin door ajar. Anyhow she was gone. She must have braced her back against one side of the box, her feet against the other, and burst it open. I had most certainly underestimated her strength and resources.

The crew, warned of peril, searched the whole schooner over, slowly and methodically, lighted by lanterns. We could not find her. Well, swimming comes natural to snakes.

I went ashore as quickly as I could get a boat manned and rowed. I took Don on a leash, a shot-gun loaded, and both pockets of my jacket full of cartridges. We ran swiftly along the beach, Don and I, and then turned into the grass to make a short cut for Graves's house. All of a sudden Don began to tremble with eagerness and nuzzle and sniff among the roots of the grass. He was "making game."

"Good Don," I said, "good boy — hunt her up! Find her!"

The moon had risen. I saw two figures standing in the porch of Graves's house. I was about to call to them and warn Graves that Bo was loose and dangerous — when a scream — shrill and frightful — rang in my ears. I saw Graves turn to his bride and catch her in his arms.

When I came up she had collected her senses and was behaving splendidly. While Graves fetched a lantern and water she sat down on the porch, her back against the house, and undid her garter, so that I could pull the stocking off her bitten foot. Her instep, into which Bo's venomous teeth had sunk, was already swollen and discolored. I slashed the teeth-marks this way and that with my lancet. And Mrs. Graves kept saying: "All right — all right — don't mind me — do what's best."

Don's leash had wedged between two of the porch planks, and all the time we were working over Mrs. Graves he whined and struggled to get loose.

"Graves," I said, when we had done what we could, "if your wife begins to seem faint, give her brandy — just a very little — at a time — and — I think we were in time — and for God's sake don't ever let her know *why* she was bitten — or by *what* —"

Then I turned and freed Don and took off his leash.

The moonlight was now very white and brilliant. In the sandy path that led from Graves's porch I saw the print of feet — shaped just like human feet — less than an inch long. I made Don smell them, and said:

"Hunt close, boy! Hunt close!"

Thus hunting, we moved slowly through the grass toward the

interior of the island. The scent grew hotter — suddenly Don began to move more stiffly — as if he had the rheumatism — his eyes straight ahead saw something that I could not see — the tip of his tail vibrated furiously — he sank lower and lower — his legs worked more and more stiffly — his head was thrust forward to the full stretch of his neck toward a thick clump of grass. In the act of taking a wary step he came to a dead halt — his right forepaw just clear of the ground. The tip of his tail stopped vibrating. The tail itself stood straight out behind him and became rigid like a bar of iron. I never saw a stancher point.

"Steady, boy!"

I pushed forward the safety of my shot-gun and stood at attention.

"How is she?"

"Seems to be pulling through. I heard you fire both barrels. What luck?"

ASABRI

Asabri, head of the great banking house of Asabri Brothers in Rome, had been a great sportsman in his youth. But by middle-age he had grown a little tired, you may say; so that whereas formerly he had depended upon his own exertions for pleasure and exhilaration, he looked now with favor upon automobiles, motor-boats, and saddle-horses.

Almost every afternoon he rode alone in the Campagna, covering great distances on his stanch Irish mare, Biddy. She was the handsomest horse in Rome; her master was the handsomest man. He looked like some old Roman consul going out to govern and civilize. Peasants whom he passed touched their hats to him automatically. His face in repose was a sort of command.

One day as he rode out of Rome he saw that fog was gathering; and he resolved, for there was an inexhaustible well of boyishness within him, to get lost in it. He had no engagement for that night; his family had already left Rome for their villa on Lake Como. Nobody would worry about him except Luigi, his valet. And as for this one, Asabri said to himself: "He is a spoiled child of fortune; let him worry for once."

He did not believe in fever; he believed in a good digestion and good habits. He knew every inch of the Campagna, or thought he did; and he knew that under the magic of fog the most familiar parts of it became unfamiliar and strange. He had lost himself upon it once or twice before, to his great pleasure and exhilaration. He had felt like some daring explorer in an unknown country. He thought that perhaps he might be forced to spend the night in some peasant's home smelling of cheese and goats. He would reward his hosts in the morning beyond the dreams of their undoubted avarice. There would be a beautiful daughter with a golden voice: he would see to it that she became a famous singer. He would give the father a piece of fertile land with an ample house upon it. Every day the happy family would go down on their knees and pray for his soul. He knew of nothing more delicious than to surprise unexpecting and deserving people with stable benefactions. And besides, if only for the sake of his boyhood, he loved dearly the smell of cheese and goats.

A goat had been his foster-mother; it was to her that he attributed his splendid constitution and activity, which had filled in the spaces between his financial successes with pleasure. As he trotted on into the fog he tried to recall having knowingly done harm to somebody or other; and because he could not, his face of a Roman emperor took on a great look of peace.

"Biddy," he said after a time, in English (she was an Irish horse, and English was the nearest he could get to her native language), "this is no common Roman mist; it's a genuine fog that has been sucked up Tiber from the salt sea. You can smell salt and fish. We shall be lost, possibly for a long time. There will be no hot mash for you tonight. You will eat what goats eat and be very grateful. Perhaps you will meet some rural donkey during our adventures, and I must ask you to use the poor little beast's rustic ignorance with the greatest tact and forbearance. You will tell her tales of cities and travels; but do not lie to excess, or appear condescending, lest you find her rude wits a match for your own and are ashamed."

Asabri did not spend the night in a peasant's hut. Biddy did not meet any country donkey to swap yarns with. But inasmuch as the pair lost themselves thoroughly, it must be admitted that some of the banker's wishes came true.

He had not counted on two things. At dinner-time he was hungry; at supper-time he was ravenous. And he no longer thought of losing himself on purpose, but made all the efforts in his power to get back to Rome.

"Good Heavens," he muttered, "we ought to have stumbled on something by this time."

Biddy might have answered: "I've done some stumbling, thank you, and thanks to you." But she didn't. Instead, she lifted her head and ears, looked to the left, snorted, and shied. She shied very carefully, however, because she did not know what she might shy into; and Asabri laughed.

There was a glimmering point of light off to the left, and he urged Biddy toward it. He saw presently that it was a fire built against a ruined and unfamiliar tomb.

The fire was cooking something in a kettle. There was a smell of garlic. Three young men sat cross-legged, watching the fire and the kettle. Against the tomb leaned three long guns, very old and dangerous.

"Brigands!" smiled Asabri, and he hailed them:

"Ho there! Wake up! I am a squadron of police attacking you from the rear."

He rode unarmed into their midst and slid unconcernedly from his saddle to the ground.

"Put up your weapons, brothers," he said; "I was joking. It seems that I am in danger, not you."

The young men, upon whom "brigand" was written in no

uncertain signs, were very much embarrassed. One of them smiled nervously and showed a great many very white teeth.

"Lucky for us," he said, "that you weren't what you said you were."

"Yes," said Asabri; "I should have potted the lot of you with one volley and reported at head-quarters that it had been necessary, owing to the stubborn resistance which you offered."

The three young men smiled sheepishly.

"I see that you are familiar with the ways of the police," said one of them.

"May I sit with you?" Asabri asked. "Thanks."

He sat in silence for a moment; and the three young men examined with great respect the man's splendid round head, and his face of a Roman emperor.

"Whose tomb is this?" he asked them.

"It is ours," said the one who had first smiled. "It used to hallow the remains of Attulius Cimber."

"Oho!" said Asabri. "Attulius Cimber, a direct ancestor of my friend and associate Sullandenti. And tell me how far is it to Rome?"

"A long way. You could not find the half of it tonight."

"Brothers," said Asabri, "has business been good? I ask for a reason."

"The reason, sir?"

"Why," said he, "I thought, if I should not be considered grasping, to ask you for a mouthful of soup."

Confusion seized the brigands. They protested that they were ungrateful dogs to keep the noble guest upon the tenterhooks of hunger. They called upon God to smite them down for inhospitable ne'er-do-weels. They plied him with soup, with black bread; they roasted strips of goat's flesh for him; and from the hollow of the tomb they fetched bottles of red wine in straw jackets.

Presently Asabri sighed, and offered them cigarettes from a gold case.

"For what I have received," said he, "may a courteous and thoughtful God make me truly thankful. . . . I wish that I could offer you, in return for your hospitality, something more substantial than cigarettes. The case? If it were any case but that one! A present from my wife."

He drew from its pocket a gold repeater upon which his initials were traced in brilliants.

"Midnight. Listen!"

He pressed a spring, and the exquisite chimes of the watch spoke in the stillness like the bells of a fairy church.

"And this," he said, "was a present from my mother, who is dead."

The three brigands crossed themselves, and expressed the regrets which good-breeding required of them. The one that had been the last to help himself to a cigarette now returned the case to Asabri, with a bow and a mumbling of thanks.

"What a jolly life you lead," exclaimed the banker. "Tell me, you have had some good hauls lately? What?"

The oldest of the three, a dark, taciturn youth, answered, "The gentleman is a great joker."

"Believe me," said Asabri, "it is from habit — not from the heart. When I rode out from Rome today, it was with the intention never to return. When I came upon you and saw your long guns and suspected your profession in life, I said: 'Good! Perhaps these young men will murder me for my watch and cigarette case and the loose silver in my breeches pocket, and save me a world of trouble —'"

The three brigands protested that nothing had ever been farther from their thoughts.

"Instead of which," he went on, "you have fed me and put heart in me. I shall return to Rome in the morning and face whatever music my own infatuated foolishness has set going. Do you understand anything of finance?"

The taciturn brigand grinned sheepishly.

He said that he had had one once; but that the priest had touched it with a holy relic and it had gone away. "It was on the back of my neck," he said.

Asabri laughed.

"I should have said banking," said he, "stocks and bonds."

The brigands admitted that they knew nothing of these things. Asabri sighed.

"Two months ago," he said, "I was a rich man. Today I have nothing. In a few days it will be known that I have nothing; and then, my friends — the deluge. Such is finance. From great beginnings, lame endings. And yet the converse may be true. I have seen great endings come of small beginnings. Even now there is a chance for a man with a little capital. . . ."

He raised his eyes and hands to heaven.

"Oh," he cried, "if I could touch even five thousand lire I could retrieve my own fortunes and make the fortunes of whomsoever advanced me the money."

The sullen brigand had been doing a sum on his fingers.

"How so, excellency?" he asked.

"Oh," said Asabri, "it is very simple! I should buy certain stocks, which owing to certain conditions are very cheap, and I should sell them very dear. You have heard of America?"

They smiled and nodded eagerly.

"Of Wall Street?"

They looked blank.

"Doubtless," said the banker, "you have been taught by your priests to believe that the great church of St. Peter, in Rome, is the actual centre of the universe. Is it not so?"

They assented, not without wonder, since the fact was well known.

"Recent geographers," said Asabri, "unwilling to take any statement for granted, have, after prolonged and scientific investigation, discovered that this idea is hocus pocus. The centre of the universe is in the United States, in the city of New York, in Wall Street. The number in the street, to be precise, is fifty-nine. From fifty-nine Wall Street, the word goes out to the extremities of the world: 'Let prices be low.' Or: 'Let them be high.' And so they become, according to the word. But unless I can find five thousand lire with which to take advantage of this fact, why tomorrow —"

"Tomorrow?" asked the brigand who had been first to smile.

"Two months ago," said Asabri, "I was perhaps the most envied man in Italy. Tomorrow I shall be laughed at." He shrugged his powerful shoulders.

"But if five thousand lire could be found?"

It was the sullen brigand who spoke, and his companions eyed him with some misgiving.

"In that case," said Asabri, "I should rehabilitate my fortune and that of the man, or men, who came to my assistance."

"Suppose," said the sullen one, "that I were in a position to offer you the loan of five thousand lire, or four thousand eight hundred and ninety-two, to be exact, what surety should I receive that my fortunes and those of my associates would be mended thereby?"

"My word," said Asabri simply, and he turned his face of a Roman emperor and looked the sullen brigand directly in the eye.

"Words," said this one, although his eyes fell before the steadiness of the banker's, "are of all kinds and conditions, according to whoso gives them."

Asabri smiled, and sure of his notoriety: "I am Asabri," said he.

They examined him anew with a great awe. The youngest said:

"And *you* have fallen upon evil days! I should have been less astonished if some one were to tell me that the late pope had received employment in hell."

"Beppo," said the sullen brigand, "whatever the state of his fortunes, the word of Asabri is sufficient. Go into the tomb of Attulius and fetch out the money."

The money — silver, copper, and notes of small denominations — was in a dirty leather bag.

"Will you count it, sir?"

With the palms of his hands Asabri answered that he would not. Inwardly, it was as if he had been made of smiles; but he showed them a stern countenance when he said:

"One thing! Before I touch this money, is there blood on it?"

"High hands only," said the sullen brigand; but the youngest protested.

"Indeed, yes," he said, "there is blood upon it. Look, see, and behold!"

He bared a breast on which the skin was fine and satiny like a woman's, and they saw in the firelight the cicatrice of a newly healed wound.

"A few drops of mine," he said proudly. "May they bring the money luck."

"One thing more," said Asabri; "I have said that I will mend your fortunes. What sum apiece would make you comfortable for the rest of your days and teach you to see the evil in your present manner of life?"

"If the money were to be doubled," said the sullen brigand, "then each of us could have what he most desires."

"And what is that?" asked the banker.

"For me," said the sullen brigand, "there is a certain piece of land upon which are grapes, figs, and olives."

The second brigand said: "I am a waterman by birth and by longing. If I could purchase a certain barge upon which I have long had an eye, I should do well and honestly in the world, and happily."

"And you? What do you want?" Asabri smiled paternally in the face of the youngest brigand.

This one showed his beautiful teeth a moment, and drew the rags together over his scarred breast.

"I am nineteen years of age," he said, and his eyes glistened. "There is a girl, sir, in my village. Her eyes are like velvet; her skin is smooth as custard. She is very beautiful. If I could go to her father with a certain sum of money, he would not ask where I had gotten it — that is why I have robbed on the highway. He would merely stretch forth his hands and roll his fat eyes heavenward, and say: 'Bless you, my children.'"

"But the girl," said Asabri.

"It is wonderful," said the youngest brigand, "how she loves me.

And when I told her that I was going upon the road to earn the moneys necessary for our happiness, she said that she would climb down from her window at night and come with me. But," he concluded unctuously, "I pointed out to her that from sin springs nothing but unhappiness."

"We formed a fellowship, we three," said the second brigand, "and swore an oath: to take from the world so much as would make us happy, and no more."

"My friends," said Asabri, "there are worse brigands than yourselves living in palaces."

The fog had lifted, and it was beginning to grow light. Asabri gathered up the heavy bag of money and prepared to depart.

"How long," said the sullen brigand, "with all respect, before your own fortunes will be mended, sir, and ours?"

"You are quite sure you know nothing of stocks?"

"Nothing, excellency."

"Then listen. They shall be mended today. Tomorrow come to my bank —"

"Oh, sir, we dare not show our faces in Rome."

"Very well, then; tomorrow at ten sharp I shall leave Rome in a motor-car. Watch for me along the Appian Way."

He shook them by their brown, grimy hands, mounted the impatient Biddy, and was gone — blissfully smiling.

Upon reaching Rome he rode to his palace and assured Luigi the valet that all was well. Then he bathed, changed, breakfasted, napped, and drove to the hospital of Our Lady in Emergencies. He saw the superior and gave her the leather bag containing the brigands' savings.

"For my sins," he said. "I have told lies half the night."

Then he drove to his great banking house and sent for the cashier.

"Make me up," said he, "three portable parcels of fifty thousand lire each."

The next day at ten he left Rome in a black and beauteous motor-car, and drove slowly along the Appian Way. He had left his mechanic behind, and was prepared to renew his tires and his youth. Packed away, he had luncheon and champagne enough for four; and he had not forgotten to bring along the three parcels of money.

The three brigands stepped into the Appian Way from behind a mass of fallen masonry. They had found the means to shave cleanly, and perhaps to wash. They were adorned with what were evidently their very best clothes. The youngest, whose ambition was the girl he loved, even wore a necktie.

Asabri brought the motor to a swift, oily, and polished halt.

"Well met," he said, "since all is well. If you," he smiled into the face of the sullen brigand, "will be so good as to sit beside me!... The others shall sit in behind. . . . We shall go first," he continued, when all were comfortably seated, "to have a look at that little piece of land on which grow figs, olives, and grapes. We shall buy it, and break our fast in the shade of the oldest fig tree. It is going to be a hot day."

"It is below Rome, and far," said the sullen brigand; "but since the barge upon which my friend has set his heart belongs to a near neighbor, we shall be killing two birds with one stone. But with all deference, excellency, have you really retrieved your fortunes?"

"And yours," said Asabri. "Indeed, I am today as rich as ever I was, with the exception" — his eyes twinkled behind his goggles — "of about a hundred and fifty thousand lire."

The sullen brigand whistled; and although the roads were rough, they proceeded, thanks to the shock-absorbers on Asabri's car, in complete comfort, at a great pace.

In the village nearest to the property upon which the sullen brigand had cast his eye, they picked up a notary through whom to effect the purchase.

The little farm was rather stony, but sweet to the eye as a bouquet of flowers, with the deep greens of the figs and grapes and the silvery greens of the olives. Furthermore, there were roses in the door-yard, and the young and childless widow to whom the homestead belonged stood among the roses. She was brown and scarlet, and her eyes were black and merry.

Yes, yes, she agreed, she would sell! There was a mortgage on the place. She intended to pay that off and have a little over. True, the place paid. But, Good Lord, she lived all alone, and she didn't enjoy that!

They invited the pretty widow to luncheon, and she helped them spread the cloth under a fig tree that had thrown shade for five hundred years. Asabri passed the champagne, and they all became very merry together. Indeed, the sullen brigand became so merry and happy that he no longer addressed Asabri respectfully as "excellency," but gratefully and affectionately as "my father."

This one became more and more delighted with the term, until finally he said:

"It is true, that in a sense I am this young man's father, since I believe that if I were to advise him to do a certain thing he would do it."

"That is God's truth," cried the sullen brigand; "if he advised me to advance single-handed against the hosts of hell, I should do so."

"My son," said Asabri, "our fair guest affirms that upon this beautiful little farm she has had everything that she could wish except companionship. Are you not afraid that you, in your turn, will here suffer from loneliness?" He turned to the pretty widow. "I wish," said he, "to address myself to you in behalf of this young man."

The others became very silent. The notary lifted his glass to his lips. The widow blushed. Said she:

"I like his looks well enough; but I know nothing about him."

"I can tell you this," said Asabri, "that he has been a man of exemplary honesty since — yesterday, and that under the seat of my automobile he has, in a leather bag, a fortune of fifty thousand lire."

The three brigands gasped.

"He is determined, in any case," the banker continued, "to purchase your little farm; but it seems to me that it would be a beautiful end to a story that has not been without a certain aroma of romance if you, my fair guest, were, so to speak, to throw yourself into the bargain. Think it over. The mortgage lifted, a handsome husband, and plenty of money in the bank. . . . Think it over. And in any case — the pleasure of a glass of wine with you!"

They touched glasses. Across the golden bubbling, smiles leapt.

"Let us," said the second brigand, "leave the pair in question to talk the matter over, while the rest of us go and attend to the purchase of my barge."

"Well thought," said Asabri. "My children, we shall be gone about an hour. See if, in that time, you cannot grow fond of each other. Perhaps, if you took the bag of money into the house and pretended that it already belonged to both of you, and counted it over, something might be accomplished."

The youngest brigand caught the sullen one by the sleeve and whispered in his ear.

"If you want her, let her count the money. If you don't, count it yourself."

The second brigand turned to Asabri. "Excellency," he whispered, "you are as much my father as his."

"True," said Asabri, "what of it?"

"Nothing! Only, the man who owns the barge which I desire to purchase has a very beautiful daughter."

Asabri laughed so that for a moment he could not bend over to crank his car. And he cried aloud:

"France, France, I thank thee for thy champagne! And I thank thee, O Italy, for thy merry hearts and thy suggestive climate!... My son, if the bargeman's daughter is to be had for the asking, she is yours. But we must tell the father that until recently you have been a very naughty fellow."

They remained with the second brigand long enough to see him exchange a kiss of betrothal with the bargeman's daughter, while the bargeman busied himself counting the money; and then they returned to see how the sullen brigand and the pretty widow were getting on.

The sullen brigand was cutting dead-wood out of a fig tree with a saw. His face was supremely happy. The widow stood beneath and directed him.

"Closer to the tree, stupid," she said, "else the wound will not heal properly."

The youngest brigand laid a hand that trembled upon Asabri's arm.

"Oh, my father," he said, "these doves are already cooing! And it is very far to the place where I would be."

But Asabri went first to the fig tree, and he said to the widow: "Is all well?"

"Yes," she said, "we have agreed to differ for the rest of our lives. It seems that this stupid fellow needs somebody to look after him. And it seems to be God's will that that somebody should be I."

"Bless you then, my children," said Asabri; "and farewell! I shall come to the wedding."

They returned the notary to his little home in the village; and the fees which he was to receive for the documents which he was to draw up made him so happy that he flung his arms about his wife, who was rather a prim person, and fell to kissing her with the most boisterous good will.

It was dusk when they reached the village in which the sweetheart of the youngest brigand lived. Asabri thought that he had never seen a girl more exquisite.

"And we have loved each other," said the youngest brigand, his arm about her firm, round waist, "since we were children. . . . I think I am dying, I am so happy."

"Shall you buy a farm, a barge, a business?" asked the banker.

"Whatever is decided," said the girl, "it will be a paradise."

Her old father came out of the house.

"I have counted the money. It is correct."

Then he rolled his fat eyes heavenward, just as the youngest brigand had prophesied, and said: "Bless you, my children!"

"I must be going," said Asabri; "but there is one thing."

Four dark luminous eyes looked into his.

"You have not kissed," said Asabri; "let it be now, so that I may remember."

Without embarrassment, the young brigand and his sweetheart folded their arms closely about each other, and kissed each other, once, slowly, with infinite tenderness.

"I am nineteen," said the youngest brigand; then, and he looked heavenward: "God help us to forget the years that have been wasted!"

Asabri drove toward Rome, his headlights piercing the darkness. The champagne was no longer in his blood. He was in a calm, judicial mood.

"To think," he said to himself, "that for a mere matter of a hundred and fifty thousand lire, a rich old man can be young again for a day or two!"

It was nearly one o'clock when he reached his palace in Rome. Luigi, the valet, was sitting up for him, as usual.

"This is the second time in three days," said Luigi, "that you have been out all night.... A telegram," he threatened, "would bring the mistress back to Rome."

"Forgive me, old friend," said Asabri, and he leaned on Luigi's shoulder; "but I have fallen in love. . . ."

"What!" screamed the valet. "At your age?"

"It is quite true," said Asabri, a little sadly, "that at my age a man most easily falls in love — with life."

"You shall go to bed at once," said Luigi sternly. "I shall prepare a hot lemonade, and you shall take five grains of quinine.... You are damp.... The mist from the Campagna. . . ."

Asabri yawned in the ancient servitor's face.

"Luigi," he said, "I think I shall buy you a farm and a wife; or a barge and a wife. . . ."

"You do, do you?" said Luigi. "And I think you'll take your quinine like a Trojan, or I'll know the reason why."

"Everybody regards me as rather an important person," complained Asabri, "except you."

"You were seven years old," said Luigi, "when I came to serve you. I have aged. But you haven't. You didn't know enough then to come in when it rained, as the Americans say. You don't now. I would not speak of this to others. But to you — yes — for your own good."

Asabri smiled blissfully.

"In all the world," he said, "there is only one thing for a man to fear, that he will learn to take the world seriously; in other words, that he will grow up. . . . You may bring the hot lemonade and the quinine when they are ready."

And then he blew his nose of a Roman emperor; for he had indeed contracted a slight cold.

THE END